I0690505

SWORDS
&
SORCERIES

Tales
of
Heroic Fantasy

Volume 11

OTHER ANTHOLOGIES AVAILABLE

from

PARALLEL UNIVERSE
PUBLICATIONS

SWORDS & SORCERIES: Tales of Heroic Fantasy
Volumes 1 - 10
Presented by David A. Riley & Jim Pitts

KITCHEN SINK GOTHIC 1 & 2
Selected by Linden Riley & David A. Riley

THINGS THAT GO BUMP IN THE NIGHT
Selected by Douglas Draa & David A. Riley

CLASSIC WEIRD 1 & 2
Selected by David A. Riley

SWORDS
&
SORCERIES

Tales of Heroic Fantasy
Volume 11
Presented by
David A. Riley
Jim Pitts

PARALLEL UNIVERSE PUBLICATIONS

First Published in the UK in 2025
Copyright © 2025
Cover & interior artwork © 2025 Jim Pitts
Silence for Snakes © 2025 Harry Elliott
Midwinter © 1995 David A. Sutton was first published in
The Merlin Chronicles, Raven Books/Robinson Publishing Ltd
Tomb Robbers © 2025 Susan Murrie Macdonald
Blackshield Manor © 2025 Marc Edward Star
The Eggshell Carver © 2025 Tais Teng
The Eternal Assassin: The Man Who Hunted Death © 2025
Andrew Darlington
The Gwailou Ship © 2025 Geoffrey Hart
Good Fortune © 2025 Ũũmbi (Mungai M'mbogori)
The Wyrm's Tongue © 2025 Daniel Mahoney
Wardark and the Sands of Serpanam © 2025 Craig Herbertson

All rights reserved. No part of this publication may be reproduced,
stored in a retrieval system, rebound or transmitted in any form or
by any means, electronic, mechanical, photocopying, recording or
otherwise, without the prior written permission of the author and
publisher. This book is sold subject to the condition that it shall not
by way of trade or otherwise be lent, resold, hired out or otherwise
circulated without the publisher's prior consent in any form of
binding or cover other than that in which it is published.

ISBN: 9781739367497

**Parallel Universe Publications, 130 Union Road,
Oswaldtwistle, Lancashire, BB5 3DR, UK**

Dedicated as always to the memory
of writer, editor,
and publisher,
Charles Black
who inspired this anthology series

CONTENTS

INTRODUCTION

Welcome to our eleventh volume of sword and sorcery stories, which as usual is a mix of brand new names and the return of some longtime favourites.

Regular contributor Harry Elliott is a British author with a passion for the fictional and the fantastic. When faced with the question "What is best in life?" in regard to his writing, to read his work it may seem that he has decided thusly: *To crush your characters, see them driven before you, and to hear the lamentation of the readers!* The truth, fortunately, is not so harsh. Across his written

works you may often fear for the characters throughout many perils, from the war-torn worlds of his military science fiction novel, *Warrior Errant*, across the neon-splashed quest for vengeance in his short cyberpunk series, *DataJack*, to the mysterious and mythic setting of the Undervalley, explored in this very book that you now hold in your hands. Herein you will find the short story "Silence for Snakes", but there are tales that have come before, in Volumes 5, 6, 7 and 10, where respectively you will find "Skulls for Silver", "Trials for Treasure", "Blades for a Bounty" and "Masks for the Madness". In these tales of the Undervalley beasts of legend lurk, and warriors do battle by strength and steel, so long as there's coin involved or feuds to be fought. However dire the events of these tales may become, this author would have you read on, always and forever, for through the thrill and the fear, he hopes that you will find at the very least some small measure of escape from your own trials and, just maybe, a happy ending too.

David A. Sutton lives in Birmingham, England and this is his first story in *Swords & Sorceries*. He is the recipient of the World Fantasy Award, The International Horror Guild Award and twelve British Fantasy Awards for editing magazines and anthologies (*Fantasy Tales, Dark Voices: The Pan Book Of Horror* and *Dark Terrors: The Gollancz Book Of Horror*). Other anthologies include *New Writings in Horror & The Supernatural, The Satyr's Head & Other Tales of Terror, Phantoms of Venice,* and *Haunts Of Horror.* He has also been a genre fiction writer since the 1960s with stories appearing widely in anthologies and magazines, including in *Best New Horror, Final Shadows, The Mammoth Book Of Merlin, Beneath*

The Ground, Shadows Over Innsmouth, The Black Book Of Horror, Subtle Edens, The Ghosts & Scholars Book Of Shadows, Psychomania, Second City Scares, Kitchen Sink Gothic, Phantasmagoria, Gruesome Grotesques, The Ghosts & Scholars Book Of Hill Figures and *The Ghosts & Scholars Book Of Folk Horror*. His short stories are collected in *Clinically Dead & Other Tales of the Supernatural, Dead Water and Other Weird Tales, En Vacances* and *The Evil Bones: Stories from the Dark Side*. He is also the proprietor of Shadow Publishing, a small press specialising in collections and anthologies.

"Midwinter" was first published in Mike Ashley's *The Merlin Chronicles* in 1995.

This is Susan Murrie Macdonald's fourth story here. Susan is a free-lance wordsmith: ghost-writer, blogger, journalist. She has published roughly twenty short stories, mostly fantasy, but also some science fiction, westerns, romance, and children's stories. She is the author of *R Is For Renaissance Faire*, a children's book based on her four years as a

volunteer with the Mid-South Renaissance Faire. She is a stroke survivor, although she has been out of the wheelchair almost three years and can limp half a mile with the help of a cane. She is an ex-copy editor and an ex-teacher. She still works as a freelance proof-reader. She is a staff writer for SciFi. Radio with over a hundred articles posted on their website. She is, of course, working on a novel; 'isn't everyone?'

Susan lives in a small town in Tennessee about twenty kilometres from Memphis. She is married to a travel agent and has a son and daughter of university age. She has had stories in *Tales from OmniPark*, *Under Western Stars*, *Space Force: Building a Legacy*, *Cat Tails: War Zone*, *Wee Tales*, *The Caterpillar*, *Sirius Science Fiction*, *Itty Bitty Writing Space*, *Bumples*, *Alternative Truths*, *More Alternative Truths*, *Paper Butterfly*, *Sword and Sorceress*, *Knee-High Drummond and the Durango Kid*, *Barbarian Crowns*, and *Supernatural Colorado*.

First timer here, Marc Edward Star is the author of *Mirror of Malatesto*, a role-playing game adventure setting of ancient cults and dark conspiracies inspired by the Medieval European witch hunts, the Inquisition and the Salem witch trials, twisted so that warlocks replaced witches and inverted by a world not induced into panic by mere paranoia, but actually infected by a conspiracy so covert and so comprehensive that the foundational institutions of the realm — political, commercial and spiritual — have been covertly subdued to serve an ages-old sinister plot to waken an ancient evil. "Blackshield Manor" is the first work of fiction inspired by this world. Star lives in Los Angeles, California where he currently is studying for his law degree yet dreams at night of dark worlds and sorcerous tales.

Frequent contributor, Tais Teng writes: "Good to be in *Swords & Sorceries* again! I keep writing S & S regularly, though mostly in Dutch, because my publisher really likes heroic fantasy and is willing to publish my collections. Most publishers only want novels, and right now I like writing short stories and novellas more than 600 page tomes. Every year some of my English stories end up in *Cirsova*, though, and often in other collections. Right now, I am working on a manual for writing fantasy stories."

During a recent birthday trip to the Lake District, Andrew Darlington slipped and fell heavily on his shoulder, fracturing the humerus bone in his arm – and that's not humorous in the least! But fortunately, although his left arm is currently in traction out of action, he can still peck out stories on the laptop keyboard with his right hand! And his music journalism for *RnR* magazine subsequently featured a Zoom! interview with Hilda, the 83-year-old singer with the South African Mahotella Queens trio! A hugely entertaining interview to do. Meanwhile, the exploits of the Eternal Assassin continue in different guises...

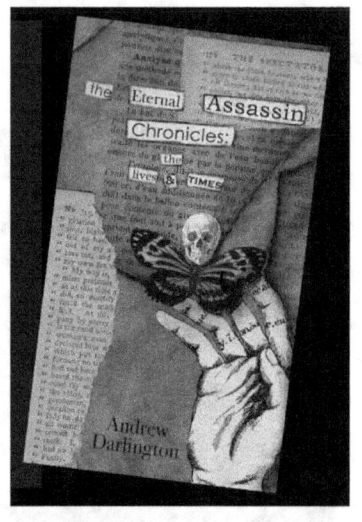

Meanwhile, taking a break from his popular Freya and Mouse stories, Geoff Hart has this time written a supernatural story set in the real history of China, with suitable modifications to make it a story rather than a history.

Geoff Hart works as a scientific editor, specializing in helping scientists who have English as their second language publish their research. He's the author of the popular *Effective Onscreen Editing* and *Write Faster With Your Word Processor*. He also writes fiction and has sold 85 stories thus far. Visit him online at *www.geoff-hart.com*.

Newcomer to our series with "Good Fortune" is Mungai M'mbogori, who uses the pen name Ũũmbi. Mungai M'mbogori is a young and emerging writer, based in Nairobi, Kenya. His last formal occupation was at a local publishing house called

Storymoja, also based in Nairobi, as a writer and editor. After leaving the company in August 2024 to be an independent artist, he has since been published by Qwani, a youth led publication based in Nairobi and is a graduate of the Sanara program for scriptwriters, which was facilitated by the Mastercard Foundation, in partnership with Heva Fund, Baraza Media Lab, SNDBX Ubuntu and The GoDown Arts Centre. Under his pen name "Ũũmbi" he likes to write poetry, fiction and sometimes essays. When he is not writing, he enjoys reading books, comics, watching anime and listening to music.

Another newcomer here, Daniel Mahoney writes character-driven dark fantasy and speculative fiction that explore the boundaries between myth and memory. His stories often centre on the cost of power and the weight of choice, blending the atmosphere of folklore with a modern emotional edge. His work has appeared in *Kelp Journal*. He lives in the Pacific Northwest, where he says the fog and forests provide endless inspiration.

Craig Herberston was born at home in Edinburgh, Scotland in 1959 and after a period of wandering now lives in a small town in Perthshire where he practices his fiddle and writes.

"Obsessed with fantastic worlds from the moment that I bought *Tarzan and the Forbidden City* as a ten year old boy, my bookshelves are still lined with journeys from Lemuria to Hyperboria.

"Despite my love of the genre, my first mainstream publication was actually a novelette in the *Pan Book of Horror Stories* in 1987. Nearly fifty short stories, two collections of horror stories and two dark fantasy novels have followed. My dark fantasy, *School: The Seventh Silence*, has been compared to Franz Kafka and Lewis Carrol but Wardark the reiver has simpler motives. Doomed by the sorcerer Xianthus, Wardark has appeared three times in *Swords & Sorceries* and now returns to battle his way across the desert of Serpanam."

Check out Craig's website *https://heavenmakers.com* for reviews and observations on fantastical worlds.

And, as usual, this book is favoured with the amazing artwork of Jim Pitts. As well as having been busy on the collection of Elak of Atlantis tales by Adrian Cole, Jim is regularly featured in the pages of *Phantasmagoria Magazine*, *Lovecraftiana*, and *Schlock! Webzine*, and elsewhere.

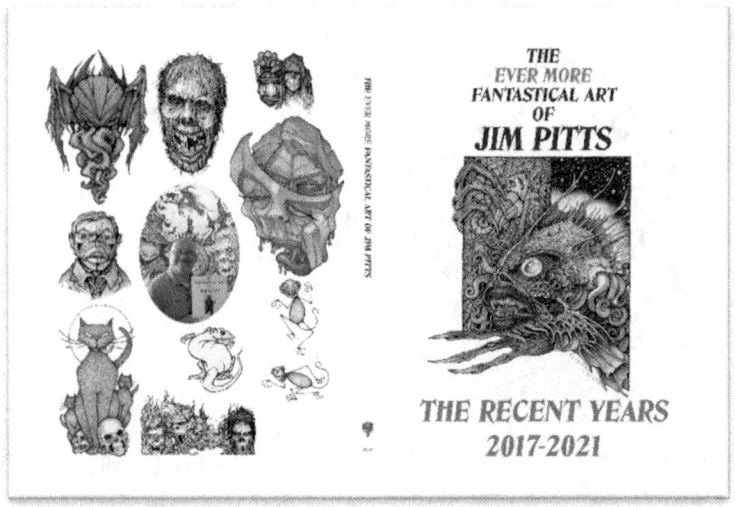

These then are the authors and artist whose work is included in the pages of this, our eleventh volume of sword and sorcery stories. We look forward to you joining us for *Volume 12* next year!

David A. Riley
Oswaldtwistle, November 2025

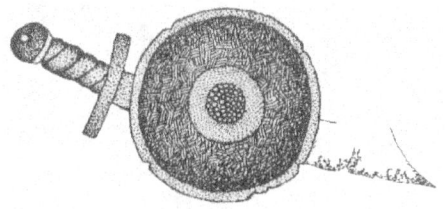

SILENCE FOR SNAKES

Harry Elliott

I. The Way West

A wall is not raised to make a friend.

A gate is not built to welcome guests.

Here was a wall, and a gate to boot. It was not a very long wall, because it had no need to be. Here in the Skathar Pass, where the flint-black cliffs came within three hundred feet of touching, the Red Men of the West had built a bastion to shut the way.

Presumably they had not built this gate to entertain guests, but guests had come nonetheless. Very angry guests, thought Mann Silver, if the trailing arcs of fire were anything to go by. Streaks of ember-orange in the deep blue of night, rising up from a siege camp in the valley below to fall upon the bastion, where they splashed on stone and rained tears of flame. A dazzling sight, to be sure, if entirely impotent. It would take more than clay pots of burning tar to breach those walls.

"Shit," said Hel Strumm, crawling through the wild grass to meet Silver at the ridge. "It's never easy."

"Two weeks," spat Gul Hakker, elbowing his way between them. "Two weeks of miserable foot slogging and empty wineskins, for this?! And now what? Two weeks retracing our steps!"

"We don't have the provisions for that," said Silver, tracing his eyes along the flame lit bastion.

"Well, we'll just have to kill them all," Gul said, a weary resignation in his voice.

"Which ones?" asked Silver, looking from bastion to siege camp.

"All of them," said Gul simply, "but preferably the ones with the most food first."

"Every war has at least two sides, surely we can find common cause with one of them," said Hel.

"I know those banners," said Silver, nodding to the colours arrayed atop the battlements, red cloth rippling in the fire-heat. "We've killed too many Westmen to be welcome by anything but arrows there, which leaves us one choice."

"We kill more Westmen," said Gul decisively.

Hel sighed. "If it comes to that."

"It always does," said Silver.

"Do we know them?" asked Hel, pointing at the nest of warm lights amidst the scrawny wilderness.

"Too dark to say for sure," said Silver, squinting. "They're organised though. Organised enough to have siege engines and provisions two weeks from the nearest settlement."

"Is that good?" asked Gul, licking his lips at the mention of provisions.

Silver gestured to the bastion with a small nod of his head. "The Westmen too are organised. They like their rules, their *uniformity*. Order is the tyrant's excuse for peace."

"We're back to killing them all then, are we?" said Gul, and sounded almost relieved.

Hel elbowed the stout Gul. "I think what good Silver means to say is: a common enemy doesn't always a friend make."

"But perhaps allies of necessity," muttered Silver. "Worst case, we steal some supplies and retrace our steps, find another way west."

"Best case?" asked Hel, raising an arched eyebrow.

Silver pushed himself over the ridge and began stalking through the wild grass towards the lights of the camp below. He drew his twin swords.

"We make a friend."

II. Undervalley Unrest

The siege camp had become a fortress in its own right. The surrounding trees – which grew tall and straight to reach longingly for the distant sun – had been felled, and now reformed as a palisade wall and watchtowers and sharpened lines of stakes.

They were met across a ditch by torches blowing in the night wind, and the low creak of nocked bowstrings. Tired, suspicious eyes regarded them, and questions came loaded and quick. Then, permitted further into the pulsing rings of firelight, some of those eyes widened, first with recognition and then with awe.

Guards were lowered and gates opened, and the three were welcomed within the walls of sharpened tree trunks. Mann Silver remembered the war camp of the Red Men, back east where they had laid siege to the giant's cave. They had set their tents like pieces on a playing board, equally spaced in ordered ranks. The present camp was by contrast a wild patchwork of shelters, tents of different sizes and styles and colours, with distinct fetishes and talismans and badges.

That motley was reflected too in the warriors gathered here. Where the Westmen were indistinguishable in red-dyed armour of lamellar make, faces homogenised by domed helmets and long cheek guards, the presently gathered force adhered to no such uniformity. Each warrior was unique. Here, a man in beast fur, with a horned helm and battleaxe. There, a woman in scales, a longsword in hand. And on it went as they were led through the camp, beholding fighters of every stripe, no doubt drawn from a hundred different hearths.

At the hub of the camp they came to the largest tent yet, the unmistakeable command post. They ducked beneath the awning and into the flickering shadows of burning braziers. Through the smoky air they discerned a man, draped in a plain, white chiton with a zoster fastened beneath the chest, a wide belt of leather studded with bronze plates. He had a thick horseshoe moustache, and long hair drawn into a topknot.

He regarded their entry, and his eyes filled with a savage light that lifted to his face a tight smile.

"Be most welcome. I am Kirhon, lochagos of these forces, and I think I know you," he said, pointing a finger at each of them in turn. "The one built like a barrel, stout and thick, with a horsetail plume of reddest hair. The spear maiden, golden haired, lean and sharp. And the shrouded one, black mane 'neath black hood. You will know him by his blades, twins of mirror steel. Your deeds have outpaced you."

"Someone's been telling tales," said Hel, a flash of teeth beneath curved lips. She fanned herself mockingly. "I wonder who."

Lochagos Kirhon stepped closer. "The tales failed to do justice to your beauty."

Hel gave a practised laugh, the one that said: *not in a thousand full moons, not if I was in heat and you were the last man in all the Undervalley, now step away before my boot finds something delicate.*

Kirhon cleared his throat and Silver came to his rescue.

"We share a problem." He nodded west, where beyond this tent, and the camp around it, the bastion stood. At that moment, as if to punctuate his point, the thud and clang of catapults, loosing their fury into the night. In the firelight they paused, eyes raised, heads tilted, and listened to the deep roar of flaming tar exploding on the enemy rampart, some thousand feet distant.

"The Red Men are not content in the west, it would seem," said Kirhon. "They push into our corridors and seal them off, one at a time. Well, enough is enough. Every Demarch from Skathar to Kresh has raised the levy, and so you see before you the resistance of the Heartscars. If the Eastmen will not oppose this expansion, then it falls to us - the Men of the Middel - to show the Undervalley the face of courage."

"Very impressive," said Silver, and gave a shallow bow of his head to show his sincerity. He left unsaid how this act of resistance was sorely overdue.

Gul was decidedly less diplomatic. "It's good to see the Middel no longer welcomes cohorts of Red Men to trample unchecked through their valleys. We've made a mountain of their bodies in the East, and the only fast way East is through the Heartscars. Did you wave as they marched you by? Did you offer meat and ale?"

Kirhon stiffened, then sighed. "You'll have no argument from me, slayer. Long have I petitioned my own Demarch for action. As the mule must feel the lash before it moves, so too did our people have to suffer before they were roused to action. It is the sad way of things, that so few can see the storm before they feel the rain."

"Our path is through that bastion, Lochagos," said Silver. "When do you make your assault?"

"We have made it," Kirhon said. "I lost fifty men before we even reached the gate. That was a week ago. Now we throw fire at stone to mask the sting of our losses, but before long we'll have neither clay pot nor tar to fill, and then I imagine we'll make a home of this place."

"That is your plan?" barked Gul. "To sit here and do nothing?"

"We cannot rout them," said Kirhon, resigned. "What we *can* do is make a garrison here, a line beyond which no Westman will prevail."

"You would stall after a single effort?"

"I was in that effort," snarled Kirhon. "I saw it with my own eyes. That wall is impenetrable."

"If it was meant to be impenetrable, they wouldn't have put a door in the front," said Silver.

"Hah!" Kirhon fell silent, studying them intently. "Well, here you are. Slayers of Westmen! The famous three. Who has not heard of your exploits? The three who stood against an army, and triumphed! Perhaps this is a gift? Perhaps this common cause is in fact a good omen? A sign of the turning tide. How would *you* clear the Skathar Pass of this most noisome blockage?"

"You say you took heavy losses on the approach," remarked Silver, dark eyes narrowing in thought beneath a creased brow. "What defences did you note?"

Kirhon sighed. "Many bowmen upon the walls, and ballistae too. They have cleared the land before the bastion, so no man may approach unseen, and by night they light pyres in the clearing to illuminate the approach."

"Then simply put out those pyres and let darkness shroud your assault!" Gul said, curling his thick fingers into an angry fist.

"And I suppose the Red Men would think nothing of

mysteriously extinguished fires?" Kirhon asked, making no effort to hide his sarcasm.

"We share a problem," Silver repeated, "and I do not deny it is a hard one. We would join your effort, and if there is a timely solution, we would help you in the solving."

"Sieges are rarely swift," Kirhon warned.

"As you said, we are here now," smiled Hel.

"In the meantime, give us your hospitality," said Silver. "We have been long on the walk, and have need of resupply."

Kirhon spread his palms, a conciliatory gesture. "I am sure you have noticed, we are a long way from resupply. My own provisions are limited, my caravans few and far between, and I have many soldiers whose strength must be maintained. I cannot spare something for nothing, you understand? But should a plan be brought before me, an actionable path delivered to crack the Red Men shell, well, then I believe we would all feast together, with plenty to spare."

Silver's mouth tightened. "We'll think of something."

"Tonight," stressed Kirhon, unblinking. "You'll think of something *tonight*."

"Why the sudden haste?" asked Hel, and Silver could tell she was reigning in her frustration.

"As I said, my stores are precious." Kirhon's eyes hardened, his ultimatum delivered there if not in words. "I cannot afford to keep the unhelpful."

Mann Silver could sense Gul's bristling. Tired feet and two weeks of sleeping rough were almost motivation enough to let the man do something stupid, but this would be a pointless place to die. He considered too wishing this Kirhon the best of luck and turning his back on it, but the thought of another two weeks retracing their steps was even less appealing.

Silver gave a nod, a promise to himself as much to anyone else. "When next the Skathar Pass feels daylight, those gates will part, and you'll get your blood."

III. Mad Pilgrims and Bad Plans

"Do you remember how this all began?" asked Hel.

They had climbed to a walkway behind the palisade, and stood watching the occasional catapult launch. The artillery crews were sluggish in their loading of the clay pots, tired of the weight and the repetition, failing to keep up any sort of regular interval, but persisting all the same. The fire pots soared through the night, scorching tails leaving afterimages in their eyes.

"Gul's insatiable need for mead?"

Hel laughed, her eyes bright with firelight. "Yes, yes, I suppose it did."

Silver looked over his shoulder. Even here at the edge of the camp he could hear the hell that Gul was raising in his quest to bribe, bet or beat his way to a drink. He wondered how quickly that would sour the good favour bought by their reputation, and then shrugged to himself.

"At least, looking back, that was the first step on this road," Hel continued. "But we didn't know it, at the time. We might have taken a different direction at any point after that. Circumstance may have diverted us a hundred times between then and now. An adventure doesn't begin by chance, not really. It begins with a choice. It began when we chose to help someone in need."

"Actually, I think our first choice was to rip off some slavers," said Mann through a half smirk.

Hel elbowed him playfully, then sighed. "Those crazy Climber Pilgrims. A strange belief can make people do a terrible thing."

Mann paused halfway through rubbing his ribs. His gaze travelled unbidden, out towards the black cliff walls that enclosed their world. His next word was thoughtful and distant. "Climbers."

Hel followed him. "Oh no, no, no, no."

"It could work," he said, his voice low with calculation.

"Climber Pilgrims aren't famous because they reach the top, Silver, they're famous because they fall."

"We wouldn't need to reach the top," he said, and now the excitement of possibility was infusing his words. "Not even close. Just high enough to get onto the wall. It can't be more than thirty feet tall, maybe forty."

"Some Climbers don't even make it that far," said Hel. "This is a bad plan, Silver. Only the mad climb."

"That's why they won't be watching the cliffs." Excitement had given way to confidence now, and Hel could feel her gut knotting into a tight ball of fear. Silver caught her expression, turned to face her. "Think of everything we've survived, assassin's blades, beast claw and serpent fang. This stands trivial by comparison. We begin our ascent as close as we can, a short climb, just high enough to be above the wall, then a traversal, across the face and onto the top. Hit the archers sidelong, and we'll be at the gatehouse before they so much as know they're dead. Then the gate, and a flaming arrow to bring the army."

"You make it sound easy, but have you ever climbed so much as your own height on those cliffs?" asked Hel, and Mann had never seen her so rattled, this woman who he had watched cut down beasts three times her size.

"Not the cliffs, no," he admitted, "but how many rock faces and hills have we overcome in these valleys? How different could it be?"

"I don't like it, Mann," she said, her voice low.

Silver frowned, then set his jaw. "Alright. I won't ask you to do it."

Hel could not contain the tight sigh of relief. "There will be another way."

"Stay with the army, and when you see my signal, lead them in. I'll meet you on the other side." He had to catch Hel's fist almost before the last words had left his mouth. This blow he would not have described as playful.

"I like that even less," she said through gritted teeth, her fist still balled in Silver's palm. Gently, he folded it against her chest.

"I can do this," he pressed, holding her stare.

Hel did not blink. Did not so much as swallow. "Not alone. We go together. You bastard."

"By morning we'll be laughing about this," said Silver, and it had the ring of a promise.

"You tell Kirhon. I'll find Gul before he drinks too much. Oh, he's going to love this," Hel said, turning to climb down from the palisade.

Silver caught her wrist. She found his eyes, soft where usually they were serious. "Thank you, Hel."

She pulled her hand free. "Thank me if we're still alive at the end of this."

"Hel?" She stopped again, this time with her hands on the rungs. "Maybe don't give Gul all the details right away. I'll let him know the full plan later."

"Later when?"

"When we're climbing?" he suggested.

Hel laughed and disappeared below the lip of the palisade walkway, but Silver breathed his own sigh of relief. Her laugh had been genuine. He looked back into the night. The valley was frosted blue by starlight, and then streaked with orange as an oil pot launched, briefly lighting the space between like a torch dropped into a well. The crump of explosive impact rolled back across the distance.

Silver wondered how much more he could ask of his friends. He wondered what would break first: the limit of their loyalty, or their lives?

IV. Only the Mad

"Are you sure this was the only plan?" shouted Gul, hanging from a rock ledge six feet below. Mann looked down and regretted it immediately. He was only twelve feet above the ground, the height of two men, but that looked a lot worse from the top than it did from the bottom. A man could still break his spine from a fall at this height.

"Quiet," he hissed, face pressed close to the cold stone. That was the other thing that had looked easier from the ground. Even in the silver light of moon and star, Mann had made note of a series of handholds to a reasonable height. It had looked trivial, even. When the climb had begun, and his view of the world had been reduced to dark stone an inch from his nose, that simple path had disappeared. Now every finger-wide hold was a sharp and treacherous ledge a world away, each new grip demanding a greater cost in courage against a rapidly diminishing chance of survival should the hand slip.

The Climber Pilgrims were not well regarded by the disparate city-states of the Undervalley, but Mann was discovering a newfound respect for the insane courage that drove them to brave the black cliffs. This night their goal was little greater than a height of thirty feet, a height that seemed impossible just halfway up. The Climbers aspired not to thirty feet, not even to three hundred, but to surmount the ten thousand feet to those mythical lofts, and to discover what existed of the world above the enclosures of the Undervalley.

Knowing that his own target was paltry by comparison brought much needed resolve, and in that moment the long climb to little heights was behind him. He cast about, straining to find the others without slipping from his perch. Hel was to his left, and Gul was just below, hefting his bulk with angry grunts of exertion.

"I think we're in line," he gasped, looking across the dark verticality towards the bastion, though he could see little of it from this angle.

"We should go higher," came Hel's voice, urgent and reluctant at the same time. "We don't want to be at their eyeline."

Mann nodded, but could summon no words. Hel was right. If they were spotted on the approach, they would be helpless against the cliff face as arrows pinned them to the stone or sent them plummeting like sacks to burst on the ground below. Their best bet would be to descend upon the wall, above the expectation of the sentries.

"Or we could go back down," said Gul. "A frontal assault is beginning to feel like the safer choice."

They pressed on, and that extra effort rewarded them with a ledge wide enough to stand on with more than just their toes. Mann pressed his back to the chipped stone face and allowed himself a steadying breath. His fingers were cramped into claws from the pressure of bearing his weight, and his thighs burned from the ascent. He shot a half smile at Hel.

"Easy," he said, and from her scowl Mann could tell she was weighing the risk of losing her balance against the reward of kicking him off the edge. He swallowed his smile and gestured along the rock face. "Now across. With luck, this ledge will persist until we're above the wall, and then the fun begins."

Careful, shuffling steps made for a painful pace across the dark facade. In places, the stone had a glassy quality about it, and seemed to collect in its dark depths the cold light of the heavens, wherein it was kept trapped, like swirls of milk in oil. Mann had heard many tales as to the nature of their jailors, these immovable titans in which their lives were hemmed. Some said they were sorcerous in nature, a product of that dreaded force: *magic*.

The slow and methodical advance left room for his thoughts to wander. Perhaps for the first time, Mann reflected on how little they knew of their world, and of how much of that mystery they accepted unquestioningly in their daily lives. Were the Pilgrims in fact the wisest of them all? The only ones who dared to challenge the boundaries of their existence and seek the hidden truths beyond.

"There's a tunnel." Hel's voice snapped Mann from his reverie. "Not large. Enough to crawl through, maybe."

"And another, here," said Gul, and uncovered the spiked head of his morning star.

"Keep your hands free," Mann cautioned, but felt the beckon of his own weapons, as his gaze now was drawn to what he had – lost in thought – overlooked. There were holes all about the cliff face, worn strangely smooth at the edges. In places, the moonlight caught traces of some residue coating the shiny black stone.

"Wind does not carve such hollows," whispered Hel, and the rising alarm in her voice sent Mann's skin to prickling.

"Keep moving," said Mann. He returned to the way forwards and froze in front of a quivering mouth, a toothless slit slick with strands of thick saliva, and a pair of sickle-moon mandibles that clicked as they gnawed against one another.

From a burrow ahead of Mann, a long body of glistening segments had curved out into the night and twisted towards him. Twitching insectoid legs lined the length of its articulated mass. There were no eyes visible in its face, if it could be said to possess such a thing. Just a rectangle of hungry darkness, and shiny black pincers to feed it.

It drove into him – flattening him onto the stone – faster than he could draw his swords, so instead he caught its trembling mandibles, one in each hand, and pushed against their fervent attempts to draw him into that tunnel of stinging acid.

"Hah!" cried Gul, and crashed his morning star upon its head. It released Mann at once, its bulk slapping against the ledge and writhing side to side, thick and stinking ichor spilling from its split chitin.

Gul cried out again – not the triumphant war cry of before – now full of hurt and rage. Mann twisted, scrambling to free his swords, and watched as Gul was yanked from his feet, his face cracking on hard stone. A second burrow behind him had extruded its own hidden horror, and sickle pincers were now dragging Gul's feet into the hungering void.

Mann found his footing, twin blades half drawn, when the blind flailing of the wounded worm smashed him against the cliff. His swords clattered on stone, and Mann slipped from the edge. His feet went out from under him, into the high chill of the night, out over the soaring depth. He caught the ledge, split his cheek against the stone, felt the shock crash through his body at the sudden stop.

The worm waved its segmented length above him, its pincers like devil horns silhouetted against the moon. Its cry was shrill and sorrowful, a lament for those soon to be consumed. Then it choked and went rigid, a beam transfixing its body. The shaft of a spear, its moon-washed tip punching through and through.

Hel Strumm wrenched the spear clear. The worm collapsed, like a taut chain loosed of its tension, one link crashing down after the next, and its bulk slithered over the edge, its hidden length spilling from the burrow like a magician's ribbon, until it was expended, and burst apart on the ground below.

The spear spun in Hel's grip, and came down like a stake through the head of the second worm, right between Gul's legs and out through the bottom of its mouth. Freed from the ravening of its jaws, Gul twisted and grabbed hold of its still quivering mandibles. His arms bulged, and he tore the pincers apart, splitting the worm's skewered head down the middle.

Hel loomed over Mann's dangling body, and returned his half smile.

"Easy," she said, and then membranous and bony wings extended out behind Hel, framing her against the starry night sky. She saw the warning in Mann's eyes a fraction of a second before two talons folded over her shoulders, and those wings beat the air, and she was carried off the edge of the cliff face and out over the valley below, thrashing in the grip of something huge and winged.

"Hel!" Mann roared, but his hands were pressed white and bloodless to the ledge.

Gul kicked his way clear of the dead worm, ripped a spike of rock from the cliff and launched it after the winged thing, but it was already too far, and the stone tumbled aimlessly out of view. So he bellowed his rage into the dark.

"Help me, damn it!" yelled Mann, and Gul reached

down and pulled him bodily onto the ledge. Mann found his swords and rose to his feet on unsteady legs.

"I can't see her!" cried Gul, and Mann barged into the stout man, flattening him against the cliff as a second set of talons sliced through the night where Gul had been a second before.

The crack and howl of wings was all around them. Something screeched and tore against the rocks, flapping to arrest its errant momentum, but it was not alone. From above and below, crooked talons clipped and cracked against the stone, and winged forms larger than a man lurched along the jagged cliff face, their slender bodies thick with wiry bristles, their bulging black eyes glinting in the silver light.

They snapped with jutting lower jaws, and swiped with claw tipped wings, enclosing the two men in a web of veiny wings. Mann and Gul were pressed back to back, swatting and slashing against the fang-filled darkness.

Something was squelching and shifting by their feet. Mann spared a glance, even as claws clattered from his crossed blades. The other dead worm was being dragged from its burrow by one of the winged creatures, its hungry attempts to free the meal thwarted by heavy swings from Gul's morning star.

"Leave them to it," roared Mann, gesturing along the ledge. "Break for it!"

They barged clear of the enclosing wings, leading with the unfriendly edges of their weapons, but the creatures did not follow. As the two men staggered free across the ledge, they could hear the crunching and snapping of the winged beasts as they tore into the slain worm. Mann did not stop, not until there was neither sound nor sight of the feast. Only then did they allow themselves respite, and even then warily so, for they were still suspended forty feet above the ground, on a narrow walkway of crumbling stone, and surrounded even here by hungry mouths lurking in hidden lairs.

"Damn it, Silver," Gul said, breathing out through his nose like an enraged bull.

Mann felt that same bottled rage burning in his veins. He wanted nothing more than to go back, to slash the wings from every devil out there, to find their nests and set them to the flame, for all the good it would do. All that anger, worthless in its attempt to mask the wretched truth. They would never find Hel. Not under the blinding sheath of night. Not across the impossible verticality of the cliffs. Not against the speed and freedom of the wings of her captor.

He saw her face then, uninvited in his mind's eye. He saw the fear in her eyes at the prospect of the climb, the uncertainty at the mad confidence of his plan. His stupid, mad plan. Mann grit his teeth.

"We press on."

V. The Blood You Wanted

It would be insanity to attempt an assault by way of the cliffs. Everyone knew that only the Pilgrims dared to climb, and they were, well, insane. Even if someone did have the stones to brave such an approach, the logistics of it were simply impractical. To equip and train a force to scale the treacherous heights, and to do so in large enough numbers to make an attack effective? Such a manoeuvre would hardly be cost effective, and surely would be spotted well in advance. Unless it was executed by night, but who would countenance making that climb in the dark? Not to mention the things that lived in the cliffs. Things that were easily enough kept at bay by torch and pyre, but less easily deterred in their own territory.

The whole prospect was unthinkable, and therefore went unthought. So when Gul dropped off the cliff face from ten feet above the top of the wall, and landed boots first on the head of the closest archer, that man died entirely without expecting it.

Silver came down behind him, hit the walkway in a roll to break his fall, came out of it with twin blades thrust forward. He impaled the next red-armoured archer through the chest, and killed the cry of alarm that was rising from his lungs.

They did not stop. They were full of fury. Fury that, like a flood, sought release, a ruddy red release that would sweep away all before it until its force was expended. That relief was a long way off.

Across the top of the wall they went, with all the crippling force of surprise, leapfrogging from kill to kill. The sentries died quickly, stunned by shock. Gul drove upwards with his morning star, crashed it into one man's chin, lifted him off his feet and onto his back. Silver took the lead, one slash following the next, sending little squares of red-dyed lamellar spilling into the air as armour sundered under steel. Then back to Gul, who, with a wide swing, bludgeoned a sentry in the side of the head and sent his senses permanently to flight. Back to Silver: a precise decapitating strike that sent a helmed head toppling from the rampart. On and on, step by step, a bloody path towards the gatehouse.

This was a weakness of the wall. Against an enemy who approached in a frontal assault, the wall provided for the defender elevation and surface area from which a row of archers could rain death, side by side. If that enemy approached side-on, however, the narrow walkway of the wall became its own enemy. The archers could no longer shoot upon the same target, not without risking the ally who had once been beside him; now in front of him, blocking his sight. In this way the wall ceased to be a force multiplier, diminishing the advantage of numbers, and became instead a channel of death, forcing the archers to face the melee one by one, ill-equipped for such close combat and reeling from surprise in the drowsy hour before dawn.

It did not take long. Speed, surprise and the cover of darkness got them to the upper gatehouse with little more than a muffled cry from the sentries. The last archer on this half of the wall turned to flee at the sight of his slain comrades. He pulled open the barred door that led into the gatehouse, then threw up his hands as Mann's sword came spinning out of the night and buried itself in his spine.

Mann leapt over the body, unsheathing from it his blade in the same movement. Under the roof of the gatehouse was a walkway that overlooked the inside of the gate. The gate itself was two feet of solid wood, not secured with bolt or bar, but by a winch attached to a chain. When turned, the winch could hoist the entire gate off the ground. It was no wonder Kirhon's host had failed to breach. This gate could not be forced wide or battered apart. It would have to be split open, and Kirhon had no tools to that effect.

There were five servants here, hunched on the walkway around the winch. They were dregs of men, clothed in rags, bedraggled and filthy, hugging their knees or curled foetal on the floor. They had been sleeping, but Mann's last kill set them to stirring.

"To work with you, wretches," threatened Gul, brandishing his club towards the winch. The servants dragged themselves up, their backs bent and arms hanging slack. They lurched and twitched, strange noises grating in their throats.

"These are no men," said Silver.

The closest servant flicked up its head. Milky membranes slid sideways across eyes that were yellow and slitted. Its lower jaw unhinged, and it hissed through a mouth that opened wider than any should. There were fangs in that mouth, needle hooks that had split through human teeth.

Mann cut off its head. The others pounced, clawing with half-reptile hands, patches of scale glistening in the flickering torchlight. Gul swung his morning star two-handed and knocked the next snake-man over the edge of the walkway. Its body fell limply to the ground below. His return swing bounced the third servant off of the wall. Mann cut down the fourth with a flurry of three overlapping slashes, and impaled the fifth on the blades of both swords. It leaned in close, drawing itself along the steel to hiss at Mann's face. Gul crushed its skull with a hammer blow.

"Who's going to open the gate now?" Gul complained.

Mann looked sideways at him and shrugged. "You're a big man."

Gul grunted and dropped his club, grabbing hold of the huge winch with both hands, his arms spread wide, the muscles of his back bunching tight. It was a mechanism designed to lift the great weight of the gate, and five creatures had been stationed here to that sole purpose, but when Gul pushed, the winch creaked and began to turn. The chains screeched and rattled, and the slab-like gate inched up from the ground.

"I'll send for Kirhon," said Mann. He turned to salvage a bow from the slain archers, when the door at the other end of the gatehouse opened, and a sentry poked in his head.

"What are you half-wits doing in here," began the man, then froze. His widening eyes travelled from the slaughtered half-men up to the straining Gul. A warning cry was rising to his lips. Mann surged across the walkway and rammed shoulder first into the door. The sentry's head was hammered between stone frame and iron-banded door. His eyes rolled into his skull and he slumped face first into the floor.

"Hurry along now, Gul, we're about to have company."

Gul's neck was taut with hard tendons, his teeth barred. "I don't see you pushing!"

"I have to entertain our guests," said Mann.

Two more sentries resolved out of the darkness, drawn by the rattling of the rising gate. There was barely space on the wall-top for two men to stand abreast, and Mann could see them jostling for a better view, squinting against the torchlight. They came within five feet before their fire-blind eyes recognised that the man approaching them was not one of their own. Mann was hindered by no such confusion. Gul was in the gatehouse, which meant that anyone else he saw was an enemy. That clarity of information gave him a two second advantage over the guards, who were slowed by the unexpected.

The difference of two seconds meant that Silver had closed the distance before the first archer even had his bow up. He drove in with a blade, but the point snagged against the lamellar armour and turned aside. The guard behind angled a dagger over his comrade's shoulder and drove it at Silver's neck. He parried it with his second sword, and the fight became an awkward grapple as the three men were caught tangled in the narrow space.

Behind him, Silver could hear the ongoing rattle of Gul's labours. As loud as the rising gate sounded here, there was no guarantee that Kirhon's men could hear it wherever they were, hiding somewhere in the night beyond the perimeter of warding pyres. Their assault relied on the signal that Silver had promised, but the element of surprise was fading, and even now the garrison would be rousing to the clamour. Then, out of the crisp night air, two balls of fire came howling down towards them. It would have been suspicious, of course, for the besiegers to cease their otherwise routine bombardment. Such a change would have suggested to the besieged that plans were afoot, and sharpened their senses against surprise. So Kirhon had left behind his artillery crews to continue their routine.

One of the clay pots struck the other half of the wall, where dead archers lay unbothered. The second pot – because the universe was nothing if not unfortunate – struck the wall six feet below Mann, and washed the three entangled men with a wave of burning tar. Fat globules of sticky fire splattered their armour, and sizzled where it found uncovered flesh. Naturally, this did not stop them from trying to kill Mann.

The first archer was still trying to nock an arrow, which had become slightly more difficult now that he was on fire, while the second was relentless in his attempts to land the dagger over his comrade's shoulder. Mann caught the repeated blows against his sword, but the closeness of the melee was working against the reach of his blades.

In moments of action, the man who kept his wits was the man who survived. It was all too easy to give in to the mindless rage of instinct, to become locked into a single panicked course of repetition. Against the scorching flames and killing fury, Silver stayed calm. He timed the frantic stabbing of the foe's dagger, let his sword drop, and caught the sentry's wrist, dragging him off balance and slamming his arm against the battlements. The dagger spun away over the edge.

Silver twisted the arm, looped it round over the other archer's neck, locked the two men against one another, using their imbalanced weight against them. He relinquished his second blade, and instead grabbed hold of the arrow in the archer's hand. The man looked at him, eyes wide, caught somewhere between sheer panic and utter confusion. Silver forced the tip of the arrow into a patch of burning tar, and helped the archer nock it to the bowstring.

Between the close press of their three bodies, there was no space for a full draw, so Mann strapped the bow across the archer's face, and pulled back on the bowstring with his free hand, using the poor man's head as the point of resistance. He released the string, heard the crack of it slapping the back of the archer's head, and watched as the nocked arrow scored a red line across his cheek and flew wobbling into the night sky.

Weighted with burning tar and strangely sent, the arrow flew poorly, listing off to one side and turning into a spinning descent, but it had still flown, a burning arrow against the dark. A signal to bring the army.

Mann, still grappling either man, braced his boot heels against them and pushed off hard, sending them toppling over one another into an ungainly and burning heap. Mann landed on his back and thrashed against the stone to extinguish the flames clinging to his clothes. Then, kicking off the floor onto his feet, he recovered his blades and backed away towards the gatehouse. Arrows whistled out of the night and snapped against the battlements around him. The remaining archers were now fully aware of his presence.

Slipping around the door in time to hear a half dozen arrows stick fast in the wood, Mann pulled it shut and slammed the locking bar into place. Gul was still here, his full weight thrown upon the winch, his veiny arms bulging as he forced one rotation into another. Mann joined him, sheathing his swords and hauling on the winch.

Then came the thunder of boots, and Mann looked over the walkway to see Kirhon's host charging in under the gate and towards the encamped garrison on the far side. Mann locked the winch in place with its iron bar, and slapped Gul on the back. The stout man slumped against the winch, breathing hard, skin glistening with sweat.

"Let's go," Mann said, as heavy blows rattled the barred door. Gul nodded, and they picked their way over the snake-men bodies and out onto the half of the wall along which they had come.

From the battlements, they watched as Kirhon's host drove into the ordered rows of tents, where the garrison had been scrambling from their slumber. They were a wild bunch, this motley of warriors drawn from across the Heartscars, savage and undisciplined. They made a terrible mess of things, collapsing tents over half-dressed soldiers and setting them alight, swinging and slashing their way through the reeling resistance.

It would bring swift defeat to underestimate the martial doctrine of the Red Men. Their armies fought lock-step, protected by overlapping ranks of shields, and driving down their enemies against a wall of spears. When the Red Men chose to make war, history recorded few losses. Their strength was in discipline and order, and this night that was the cause of their defeat. Caught by surprise, unable to close their formations, these perfectly drilled soldiers were overcome by Kirhon's unruly band of warriors. The generals of the West would flinch, no doubt, to hear of this defeat at the hands of fighters who, if asked, would trip over themselves trying to form a straight line.

Mann scanned the battlefield by the warming light of dawn, and noted a larger tent at the rear, furthest from the wall, staked upon a shelf of land that overlooked the encampment.

"We should find their commander, before Kirhon's butchers make meat of him," said Mann, moving towards the steps that led down the inside of the wall.

"Why?" asked Gul, a note of petulance in his voice. The loss of Hel was fresh, and Mann knew he would have to address that before long, but to stop now – in the midst of battle – would be a fatal folly.

"Information," said Mann, flying down the stone steps two at a time. "Answers."

"You should have said vengeance," said Gul, following close behind.

They made a beeline through the carnage, following the wake of Kirhon's host to avoid any of the stiffening resistance along the edges of the battle. When they reached the ridge, they followed it away from the main concentration of the encampment, and used roots and rocks to clamber to the top. There they found the command tent, much larger than it had appeared from the wall, more of a multi-sectioned marquee.

At the front of the structure they caught a glimpse of Red Men marshalling, those furthest from the wall who had not suffered the immediate rampage of the attack. Their response was good, their recovery from shock admirable, but Mann thought there were too few of them now to make a difference. At the least, they would put up a good fight holding the ridge, but Kirhon would win this day all the same.

Mann had no interest in that particular fight. With Gul in tow, they slipped around the back of the marquee and carved through the thick fabric. They ducked in through the opening, and at once wished they had not.

VI. Sorcerer of Scales

There was a woman, naked and spread-eagled. She was affixed within a hoop of brass, itself supported upon a stand, its legs carved to appear as coiling serpents. Her eyes were wide with terror, but her mouth had been covered to contain her fear. An incision had been made, down the seam of the ribcage between the breasts. The parted skin had been pinned open, revealing a square of slick flesh over bone.

"What depravity is this?" asked Gul, circling the tilted hoop and its prisoner.

"The bindings," said Mann, pointing to where the woman was fastened to a crossbeam within the hoop. "We free her."

"Freedom is paltry when put before purpose."

The voice was deep but soft, and at once commanded their attention. From the partition into this section of the marquee had come a woman, tall and flowing in robes of emerald and red. In one hand she gripped a staff of ebony, topped with the skull of a serpent. In the other she balanced a small platter of polished silver, and upon it a single black scale.

Mann's gaze flicked from the platter to the prisoner, her flesh precisely laid bare, an incision made to purpose.

"You are the architect of this corruption," he said, circling towards the robed woman.

"Such flattery." She laughed, a rich and sultry sound, and bowed her head in formal greeting, though her bright green eyes never left them. "I am Kashiva, and I am but humble servant."

"I would reckon with your master," growled Gul.

"And you shall," she declared with confidence. "As all men will."

"Surrender yourself," said Mann. "Your soldiers fall as we speak."

"I have a greater force still," she countered, her demeanour unwavering.

"We have faced your wretches already," said Gul. "They offered no sport."

Kashiva raised a contoured eyebrow, amusement plain on her pursed lips. "The gatehouse? Poor offcasts. Transformation is a divine process. Not all are worthy, though lesser purpose is purpose still. Perhaps you would like to see a purer form?"

She closed her eyes, and a low whisper filled the room, sourceless and sibilant. Mann knew sorcery when he saw it. He charged Kashiva. Gul did the same on the far side of the hoop. The curtain at Kashiva's back parted, and a blur of black and yellow scales swept forth, covering her as she withdrew from the room.

They had seen beasts such as this once before. At the carnival in the Galgath Crux, though then there had been but one of them. Now there were three. Hideous amalgams of man and snake, smaller than the carnival hybrid, but no less vile. Their shapes were not uniform. One rose on a serpent's tail, without legs, its vestigial arms held close beneath a snake head that was grossly enlarged. The second had retained its human form, but skin had given way to scale, and tooth to fang. The third could no longer stand upright, and had almost entirely abandoned its origins, save for the eyes, still human, looking wide and trapped in its new serpentine form.

The chorus of disembodied whispers had not faded, and the snake-men danced to its call, striking towards Silver and

Gul with whip-like speed. The first slithered towards Silver, leading with the fangs of its slack jaw. The second leapt at Gul, while the third looped around the base of the hoop and turned its head from side to side, seeking opportunity.

Gul met the leap with his morning star, batting the snake-man to the ground. It bounced up and straight back at him, as though it felt no pain. He bludgeoned it a second time, then a third, each blow throwing it aside, only for it to snap back like elastic.

Silver dropped into a side-roll to evade the open mouth. It went past him, then spun on its coiled tail, just in time to meet crossed blades. Steel met scale. They were tougher still than lamellar plates, and recorded little damage. Silver drove into it, a whirlwind of practised strikes, one slash feeding into the next. The snake-man recoiled, slipping away on its whipping tail, screeching displeasure from a hanging jaw.

Across the room, Gul caught his opponent on the skull with a hammer blow, and flattened it face first into the ground. The third snake-man saw its moment, and pounced from the hoop. Its jaws closed around Gul's shoulder, and its tail coiled around his body, locking his weapon arm flat against his side. The other snake-man staggered from the ground, blood running down its scaled human face, and leapt onto Gul, dragging them all into the dirt.

Silver saw it happen in the corner of his eye. He needed distraction, some moment to create space so that he could free Gul before the snake-men tore him to pieces. There were a collection of tables around the edges of the room, some long and narrow, others small and round, all of them cluttered with bottles of different shapes and sizes. He darted towards the closest, to scoop up something that would hopefully break horribly in the snake-man's face.

The thing about combat, alas, was that your enemy was rarely happy to let you act unopposed. The snake-man's tail felt like an iron bar as it whipped into Silver's back. Such was the force that it lifted him from his feet and dropped him through the closest table, breaking it in half and smashing every bottle beneath him. The snake-man wormed towards him, giving no pause, lowering its misshapen head to enfold him within its mouth.

So Silver did the worst possible thing that a swordsman could do. He disarmed himself. From the ground, he threw his first blade. It went end over end, and because such a weapon was not designed to be thrown, it struck the snake-man pommel first, square in the nose. Its head snapped back, and the uneven weight of its malformed skull dragged its upper body with it, so that its spine folded over its tail, as if it had been snapped in two.

Silver knew better than to hope it was anything but fleetingly stunned. He leapt to his feet, and with both hands over his head, threw the second blade. This time the throw was sublime. It struck the scaled man clawing over Gul. It struck the wretch point on. The force of it drove the sword into the scaled man's midriff, beneath the ribcage, and knocked it sideways.

An almighty bellow shook the air. Gul hauled himself to his feet, dragging the weight of the constricting serpent with him, and forced his arms outwards, like a man straining against a coil of rope. He broke the snake-man's grip, took hold of its tail, and spun on his heel, swinging the creature like he was performing a hammer throw. Gul released and sent it crashing through a row of tables.

The scaled man was rising to its feet, sword still jutting from its flank. The grotesque was rising too, its bulbous head hanging like a dead-weight as the rest of its serpentine body straightened. They were no less resilient than the carnival hybrid it seemed, despite their smaller stature. Perhaps, Silver thought with growing dread, they still had room to grow.

He dived into a roll to scoop up one fallen sword, and caught the second as Gul freed it from the snake-man and tossed it back to him. They were having the same thought. Both men ducked out of the marquee and into the smoke-wreathed dawn. Below them, the camp was ablaze. At the foot of the ridge, Kirhon's host was crashing against the last stand of the Red Men.

Their escape routes were equally bad. An ankle-breaking drop from the top of the ridge, or almost certain death through the back of the Red Men line. Their hesitation ate their head start, and they turned back to the marquee as the three snake-men tore through the slit fabric. They were slowed and bleeding, but the hunger in their eyes was no less bright.

"I really hate these things," said Mann, widening his stance and flourishing the twin blades. Gul stepped up beside him, morning star clutched in both hands. He shared a grim nod with his friend.

"I would say otherwise, but this is a shit place to die," Gul said, and they both laughed as the snake-men charged.

The shadow of wings swept overhead. It came with the sharp whistle of sliced air. They gave pause, man and snake alike. Then the whistling grew yet louder, but this time it was not wings cutting the air, but the point of a spear. Cast from above, with all the speed and force of its fall, the spear hit the scaled man dead centre. The spear punched through its chest like a nail delivered by godly hammer blow, and stuck fast in the ground, staking there the scaled man into the earth, still half upright against the shaft.

Turning fearful eyes skyward, the snake-men had only a second to realise their doom. Black talons flattened them against the dirt and curled tight against their scaled flesh. With the heavy beat of wings, the cliff-haunter took to the air, hefting with it the dangling snake-men in either talon. In the second before it fled to the shadows of the cliff, a figure dropped from its back.

"Hel!" roared both Silver and Gul, and they tore across the ground towards her, throwing around her their arms.

"You both stink," she said, laughing even as she reeled from their crushing embrace. They broke away, staring at her with staggered awe.

"How did you do that?" demanded Gul, almost indignant.

Hel looked up at the sky, where the winged creature was just visible against the black cliffs, dipping in the air as it struggled with the greedy weight of its catch. "Oh, that? The motivation of food and sheer fucking will."

"Hel," said Silver quietly, his voice strained.

She regarded him kindly, her eyes caught somewhere between sorrow and sympathy. Then she frowned and brushed at his dark leather armour. "You look terrible."

"I might have been on fire," he said, "very briefly."

They laughed, the three of them, clutching at each other's shoulders.

"Never again," promised Silver, glancing at the towering height of the cliffs.

"Oh, I don't know," said Hel. "It wasn't that bad."

They shared a look, Mann Silver and Hel Strumm, enough to communicate between them every unspoken thing.

Gul broke away to inspect the scaled man, still impaled by the marquee. It was still twitching. "These things die hard."

"Just like the one at the carnival," said Hel, her eyes wide as she studied the creature.

"Yes," said Silver, "and now we know they fight for the Red Men."

"How?" asked Hel.

"Sorcery," spat Gul.

"A witch by name of Kashiva, who possesses the means to make more of their kind."

"Here?" Hel asked, and gripped her spear.

Mann stayed her with a hand on her shoulder. He looked down to the ramp of the ridge, where the last of the Red Men were breaking before Kirhon's host. "Long gone, I imagine. Fled on the time bought by dead men."

Silver sheathed one sword, and took the other in a two-handed grip. Affixed in place, the scaled man made for a much easier target, and Silver took off its head with one mighty swing. Hel braced her boot on its lifeless husk, and ripped free the spear. As its head rolled to a stop in the dirt, Mann noticed that low and sibilant whispering fall to silence.

"It would be bad for everyone if they made more of these things," she said.

"Just another reason to go west," replied Silver.

"I remember when we used to get paid for this sort of thing," said Gul.

"They made it personal. First with assassins, now with... these."

"Besides," said Hel, slapping Gul on the back. "Whoever has coin enough for assassins *and* sorcerers likely has lots to spare for us, too. Willingly or otherwise."

"Yes, yes," Gul said, swatting away their persuasions. "But first, Kirhon promised us a feast, and I intend to collect!"

"I'll drink to that," said Silver.

The three of them set off, towards the cheers of the victorious, and into the new dawn.

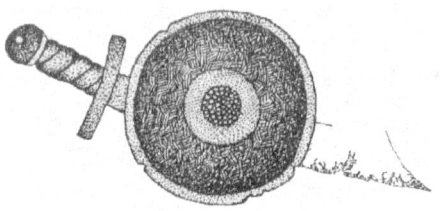

MIDWINTER
David A. Sutton

The winter was *cold* that year.

I had come to my place during autumn, when the trees were wreathed in a mist that brought to mind harrowing memories. Their branches dripped with sorrowful tears as if they were aware that some great disaster had befallen man. Only the apple trees in the grove were still joyous with fruit and I was able to feast in that sacred place, and lick my wounds.

I arrived with the furs of my raiment torn and stained with dried blood, and I likened myself to the living roe deer that is spiked with spears and struggles in its death throes. My ritual feathers were scalped, my headdress resembling an inexpertly plucked hen. Across my shoulder I clutched my leather satchel, but no longer was there left in it any of the apparatus of my profession.

But the cavern beyond the sacred grove on Hart Fell gave me shelter and the fruits and berries of the forest were my succour.

And winter came...

The solstice night was marked by a blizzard that left a deep carpet of glistening snow throughout the spinney, and the pines on the mountain slopes bowed from the pressure of their fresh, thick white coats. The night should have been one for celebration. Ah, those past years, when I played to my audience with tricks and truths, and brought in the new season. There would be feasting and drinking; there would be the sacrifice and magic... Now no one visited the hallowed grove of apple trees and I spent that night at the mouth of my cave in sombre mood, transfixed as the crescent moon scooped away silver snow-clouds before it, as if it were a giant's spoon. Although I shivered, I hoped someone would come this way and visit me. Anyone, with whom I might celebrate. They could sit at the fire which burned still within the cave and I would feed them the divine mushrooms and broth and tell them old stories. Even a Christian, yes, I would welcome even a disciple of Gildas on that loneliest of nights. For I had not seen a living human soul since the eighth month.

By dawn my limbs were ready to crack and my beard was stiff with freezing air. Behind me the fire had died and I too wished to allow myself that luxury. If I sat a little while longer and allowed sleep to overcome me, I might become my spirit self. Then I should fly, fly as the peregrine with its keen eye. Soar as the gull on broad motionless wings, buoyed by currents of air. Streak as the swift and journey to a far country where death might at last claim my soul. Instead an eternity of sour memories left me distraught and wide-awake.

As I pondered upon my desires, I became aware of movement among the fruit trees and my mood was disturbed. Yet there was no lumbering human form about to greet me.

Unexpectedly, a stag came and gazed quietly upon me, motionless except for the cloudy tempest from his nostrils. He was a giant, his brown fur shaggy in winter cloak, his antlers convoluted and rearing above the tallest frozen branches of the apple trees. Presently, he passed by. When the wolf followed the stag and gleamed his yellow eye upon me, without fear, yet without malice, I knew not to disregard the omen. He was so large a wolf I thought I might have fitted into his belly with little discomfort. But if he was hungry, it was not for human meat, and the wolf went about his business.

The strange behaviour of the two lords of the forest galvanised me into standing up so that I could warm my limbs with activity, and presently I set off to collect wood to re-light the fire.

The foot-worn track, leading from the glade down the slope of the mountain, was invisible beneath the snow. I was forced to use trees to mark my way, and eventually came to the naked bluff which overlooks the pass between the high peak of Hart Fell and its distant cousin. A hundred feet below me a stream cascaded, deep cut into the rock and overhung with icicles. Beside it a path mimicked its course, but hidden beneath snowdrifts. Further down the pass, in more clement weather, could be seen where the track diverged, one fork leading up here, to the sacred grove.

I stood for a moment and gazed gloomily across the ravine to the distant snow peak. The wind was sharp, carrying with it tiny ice crystals that stung my face. Ice sculpted one massive slope and drew the eye down along its grandeur. And my eye was thus caught by movement deep in the valley.

Seeming no larger than a blackbird at the distance, its clothes flapping as though the bird was injured, someone was laboriously struggling up the valley. He bore a staff with which he prodded the snow before attempting to take a step into what might be a deep crevasse. A wise precaution, even though I knew the route was safe.

I watched for a considerable time as the wanderer strove up the valley towards the higher slopes. I wondered where he was heading with such determination. Stopping for a while, he lay on his stomach before the stream and reached out his hands to cup a drink of water. He took several. The weather was bitingly cold, but the man must have been thirsty with so difficult a task manoeuvring himself through the drifts. My thoughts were on the whole quite idle and so it was a great surprise when I saw the traveller veer away from the stream, which gave him at least guidance, and head up the incline which led to the apple grove. Within minutes he was hidden among trees, but I did not doubt his intention. Unless he was mad and had wandered off the path through the blinding effect of the snow, the man was *intending* to come this way.

The traveller must know of the hallowed glade of the apples in the mountains of Caledonia.

Realising I had held my breath in astonishment, I exhaled a cloud of mist, which turned to minute droplets in the wind and was carried off. Hastily I moved away from the crag and began to scour for dead branches. In a while I had a bundle of wood, which I tied together with some strips of leather I had brought with me. I then returned to the cave, staggering under the weight of my burden.

Although in my misery I had allowed my fire to dwindle, I found that there remained an ember, bright under charred timbers. With the few dry twigs that remained I coaxed a flame and hunched shadows of myself were cast familiarly about the walls of the cave. I unstrapped the bundle of wood and selecting the least sodden pieces, I placed these close to the fire to dry. I busied myself and felt curiously nervous at the thought of welcoming a visitor into my lonely existence.

As I tidied my living quarters and immersed myself in commonplace thoughts, the traveller approached unnoticed. Only when his shadow momentarily screened off half the daylight from the cleft of the cave's narrow opening did I realise he had entered.

I turned.

The being before me was dressed from head to foot in rags. No warming furs covered shoulders or legs or feet. And his head was completely hooded from the weather with simple cloth, its weave impossible to have held at bay the ravening wind.

I shivered in horror for the dreadful torment this traveller must have suffered.

And my visitor shivered too. He was short in stature, though not as diminutive as I, and meagre of bone and muscle. Without a word he dropped to his knees before the fire, which now crackled cheerfully. The traveller stretched out his hands, which were small and quite white with the cold. A skin of ice, which had been welded by the tempest to one side of his garments, now began to fall away and melt on the floor.

I stepped towards the fire, so that the frozen being might see me better, thinking that perhaps he was unaware that I was, at that time, in residence.

"Welcome, stranger." When I spoke, I found my voice hoarse and high of pitch, so long was it since I had uttered a word to any living soul. "Welcome," I repeated, coughing first to clear my throat.

Without speaking, and with one trembling hand, the frozen traveller slowly slid back the soiled hood covering its face; and for the second time that morning I was astonished.

For my uninvited guest was a young woman.

*

After an hour she wordlessly accepted and drank some of the broth I had heated above the fire. I sat opposite to her and watched her through the flames as she shuddered and shivered away the last lingering chill that must have penetrated to her very soul. Her hunched shoulders visibly relaxed, as did her bent back. Her bone-white fingers clutching the soup bowl regained some of their natural flexibility. I saw all this, but it was her face to which my attention returned. She was noble of feature, with clear, pale skin; beneath heavy eyebrows, large, dark eyes gleamed despondently. Her cheekbones were high and her nose wide, as were her lips. She had her long black hair tied at the back.

She spoke at last, and her voice was pleasing to my ear.

"I am Olwyn," she told me. "And you?"

I hesitated. Though months had elapsed since the awful day, whose events I strove to forget, I paused to give my true name. The guilty are rarely forgotten.

"Lleu," I said, lying. And eager to know the reason for her travail to this neglected region, I continued, "You have obviously tormented yourself to the point of death reaching this place! To make such a pilgrimage in this weather..?"

"Were you at the battle of Arderydd?" she asked, ignoring my comments.

Her question stung me more that she could know, but of course I kept my emotions concealed.

"Why do you ask? It was many months ago and most would rather forget..."

"*Tell me*," she demanded. Her eyes became fierce with an inner light, but it was not an anger she aimed in my direction.

"Yes. I was," I confessed.

"They say," Olwyn continued, "that king Gwenddolau was a fool to trust the shaman in his dotage."

My heart shook with grief and horror at her words. My king, my patron, had been slain at Arderydd, by his Christianised foe, King Rhydderch. Even so, Gwenddolau's blood was on *my* hands.

"You seem to have much knowledge of the defeat of Gwenddolau" I said, struggling to maintain a voice measured and without sentiment. "Were you a fighter?"

"No." She spat into the fire and there was a sizzling explosion behind her next words. "My husband was."

I guessed the rest. "He was slain too," I said, thinking that perhaps only now had she succumbed to the need to sojourn to a sacred place, where she might mourn his passing.

"In my arms he died. He lived to tell the battle's tale, lived close to death for three months. Yet he rallied and seemed to recover a little from his wounds, and I rejoiced. But after our love was consummated anew, he faded... and never awoke to express his love again. Barely a month has passed since."

"I lament for you in your distress. But it is right that you speak of your husband. I can see that you have remained silent for too long. There will be solace in talking about him." Carefully, I then asked her, "What else did he tell you of Arderydd?"

Olwyn sat for a while, her eyes roving the fire, yellow miniatures of the flames reflected in those melancholy orbs. Wiping the dirty sleeve of her ragged coat across her eyes, to stem the first wellspring of tears, she made to speak, but stopped herself.

She was dwelling upon her husband, but try as I might to deflect my own thoughts to that subject, instead the sound of battle clamoured through my brain. The field of Arderydd, soaked in blood; Liddel Water running with blood; Gwenddolau's fortress hard by... splattered with blood...

After a while, she said, "They say *he* was a giant. But ancient."

I knew of whom she spoke. Her mind nagged at the failure of the shaman as her tongue might continually prod the iron-taste cavity of a pulled tooth. She wanted reasons, answers, redress.

"Myrddin?" I asked in a voice as innocent as I could muster.

"The same. Seven feet tall, eight maybe. My husband said—"

"Did he see him?" I interrupted, and hoped the speed with which I did so would not arouse in her any suspicion. In any event, it was clear her husband had not clapped eyes on Gwenddolau's shaman. Unless legend had fooled him into short-sightedness!

"My husband said he was a giant. That he carried sorcery like a cloak about him, but he was very old. At the end, how bitter was my man for the faith he placed in him!"

"Yes he was elderly," I conceded. "Many centuries. And actually, wise for it."

"Those long years weakened him." Her voice was waspish, yet she spoke with assurance, as if she knew her words captured the truth. And I was stabbed to the heart with how perceptive indeed they were.

"Perhaps it was not Myrddin's great age that sapped him of his powers. Perhaps it was the Romans and their priests... The new faith has made us all weak. Hadrian may have built his wall to protect his empire from the thirteen kings of the north, but still the Christians ventured beyond it, and their miasma has swept aside many of our kind."

Olwyn replied bitterly, "There were heroic stories, of

Myrddin. How could a few Christians defeat the one who raised the stones and made them fly? And who nurtured King Arthur to greatness?"

"Those accomplishments were many years ago," I responded angrily. She could not have guessed why, though perhaps she wondered at the harshness of my response.

"What of Myrddin? You seek him too, eh? Else why are you here, living a hermit's life? This was his place, you know it!"

The conversation had moved on. "Do you then seek him also?" I asked.

"To... to *kill*... perhaps."

Ah, she wished to avenge her husband. How her anguish stained me. The battle of Arderydd had been fought on the pinnacle of my confident predictions, on the promise of the gathering of a spiritual host who, emerging from a supernatural vapour I raised, would take Gwenddolau's forces through to Rhydderch's mere human host... and defeat them. But the Celtic spirits failed to materialise and the bodies on the field of Arderydd were those of the army that marched with Gwenddolau. I saw again, in my mind's eye, as the sounds of the dying lay hidden by the fog, the hill behind the fortress rise out of the mist at day's end. The setting sun gleamed on the row of stakes and human skulls I had raised there. And those death's heads glowered down with a vengeful and bloody light upon Arderydd.

And of the druid Myrddin? Should I tell her that I went mad that day? Did she need to know that I had slunk from the field in dishonour? Wounded I might have been, exhausted and scarred from innumerable fights with the enemy, but in disgrace and raving.

"To kill?" My response was sheathed in a haze of self-loathing which, before my eyes, became a wall of congealing blood. "Myrddin is already dead!" Oh how the agony of that desire drove my sad reminiscences to their height.

"*Dead?* How do you know, old man?"

Reply I could not, without admitting the grossness of my deception. Yet, to me, it was a falsehood of little measure, for in myself I *was* surely without life. And if Olwyn murdered me, what satisfaction could she gain for her husband? The satisfaction would, indeed, be all mine.

"His spirit... died in the battle."

"You play with words, Lleu," she replied. "Are you Myrddin's servant? Why else are you here, in his cave, if not to await the return of the shaman?"

My voice was lost. I stared at the embers of the fire and the glowing timbers mesmerised me as I sunk deeper and deeper in despair.

"*Old fool!*" Olwyn jumped up, turned on her heel and stormed out of the cave.

I stared at the place where she had sat and realised there were her shoes, which she had removed in order to dry them. A wisp of steam drifted from the sodden fabric as I stood up to follow her.

I found Olwyn on the crag, which watched over the valley, her bare feet buried in the snow. Her arms were hugged around her and the wind was visibly bending her towards the cliff's edge. Lunging through the snow I came within spitting distance of the strong-willed woman.

Turning to face me, she said, "*You!* I should have realised at once. *You are Myrddin!*"

I watched as her voice fought against the growing tempest. "I cannot kill you now, though my heart aches for revenge. You are too wretched a creature. You are ugly and a dwarf. My husband must have been bewitched."

And all the rest of those brave fighters too, I added to myself.

Did I see into her mind, or did I guess, that Olwyn, having failed to find the courage to murder me, intended to cast herself from the bluff? She shuffled her feet forwards and the slope of loose snow began to carry her towards the precipice. Her arms spiralled, but not to save herself. Instead they tried to propel her the faster, to bring this day to an end for her forever.

I lunged forwards but stumbled into the snow. As a flurry of snow billowed before my eyes, Olwyn tilted out of sight.

Impotently I raged against the stag and the wolf who had presaged these events. And I called to book the spirits of the dead who had failed to ignite Gwenddolau's men in battle fury, cursing them for deserting their charges. And thereby causing yet one more death this day.

After lying in the snow for a short time I lifted myself up, and followed the footprints of Olwyn to the edge of the crag. Peering down through the howling tempest I saw the stag that had earlier visited me. He was nimbly climbing a narrow ledge of rock that had been laid bare by the wind. Lying across his back and clinging on with the determination of one who has recently seen death face-to-face, was Olwyn.

The stag reached the top of the bluff and as Olwyn slipped from his hide, he trotted off into the trees. Quickly, but with some difficulty I carried the half-conscious woman to the cave. As I approached, a wolf—I have no doubt it was the same as I had before seen—came out of the entrance and sloped away.

Once inside and by the fire, I saw the blood and the still warm body of the hare the wolf had left us. That night I roasted it and the hot meat helped revive Olwyn.

"You saved my life," she cried with humility.

Not I, I thought.

"You are truly Lord of the Wild Hunt, Myrddin. If he had seen what happened this day, my husband would surely agree!"

It had been so many years. So many and I had forgotten that the animals of the forest are sometimes bid by my unconscious desires. I knew then that the magic was returned to me.

I gazed upon the woman, conscious of a wonderful certainty beyond her afflicted features. And I knew that the magic of prophecy was also restored to me as a luminous revelation made my eyes bright with tears of joy. The wolf and the stag were an omen of death, *my* death, not long hence, but my *soul* was to be recast nevertheless. And my next utterance was bold with the foreknowledge, and with unrestrained euphoria.

"Eat well and gain strength, Olwyn," I said. "For you are pregnant with your husband's child."

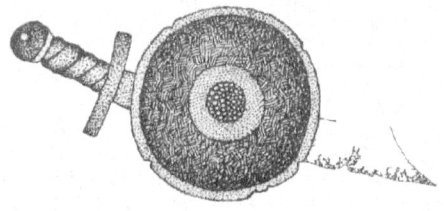

TOMB ROBBERS
Susan Murrie Macdonald

Evon and Arun loved parades. Even though at twenty summers, they were grown men now, not boys. They delighted in parades as much as any child. Military parades, holiday parades, religious parades. Evon and Arun loved the prancing horses and the musicians. The soldiers marching, the dancers, the banners flying, the jugglers. And the opportunities, especially the opportunities. Evon and Arun moved silently through the crowds. No one noticed a stranger jostling them amongst so many parade watchers. Pockets were easy to pick whilst watching a parade.

Although *this* parade was the funeral cortege for the king's favourite wife, it was still rife with opportunities. A squad of orphan girls walked before the priestesses, scattering rose petals on the road. Priestesses danced to please the Goddess … and the men in the crowd. Soldiers marched, their well-shined boots trampling on the rose petal-strewn cobblestones. Golden palomino horses drew the hearse displaying the bejewelled funeral bier.

Evon muttered an unsavoury comment about the dancing priestess. Arun smiled and nodded. An old woman in the crowd slapped both their faces.

"For shame upon you both! Those are sacred priestesses, holy virgins who have dedicated their short lives to the service of the Great Goddess. Show some respect."

"What a shameful waste that such lovely maidens should be virgins," Arun said.

"Worse that they die virgins," a man in the crowd said. "They die today, to serve the queen in the afterlife."

"Truly a waste," Evon agreed. His cousin nodded. Both were tall and slender, with wheat-blond hair and grey eyes; they looked more like brothers than cousins.

"Crude louts," the old woman denounced them. She raised her hand as if to strike them again. Arun caught her upraised arm with one hand. His other hand found her pocket and relieved it of the few coins she carried.

"Oh, no, granny," Arun told her. "Once was enough."

Evon glanced back, where the crowd was thicker. Arun took his meaning. He released the old woman and slipped into the crowd. By the time the old woman realized her pocket was lighter than it had been, both cousins had disappeared into the throng.

"Did you see the gold and rubies on the catafalque?"

"We could live for months on the price of one of those rubies."

"Alas, they're about to go to waste, locked up in the catacombs where none can see them shine."

"And those priestesses, dying to serve a dead queen. Terrible waste."

"Pity we can't go rescue them from their virginity," Evon muttered.

"Who says we can't?" Arun asked. "And maybe rescue a ruby or two while we're at it?"

"We're pickpockets, not grave robbers," Evon reminded him.

"It's past time we moved up in the world. Don't you have any ambition?"

"What I have is hunger and thirst. I need bread and ale."

"C'mon." Arun took a moment to get his bearings, since they'd moved with the crowd at least half a block from where they'd been. "We're near the Black Boar." He led the way to the tavern. Using the silver he'd stolen from the old woman who slapped them, he bought bread, ham, cheese, and ale.

The two sat and ate and quietly, very quietly, discussed the possibility of a career change.

"The catacombs are guarded by death-worms," Evon whispered. "Death-worms and demon-dogs who eat intruders body and soul."

"You're too scrawny to give them a decent meal."

"I don't want to give them a decent meal. I want to get in, grab those jewels, and get out."

Arun shook his head. "You have no ambition."

"My ambition is to die of old age in my own bed."

"I wouldn't mind dying in my own bed with one of those priestesses grateful to me for rescuing her."

"They're probably dead already," Evon suggested. "Choked to death on the foul smells of the catacombs."

Arun nodded. The canals that ran through the royal catacombs connected to the city sewers. The fetid odour kept out tomb robbers as much as the fear of death-worms.

"Death-worms don't exist," Arun whispered back. "It's just a granny-tale to scare naughty children into behaving."

"We'll need a boat," Arun said.

"My friend Bodge has boats." Evon offered.

"Will Bodge let us borrow one?"

"He rents them by the hour. But Bojo would probably give me a discount, since we're friends."

"Rent?" Arun sputtered his ale. "I'm not about to pay for a boat."

Evon reached for the last of the cheese. "We can always borrow it, without asking him."

"Now, you're talking like a thief."

Lowering their voices, they finished their meal and made plans.

An hour later, they were paddling a "borrowed" boat to the entrance of the catacombs. They had scarves tied over their faces to protect themselves from the foul stench.

A heavy iron chain lay across the entrance to the sewers. Arun picked the lock quickly.

"The gods will curse us," Evon predicted.

"The gods don't pay attention to the likes of us," Arun reminded him.

"The gods pay attention to kings and queens."

"If you're scared, go home to Granny. I'll get the jewels myself."

"I'm not scared," Evon lied.

They rowed the boat into the catacombs. Neither could tell if it was a natural river, winding its way through a cave or manmade canals. They passed a white marble sepulchre. It was short, too short for a grown man.

They threw out a rope and lassoed a nearby pillar. Once the boat was made fast, they climbed out to examine the first tomb.

'Our beloved Bojo' was carved upon the end of the sepulchre.

'Prince Bodge, son of King Davan and Queen Lutine' was carved on the long side of the marble. 'May priests offer eternal hymns and prayers for his soul.'

"Bojo. He has the same nickname as my friend Bodge," Evon said.

"Everyone named Bodge is nicknamed Bojo," Arun reminded him.

Using a crowbar, they took the lid off the sepulchre.

Within they could see a child's skeleton and a puppy's skeleton. Arun reached in and stole the jewelled collar from puppy's skull.

"Wasting diamonds on a dog's collar. Worse, wasting them on a dead dog." Arun said disapprovingly.

"Do you suppose they slit the dog's throat first, or buried it alive with his boy?"

"Probably drowned it or slit its throat first," Arun guessed with a shrug.

Evon took an emerald ring off the boy's bony hand.

Arun reached for the coronet.

"Don't bother," Evon told him. "We'd never be able to fence it."

"I thought we could shatter it and melt down the pieces," Arun suggested.

Evon shook his head. "It would only bring a fraction of what it's worth whole… if we dared to sell it whole. Don't be greedy," he admonished. "Just take the ring and the dog collar. You know what Granny says about greedy thieves."

The two quoted in unison, "I am a pig, and pigs get fat. You are a hog, and hogs get slaughtered."

They attempted to lower the lid of the sepulchre as gently as they could, but it was heavy. It slipped and cracked as they put it back.

"Nobody remembers King Davan today. I never even heard of him. No one will care we disturbed his son's tomb. Or recognize his crown."

"The priests and the royal family care," Arun corrected him. "They come down here on pilgrimage once or twice a year."

They went back to the boat and rowed further down to seek out their original goal – the resting place of Queen Galla.

They rowed past other tombs. They didn't look like

they'd been touched in years. They continued rowing until they saw a pile of white somethings on the bank of the canal. Arun held the torch up higher, so they could see better. Evon cast a rope and lashed the boat to a pillar. They climbed out of the boat.

Upon inspection, the pile of white somethings turned out to be the bodies of the priestesses in their white silk gowns. Every one of their throats had been slit.

"What a waste," Evon said. "All those perfectly good virgins gone to waste."

"It's because they were good, they died virgins," Arun muttered. "Well, if you're really desperate." He jutted his elbow at the pile of dead priestesses.

"That's sick. I'm not that desperate." Arun walked over to the pile of dead priestesses, but just to check the bodies for jewellery.

He swore. "They stink." They did, even above and beyond the stench of the sewers. When their throats had been slit, the bowels and bladders had loosened, as such organs do at the moment of death. The scarf tied around his face was not sufficient to protect his nose.

"If they're here, the queen must be close," Evon reasoned.

"There." Arun pointed to a makeshift pavilion made of crimson tapestries.

They walked over to the pavilion. Lying before it were the bodies of three temple eunuchs. Silver wine goblets lay on the floor next to them.

"They must have poisoned themselves after they killed the priestesses," Arun guessed.

"Why?" Evon asked.

"Religious zealotry? Excessive loyalty to the queen?"

Arun drew back a tapestry and revealed the queen's

catafalque. Evon joined him. They pried the jewels out of the casket. A small wooden chest lay at the foot of the royal casket. Curious, Evon opened the chest. It was full of jewellery: pearl necklaces and bracelets, ruby pendants on gold chains, rings, and earrings.

They put the pried jewels into the chest.

"Go put this in the boat," Arun ordered.

"What about the rest of the jewels?" Evon asked.

"Too many and the chest will be too heavy to lift. Worse, it'll sink the boat."

They heard a rattling sound behind them. Both turned their heads to look. They saw a long white eldritch monstrosity.

"A death-worm!" both gasped in unison.

A dozen human skulls linked together crept toward them.

"Quick, get the chest back to the boat," Arun ordered.

It weighed less than a newborn babe, so Evon picked up the wooden chest by himself. Arun followed him to the boat. The death-worm lunged for his leg. It bit him. He screamed.

"Are you all right?" Evon asked.

"No, I'm not all right. Get the crowbar. Knock it off my leg," Arun ordered.

Evon set the chest down beside the pillar where the boat was tied. He grabbed the crowbar and hurried back to his cousin. Evon brought the crowbar down on the death-worm, hard. The crowbar shattered the sixth skull in line, breaking the death-worm in two. The first skull still had its teeth firmly embedded in Arun's leg.

"I think you made it bite harder," Arun complained.

"At least I killed it," Evon retorted.

"You can't kill something that was never truly alive,"

Arun said. "Get it off me."

"If I break your leg trying to whack that thing off with this crowbar, remember you told me to do it," Evon warned.

He lifted the crowbar to swing it. "Brace yourself."

A harmless bat flew down from the roof of the catacomb. Evon swung up at it instead of down at the skull.

"You idiot! Bats are only dangerous if you're a mosquito."

Evon lowered the crowbar. He smacked the skull biting Arun's calf. The force of the blow knocked Arun to the ground.

"Blasphemers!" they heard a shout behind them. Arun and Evon turned and saw one of the dead eunuchs rising to his feet.

"The undead!" Evon cried out in terror.

"Drugged, not dead, you idiot," Arun corrected. He attempted to scramble to his feet. The skull was still attached to his left leg. The pain made it nearly impossible to move, but the fear made it impossible to stand still.

"You dare disturb My Lady's eternal rest!" the eunuch roared. "You shall die for your sins, and this will be your tomb, as well as hers."

The two thieves did not stay to argue theology, but hurried for their boat. Once he was sitting down, Arun tried to pry the jaws off his leg.

"How in the name of the Nine Hells did such a creature evolve?" Arun asked. "Or did it come out of the Nine Hells?"

"It didn't evolve, nor did the gods create them. Death-worms are not natural creatures. They were created by wizards," Arun explained.

"Seems to me that wizards need something better to do with their time," Evon mused. "Maybe they should take up knitting."

Despite his agony, Arun forced a smile at the thought of wizards knitting a long multicoloured snake.

Evon rowed. Arun held the torch, insisting he was too weak from his wounds to help row. He slowed down when they passed little Prince Bojo's tomb.

Glowing white beside the marble sepulchre, was the spectral figure of a boy with a puppy in his arms.

"He's not really there," Arun insisted. "It's only an optical illusion brought on by a guilty conscience. You know what Granny says."

"Thieves can't afford a guilty conscience," Evon quoted their grandmother. "It's too expensive."

"Demon-dogs, avenge me!" Prince Bojo called out. A second later, a huge black dog with sharp white fangs and glowing red eyes rushed out of the darkness and leapt into the boat. Arun was knocked into the cold, fetid water. Evon managed to keep his seat in the boat, and better still, save the jewellery chest. He had numerous cousins, but very few rubies.

The demon-dog grabbed Arun's arm and pulled him under. Evon hit the demon-dog on the head with the oar. It released Arun and sunk to the bottom. Evon pulled his cousin back into the boat.

"Was that an illusion, too?" Evon asked.

"Its fangs were real, at least," Arun allowed.

Evon demanded Arun help row, no matter how weak he felt. They soon escaped the canals of the catacomb. By the time they returned to their grandmother's home, Arun was burning with fever.

Bodge refused to take the boat back until Arun and Evon had scrubbed it with bleach – twice.

Just as she had taught them years ago, they handed over almost all their loot to their grandmother, keeping only a few baubles for themselves.

Arun's leg-wound festered and stank malodorously. He lay on his pallet, his fever so high his sister threatened to cook eggs on his forehead.

Granny took a pearl necklace to her favourite fence. He knew her too well to believe the tale she spun of it being a family heirloom, but he paid her for it without asking awkward questions. She used the money to hire a chirurgeon to come cut off Arun's leg and nurse him back to health. The family ate well for months. They ate meat for weeks. Granny splurged on fresh bread at the baker's instead of stale. The rest Granny put away for future needs.

One of the aunties mocked her. "What do you mean 'saving it for your old age'? How long do you expect to live, Old Woman?"

Within two months Arun was limping around the marketplace, picking pockets and begging for charity. Since he could no longer run, Granny relegated him to training his younger cousins in the craft of picking pockets.

Evon never again tried to rob tombs. Once had been enough for him. It was a full month before he could sleep at night without having his dreams invaded by demon-dogs or death-worms. He chose another of his cousins as his partner as a pickpocket and never completely escaped the nightmares, though he lived to be a greybeard, and achieved his ambition. He died of old age, in his own bed.

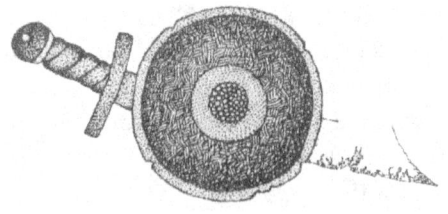

BLACKSHIELD MANOR
Marc Edward Star

1. The Road to Soulum

Blackshield Manor loomed in the distance, its fanged towers scraping the purple-tinged clouds that brushed past. Perched atop Watcher's Peak, a lone hill that soared above the dense Wyre Forest, the manor sat in judgment of the endless canopy below, or so it seemed to Ronan Morvayne, his gaze captured by the black keep that had just come into view.

A fitting home for power. Ronan's eyes, cracked and simmering with an ever-present angst, narrowed towards the manor. His moustache trailed down to his jawline, his teeth were slightly crooked but well-maintained and his full head of black hair was cut close and riddled with flecks of grey. The lines on his face suggested he had stories to tell, and his clothes, which not only fit well but were finely embroidered, gave the impression that those stories tended to end well for him.

Ronan's meaty hands clutched the reins tighter as his horse pressed forward, slowly pulling with it his cart and the heavy clang of metallic wares that chimed with every bump on the road. A road he'd never travelled before.

"And what about this one?" Jaryk emerged from inside the covered wagon brandishing a polished steel sword and sat next to Ronan. Nearly as tall as his older companion but much thinner, with scraggly blonde hair and a bright, eagerness for adventure shining behind his blue eyes, the boy noticed Ronan's gaze, then turned his head towards the forest and the ominous silhouette towering above the horizon.

"Blackshield," Jaryk muttered. The hairs on the back of his neck stiffened. "An ominous sight, indeed. The whispers of the dark heart of the Wyre Peninsula seem not so fantastic from this vantage."

"Whispers, nonetheless," Ronan replied as he took the sword and held the blade aloft, steel glinting in the scant rays of sun that broke through the darkening sky.

"Watch closely—there." The blade caught a ray of fading light, and a flash of ancient script shimmered along its length.

"What's it say, master?" Jaryk asked.

"It's written in a tongue of the middle kingdoms, before those lands fell to the warlords and nomads."

"The Savage Wastes?" Jaryk asked.

"Aye, lad."

"I'd almost rather be lost in that Deity-forsaken place than found in this land of shadow." Jaryk took another long look towards Blackshield Manor and could feel the cold, dark stone staring back. "Can you read it?"

"Dahlia."

Jaryk traced his fingers over the engraving. "Dahlia. A woman's name?"

Ronan nodded. "A queen. And a curse." He let the weight of those words settle as Jaryk leaned in for another of Ronan's wondrous tales.

"She was one of the last queens in the days before the middle kingdoms finally fell. This sword belonged to her king and he slept with it every night, fearful his keep would be stormed in the night."

"What about his guardsmen?" Jaryk interrupted.

"Paranoia is an evil mistress. No guardsmen could have saved him from the fateful night when Queen Dahlia came to his bed to give him comfort. Awakened in panic, he plunged the sword into her belly—a slow, agonizing and bloody death. She died in his arms, as did his sanity and soon after his kingdom. The sword earned its name—Nightsgrief—and became a terrifying symbol of the warlord who usurped the king's stronghold, using it to gut the spouse of any who betrayed his rule."

"Are we selling any blades that aren't tragic?" Jaryk asked.

Ronan smiled. "Without a good story, it's just cutlery," Ronan handed him the sword with a wink.

Then he felt a tug on the back of the cart. Ronan pulled on the reins, grabbed Nightsgrief from Jaryk and gave his young apprentice a disapproving look. "Did you forget to lock the end gate?" An expression of guilt washed over Jaryk's face as Ronan handed him the ropes. "Hold the reins."

Ronan jumped down and ran to the back, just as a man in worn, layered clothing slid out of the rear holding one of Ronan's wares—a curved short sword with a pearl handle. The man stood a good head taller than Ronan and smiled with one side of his mouth, displaying rotted teeth, those that weren't missing.

"Consider your toll along the Soulum pass settled," the man growled and slashed clumsily, more of a warning than a purposeful thrust, but Ronan could easily tell he lacked the skill of a practiced swordsman and likely had grown accustomed to easy pickings off religious pilgrims heading to the village of Soulum.

Ronan, however, was no pilgrim. He had grown up with the sword.

"Seems you have caught yourself in a bind," Ronan calmly replied with a smile. "For, you could turn and run, but you would find yourself with a sword in your back. Or you could back away, and end up gutted like a fish. Or," and on this Ronan placed extra emphasis, "you could actually earn your quarry and thrust like you mean it."

Ronan's toying tone enraged the brute, who roared with bluster and gracelessly lunged forward with the stolen sword.

A simple step to the side and Ronan dodged his assailant's awkward thrust. The sword in Ronan's grip felt familiar, instinctual—and with a quick manoeuvre of his arm, steel met steel. Ronan hooked the curved blade in his, rotated his wrist and disarmed his foe. The stolen weapon flew through the air and landed far enough away to leave the man frozen in shock as Ronan slashed at his face, drawing a thin line of blood.

Stumbling back, the ruffian clutched the wound, feeling the warm blood on his fingers. He growled, pulled a dagger from his belt and raised his arm. Ronan reacted reflexively, dropping into a roll that landed him beside the brute's legs as the dagger sailed harmlessly past him.

The brute reached for the rusty blade at his hip, but before he could unsheathe it, Ronan slashed at the man's ankles. He collapsed, howling strained curses.

Ronan stood and paused.

"Finish him!" Jaryk shouted, peering around the cart.

He would be justified in ending the life of an armed thief, but Ronan wanted his arrival in Soulum to be uneventful, and so retrieved his pearl handled blade, along with the dagger, as he watched the brute struggle to stand then crumple.

"I only pay taxes to the Cartel," Ronan said as the bandit groaned and crawled back towards the forest.

Ronan climbed back into the driver's seat.

"Let him tell his friends what happened," he said, resuming the journey. "We're not defenceless pilgrims."

"The zealots of Soulum would hang a villain like that," Jaryk insisted. But Ronan shook his head.

"Only if they accused him of warlockery. Otherwise they would have freely given—piously—I suspect."

"I find it so confusing, master. How can the heart of the Deitist faith in Soulum co-exist under the dark shadow of that?" Jaryk pointed towards Blackshield Manor as its red banners, each emblazoned with the clan's crest—a black shield—became visible.

The Blackshield clan. Rulers of the Wyre Peninsula. Ronan knew their sentinels executed Ahman law in the larger villages and the clan oversaw resource management for the Pentaclist Cartel.

Ronan shook his head silently as he considered the Cartel, the realm's trade organization, the bureaucracy to whom he was tethered, whose reach was so complete that Ronan needed Pentaclist documentation whether he planned to sell in the great capital city of Ahm or in a superstitious outpost village like Soulum.

Yet the Deitists were old. Entrenched. Their faith more powerful than any sword or decree.

The Clan. The Temple. The Cartel.

Ronan sighed and shrugged.

"The Deitists were here long before the Blackshields," Ronan replied. "I suspect the Blackshields were installed by the Pentaclists as proxies."

"They say the Pentaclists worship a dark god," Jaryk said quietly. "In this part of the world, I find that not so unbelievable."

Ronan gave Jaryk a stern look. "Who tells you these things?"

"Whispers."

Ronan shook his head and turned back to the road. Instinctively, his hand grazed against the metallic five-pointed star amulet hanging beneath his tunic, the mysterious relic his father handed him, still a child, along with cryptic last words about "protection."

It was heavy and intricately detailed. A reptilian eye crowned its centre. And it was the burden his father left him. What was it? Protect how? Even the maester from Ahm's Great Library only gave him vague references to Pentaclist iconography.

"Is Nightsgrief the blade that Lord Zaragoza wishes to purchase from us?" Jaryk asked, breaking Ronan's thoughts.

Ronan side-eyed the boy and smiled. He was inquisitive *and* clever, but for his own safety, Ronan committed to keeping him in the dark.

"As I told you, it's best you don't know."

Jaryk knew better than to pry. He took one last look towards Blackshield Manor as the sun descended through the clouds behind it. The outer spires seemed to curve around the perimeter of the sun, while the middle tower cut through the centre of the fiery ball, like a serpent's eye. Jaryk shuddered.

Thunder cracked from within the gathering clouds as the air around them twisted.

"How much longer?" he asked.

"Not far," Ronan replied, his gaze lingering ahead at the forest swallowing the road whole. "Soulum is just beyond the woods."

2. The Hanging Gardens

The woods were eerily silent, save for the creaking of wind through the trees. Orange and grey light from the setting sun cast long shadows across the forest floor.

"Steel yourself," Ronan said. "The Deitists take the laws of their faith most seriously in these parts."

A thick, nauseous taste of rot seeped into the back of Jaryk's throat as his eyes traced the shadows along the dirt path—shadows with twisted limbs that swayed back and forth with the wind, along the ground, against the trunks and through the crooked branches of ancient trees.

The shadows had been all around them since they entered this final stretch of woodland. Corpses, countless of them, hanging by their necks, many so old their flesh had long rotted off, their clothes in tattered shreds. A few so fresh that the bloat of death swelled their ghostly faces, stricken with terror. Around the neck of each sad soul hung a large wooden plaque upon which was painted a single word: "Warlock."

"What is this place?" Jaryk gasped, his stomach twisting in knots as the decay from this open air graveyard filled his every breath.

"The Hanging Gardens of Soulum," Ronan replied, taking in the sight with clenched jaw. His eyes lingered on the plaques, the same wooden plaques they'd used for ...

He exhaled sharply, shaking the thought away as the creaking ropes harmonized into a terrible symphony in the escalating breeze.

"Nowhere is Deitist zealotry more inflamed than here in Soulum," Ronan continued. "You wondered how can the faith operate in such a dark corner of the empire? It is fed by the paranoia and fear that is bred here in the shadows.

Everywhere they see darkness. Everywhere they see magic. And *everyone* they suspect."

Jaryk understood. Magic was outlawed in the Empire of Ahm—though it seemed an extreme measure enacted against something that didn't even exist, or if it did was little more than parlour antics, or at worst the ancient healing arts of forest recluses.

"Keep your eyes down and your tone humble when we arrive," Ronan warned. "Unless we plan to pay our respects at the temple—which we will *not*—we are bound to attract suspicion. The only strangers the Deitists welcome in Soulum are pilgrims."

"And what about guests of Lord Magnus Zaragoza?" Jaryk asked with youthful bravado.

Ronan smiled as he raised his eyebrows and grasped the boy's shoulder. "Once they accuse you of warlockery, not even the Lord of Soulum can save your soul from the noose."

The wind picked up and moaning ropes sang in agony. Jaryk looked up and felt powerless underneath the shade of rotting, swaying skeletons.

"Are they for real?" Jaryk asked.

Ronan considered for a moment. "Warlocks?"

Jaryk nodded.

"I hope so."

The dead swayed above them.

3. Arrival in Soulum

The sun faded beneath the rooftops as Ronan and Jaryk approached Soulum. The sky rumbled, clouds darkened and rain began to fall—a light, but steady downpour that mingled the scent of freshly wet soil with the aromas of charred meats from nearby hovels.

At the village entrance, two Blackshield Sentinels stood, their black hooded cloaks shrouding their faces from the fading light, while their red tabards with familiar black shield left no doubt on whose command they stood. One of them held up a hand, the rattle of chainmail reminding Ronan to tread gently.

Ronan stopped his cart.

"What is your business in the village of Soulum?" the sentinel asked, barely looking Ronan in the eye.

"Traveling merchants come to sell our wares to the pilgrims and locals," Ronan said with a forced smile as he pulled out his Pentaclist warrant. Jaryk grabbed a wooden board and held it over the document to keep it from getting wet.

The sentinel reviewed the parchment before giving way. "Welcome merchant," he said, waving them along.

Ronan nodded silently and proceeded into the village where townsfolk and Deitist pilgrims moved unhurried through the streets. A light rain was just like any other day here in Soulum.

As they approached the village square, the road thickened with pedestrians, Deitists primarily, some robed, some hooded, some carrying candles, but all heading towards the large and ornate stone edifice that dominated the centre of town—the Deitist Temple of Soulum, the Temple of the First Sage.

Ronan's breath deepened at the sight of the temple, the holiest of Deitist temples, the one constructed some two thousand years ago by the very first priest of the Cult, a prophetic figure known as the First Sage.

Ronan knew well the Cult's lore and how its superstition filled its coffers. The First Sage prophesied that a shadow of evil would one day spread upon this world, initiated by a secret cabal of warlocks and consummated by the destruction of the Soulum Temple. In the aftermath, the First Sage, mummified in the catacombs underneath, would rise again in defence of humanity. The Cult had operated on a singular premise ever since—identify and root out all sources of magic, all warlockery, and eradicate it before the evil of prophecy had a chance to take hold.

The temple's bell rang as throngs of Deitists filed towards the holy palace.

Atop the steps, a man in oversized priestly robes, decorated with trinkets and baubles, greeted each of them with a bow. The line of people took turns showing respect before entering.

Rising from a bow, the priest caught glimpse of Ronan, side-eyeing the merchant as he passed.

"Blessings of the First Sage upon you, Father Benedictus," one of the faithful said to the priest as Ronan and Jaryk approached within earshot.

Still following Ronan with an expressionless gaze, Benedictus replied, "And may his light guide you, steadfast and unerring, away from sin and heresy."

"Why is that priest watching us?" Jaryk asked.

"Because that temple is a disease."

Meanwhile, a different crowd gravitated towards the Good Shepherd Inn and Tavern, a bit livelier but just as impervious to rain.

Just where Thalos said it would be, Ronan assured himself.

Men stood outside with flagons, rolling dice and smoking pipes as Ronan stopped the cart and began to secure the canopy over his wares. Ronan breathed deeply at the smell of fresh ale and warm bread inside. He and Jaryk would spend the night at the Good Shepherd before his meeting with Lord Zaragoza the following day.

Ronan reached inside his coat to grasp Thalos's letter of introduction, the credentials to provide an audience with Zaragoza. That one piece of paper between his fingers eased his mind.

Across the square stood another imposing stone structure—the Pentaclist Cartel Lodge. Framed by grand columns and a windowless facade, the lodge would never welcome a merchant of Ronan's class. While the Cartel oversaw all trade within the Ahman Empire, access to its exclusive halls remained elusive but to the very few. Ronan's requisite Pentaclist warrant would be the closest he could ever get to the great columns that guarded the Cartel's inner sanctum.

As Ronan made one last check of wares in the cart, he pulled out a small chest, opened it and removed a vial that contained a shimmering substance, an essence of something he did not understand, but which Lord Zaragoza desired.

A worthless powder to some. Worth a fortune to a man like Zaragoza, Ronan mused to himself. *A fortune—or a death sentence. The price of an audience.*

Ronan sighed gently.

Thalos, you best be right.

Jaryk meanwhile pointed to a hilltop keep off in the distance, sitting atop the highest point in the village and asked, "Shall I guess who lives there?"

Ronan finished securing the cart and replied, "That, my young friend, is the Keep of Soulum, the home of Lord Magnus Zaragoza and the culmination of our journey tomorrow." Ronan put his arm around Jaryk. "But tonight we feast, and drink."

4. The Good Shepherd

Ronan set down two tankards of ale as he joined Jaryk at a small table in the Good Shepherd. A crowd of locals clustered throughout, brooding in colourless voices, hunched over mugs of ale. They paid no mind to strangers or traveling merchants, accustomed were they to those seeking to take advantage of the influx of pilgrims with discretionary coin.

"Lodging secured," Ronan said and held his flagon aloft. "To profitable transactions and accommodating clients."

Jaryk smiled and toasted. "May you handle their coin purses as deftly as you handle a sword."

They clinked mugs and took hearty swigs, Ronan downing nearly half in one gulp. He then let out a heavy sigh, one that smacked of a weight sliding off his shoulders.

"Two months travel to get here," Ronan said and placed his hand on Jaryk's shoulder. "You are a fine apprentice to accompany me on this journey."

"Master, I would follow you even into the fabled Abyss," Jaryk replied. Jaryk's loyalty warmed Ronan's jaded heart. Every time he set eyes on his young apprentice, he was reminded that at least he had done one good thing in his lifetime—taking this young thief off the streets of Ahm and giving him an honest life, even if was only to keep the urchin from stealing his own wares, and to use him to identify the other cutpurses before they struck. Ronan hoped he hadn't made a mistake bringing the boy along. He had warned him, Ronan assured himself, that Soulum can be unpredictable. But the boy's enthusiasm for adventure won him over.

"Mutton," a portly woman, the proprietor's wife, said

with a warm smile as she placed two steaming plates on the table. "You best eat quick if you plan to catch Father Benedictus's firebrand sermon tonight." She paused with a knowing grin. "Or is that not what brings you to our humble village of Soulum?"

"No, ma'am. Just merchants passing through," Ronan replied with a polite grin.

"Hmph," she replied, eyes lingering on the fine thread of his coat. "Ahman merchants no doubt. A long way from home." She pondered them for a moment, especially Ronan. The only profits to be had by out-of-town traders catered to the impulses of local zealots and visiting pilgrims, and the next holiday was months away. "What fine wares you must have to offset the cost of such an expensive journey."

As Ronan attempted to cleverly deflect the woman's good-natured interrogation, Jaryk fidgeted in his seat. He may not have been aware of the true reason why they had travelled to Soulum, but he knew one thing, they arrived on the invitation of the Magnus Zaragoza, the Lord of Soulum, the man whose keep sat atop the highest hill of the village and whose name, Jaryk was certain, commanded respect. His master, therefore, deserved a share of that respect, and thus, impulsively, Jaryk interjected.

"We have a meeting with Lor— ow!"

Ronan's heel reflexively stamped down upon Jaryk's foot before he could mention the name.

"Sorry, lad, was that your foot?" Ronan asked, innocently enough, as Jaryk took a deep breath, letting the pain subside.

"Keep your secrets then," the woman said with a wink and then walked away.

Ronan turned sharply towards the boy and said quietly but sternly, "They do *not* need to know our business here."

"I'm sorry, master. I just thought you deserve the respect of being associated with a man such as," Jaryk's voice fell to the quietest of whispers, "Zaragoza."

Before Ronan could prevent him from whispering the name, a raspy voice cut through the tavern's din.

"Lord Zaragoza?!?" an old man sitting by the fire pit cried out. Heads turned at the outburst. Hushed voices carried through the tavern hall.

A flash of lightning outside illuminated the tavern for a frozen moment, followed by a rumble of thunder. The eye of the storm neared. The feeble clinks of tankards and metalware, along with the patter of rain outside betrayed the room's settling silence as the old man turned towards the two travellers.

His eyes were white and long dead, but his ears sharp as a Deitist's accusation. "You plan to meet with Lord Master Magnus Zaragoza?"

All heads in the tavern turned towards Ronan and Jaryk.

Ronan eyed those around them and chuckled, dismissively. "And what matter is it of the Good Shepherd with whom I conduct my business?"

A moment's silence preceded a cascade of whispers.

"He really plans to see Lord Zaragoza." Murmuring shock rang through the tavern, then laughter spread like a contagion.

The proprietor's wife yelled out from behind the bar, "Lord Zaragoza!" before chuckling and disappearing into the kitchen.

"Nobody sees Lord Zaragoza!" the old blind man called out.

And that's how it started in the Good Shepherd, an uproar of disagreement between patrons arguing over whether Magnus Zaragoza lived or had been buried underneath his keep long ago, some even claiming the renowned lord never even existed and had only ever been a legend to deflect attention away from the true lords of the village: the Pentaclist Lodge, the Deitist Temple and the Blackshield Clan. Some claimed Zaragoza had been seen sitting as a judge on the last warlock trial, but it wasn't a public trial so who could be sure it was truly him.

"Look at what you've started, lad," Ronan whispered to Jaryk.

"I'm sorry, master," Jaryk replied.

"Lord Zaragoza lives!" A middle-aged woman with ragged curls yelled as she pounded her fist on the table. "He is one of the Marked Lords."

"Yes!" the blind man crowed. "Cursed with the blight of long life the Marked Lords are."

Ronan, a lifelong student of lore, raised an eyebrow. "And who are these Marked Lords?" he asked. "The libraries are silent on this."

The woman rose from her table and limped over to join Ronan and Jaryk.

"The Marked Lords are men of old blood," the woman began in a quiet tone as she sat down, "all but forgotten except within Deitist halls—for we are the only ones who dare to remember."

The banter of the tavern returned to a normal hum as chatter of Zaragoza faded into the background of idle conversation. The woman looked around then leaned in close, lowering her voice.

"Legend claims the Marked Lords lived eerily long lives and wielded considerable influence upon events from the shadows, guiding power from behind thick stone walls. They were named so for each carried a strange sigil etched upon their skin as if branded at birth."

"What kind of sigil?" Ronan asked.

"Perhaps a swirling eye or a crescent pierced by a fang," the woman replied. "But whatever the pattern, it is only visible under the light of the storm."

Ronan remained expressionless. A thousand tomes, a thousand scrolls in the Great Library of Ahm—never had he found any mention of the Marked Lords. How was this woman, a common villager, so certain?

"I have spent the better part of my life in the Great Library of Ahm," Ronan replied, "yet never have I heard of the Marked Lords."

"Because all records of them have been erased," she replied. "But we Deitists remember. The sigil on their hands betrays them."

"And you believe Lord Zaragoza is one of these Marked Lords?" Ronan asked.

The woman continued in a cautious whisper. "I have seen the sigil."

"What, then, is the mark that Zaragoza bears on his hand?" Ronan pressed.

The woman paused, then smiled, "That information will cost you a coin, merchant."

Ronan's hand moved towards his purse; the swirling eye sigil sounded familiar. And yes, rumours of men influencing nobles from the shadows had crossed his path. But this woman ... a Deitist. Ronan didn't trust her.

"Bah!" Ronan exclaimed. "Begone woman!"

She pointed a crooked finger at Ronan. "'Tis true. You'll see." She then stood up and disappeared into the tavern's din.

Ronan leaned back. "I don't trust these villagers."

Suddenly, the tavern door swung open with a thud. A

young man stepped through the open door, behind him the steady drum of rain and an accusatory shout: "Show yourself!" the voice outside demanded.

The young villager announced, "Acolytes are outside checking a cart and asking questions!"

The proprietor behind the bar turned to Ronan. "Merchant, that yours?"

The words had barely left the villager's mouth before Ronan stood up, cursed under his breath and moved quickly towards the exit.

Outside two young men in white hooded cloaks stood by Ronan's cart yelling, "Come out, trader!" The rain beat down upon the overhang above them as Ronan stepped forward.

"This your cart, merchant?" the shorter of the two said as he grasped the lock securing its contents. The taller one stood behind him holding a small wooden club tipped with metal studs.

"On whose authority am I compelled to answer?" Ronan asked.

"On the authority of the Deity and the Temple of the First Sage, stranger," the acolyte replied with rising impatience. "We have no tolerance or mercy to suffer the errands of fools whose aim is to infect our village with heresy or warlockery." The final word sank into Ronan's flesh as if it had claws.

"I deal in no heresy nor warlockery," Ronan replied, his tone measured but firm. "I am a simple merchant offering historical relics of the realm. Surely a man of faith such as yourself can appreciate the importance of storied artifacts."

"Open your cart then and prove your innocence," the acolyte responded.

"I am sanctioned by the Cartel," Ronan insisted. "I am not subject to the whims of the Temple."

"You are in the village of Soulum, merchant," the taller acolyte added in a deep baritone and smacked the studded club against his open hand.

Lightning struck, immediately followed by a thunderous boom that shook the ground. Patrons from inside the tavern assembled around the doorway, eager for drama.

"Just open your cart," one of the villagers said as others joined in, imploring him not to go against the Temple.

A couple of Blackshield sentinels, noticing the gathering crowd, approached.

"What is the problem here?" one of the sentinels asked.

"I am being accused by the Temple," Ronan replied.

Jaryk pushed his way through the crowd in the doorway and stood by Ronan's side.

"Accused of what?" asked the sentinel.

"We suspect the merchant is dealing in unholy substances," the first acolyte replied, his gaze firmly locked on Ronan.

"I am doing nothing of the sort!" Ronan insisted and pulled out his license. "I am a merchant of the Cartel."

"An honest man has nothing to hide," the acolyte said as the sentinel took the license and read it.

After a moment, the sentinel handed the license back to Ronan. "This man is a known trader, under the aegis of the Cartel," the sentinel said.

"That may be, but he is no exception to the laws of the First Sage," the acolyte pressed.

"Do you have evidence?" the sentinel noted.

"Open the cart and none will have reason to whisper that the Cartel offers protection to dealers of heresies," the acolyte said slowly and with finality.

Ronan looked towards the sentinels with pleading eyes.

"Are you dealing in unholy substances, merchant?" the sentinel asked.

"Of course not!" Ronan replied.

"Well if you've got nothing to hide, show them. Let's end this," the sentinel said.

"Show them," the crowd called out. Jaryk looked towards Ronan with concern. The acolytes smiled victoriously, the taller one continuing to smack the club into his hand. Ronan gritted his teeth.

"Fine."

Lightning lit up the sky in a series of stuttering flashes accompanied immediately by a booming thunder.

Ronan removed the lock and opened the cart. Swords, daggers, helms and other relics of history and war revealed themselves neatly arranged, stacked and shelved.

The acolytes hurriedly rummaged through the cart, inspecting the items.

"Careful you clumsy toads," Ronan shouted.

"There's nothing there but relics!" Jaryk shouted as the acolytes continued sifting.

Finally, the shorter acolyte pushed aside a stack of cloths to reveal a small hidden door within which he found a tiny wooden chest. Locked.

The acolyte glared at Ronan. "Open this. Show us the unholy substance."

Jaryk's eyes went wide. Never had he seen that chest before nor did he know what was inside.

Ronan sighed and shook his head before using a small key to open the chest, lifting its lid to reveal … an empty padded velvet interior.

"Waste of time," the sentinel barked. "Let the man trade."

"We have to be cautious," the acolyte insisted to the sentinel, then turned to Ronan. "After all, your parents' proclivities are still fresh in Deitist annals. It would be shame if their legacy cast a shadow on your trade."

At the mention of his parents, Ronan slammed the chest shut, placed it back on his cart and put his face nose to nose with the acolyte. "The only heresy to concern you is if I carried the Black Death."

The acolyte's eyes went wide as he took a step back, the gasps of tavern patrons louder than the pounding rain. Ronan's teeth clenched and his hands curled into fists. Lightning struck one more time, accompanied by a sudden thunderous boom.

"You should be hanged for those words," the acolyte shuddered and turned to leave, his companion smacking the club in his hand before turning to follow. As they walked into the downpour, the first acolyte turned back and yelled, "The Cartel won't always protect you!" before disappearing into the misty night.

"Carry on merchant," the sentinel ordered before they turned to leave.

The crowd dispersed, eyes lingering on Ronan as they returned to the warmth of the tavern. Alone outside with Jaryk, Ronan began arranging all of the swords and relics into a large trunk within the cart.

"Come," Ronan said, "let's store the wares in our room for the night. As pious as the town claims to be, I trust them not a whit."

Once their items were locked securely in the trunk, Ronan and Jaryk hauled the steel-laden crate through the tavern and up the stairs towards their room.

"Master," Jaryk exhaled between laboured steps, "what is the Black Death and why did those acolytes look like they had seen a ghost?"

Ronan regretted having mentioned it—and now

regretted having to explain it.

"It is a dagger," Ronan replied as they set down the trunk. "One that could bring down their entire diseased temple."

Jaryk swallowed hard. "And it exists? This Black Death?"

Ronan placed his hand on trunk and curled his fingers against the lid.

"I intend to find out," he murmured.

5. Thalos's Vault

As Jaryk settled into bed, Ronan barred the door then sat by the window to watch the storm recede. One more flash of lightning lit the village, and for a moment he saw the imposing facade of the temple cast a long shadow on the streets below. Thunder rumbled distantly.

The episode with the acolytes remained fresh in his mind—not their aggressive posture but rather his own provocative words ...

The only heresy to concern you is if I carried the Black Death.

That had been reckless. Foolish.

It was the dagger that brought him here—a journey that started long ago.

And it started with Thalos.

Ronan pushed open the door to Thalos's shop and found himself greeted by the familiar smell of aged metal relics and musty old books. Curios cluttered the shelves along with glass jars of liquids, powders and crystals. A complete human skeleton stood meticulously preserved, its monstrosity on display—an underdeveloped twin dangling from its chest cavity. In a tremendous glass jar floated the pickled head of another poor soul who had been overtaken by grotesque deformities, its skull and cheeks swollen with bulbous malformations.

Ronan shuddered.

A thin coat of dust had settled over everything. It seemed more of a storage room than a place of business— though appropriate enough, Ronan mused, for a shop named the Vault. Perhaps the door rarely opened.

Indeed, Ronan had struggled to find Thalos's Vault. No sign outside save for a placard with a crescent moon. The front door blended in with the wall—as if Thalos did not actually want customers.

"Hello?" Ronan called out to the empty shop.

An older man with scant grey hairs on his head appeared from a back room, holding on to shelves and display cases to balance himself as he walked forward. A large rat sat on his shoulder.

"How may I help you, young man?" he asked as he sat on a stool, removing the rat from his shoulder to let it crawl away. "Keeps the cats away," he said and smiled.

"Are you Thalos?"

"Who's asking?"

"I am Ronan Morvayne, a fellow merchant of storied relics. The maester of the Great Library suggested I pay you a visit."

"Well wasn't that nice of him," Thalos replied. "And what need could I possibly fulfil that the Great Library cannot?"

Ronan looked around the shop, still admiring this unique trove. Naturally he appreciated his own collection of wares and remembered each one, impressing upon his buyers that their possession of a relic added to and carried forward that item's lore. But the Vault ... Thalos packed history into every corner of this repository.

As Ronan breathed it all in, his eyes fell upon a sword that, even sheathed in a dark red leather scabbard, he instantly recognized—the pommel, a black obsidian sphere etched with a serpent's eye, and at the base of the blade, emerging from the scabbard, the five-pointed star of the Cartel. He had read about the blade but never actually seen it.

"The Stone Master's Sword," Ronan said. The only relic he knew with iconography that resembled his father's amulet. The five pointed star. The serpent's eye. However, seeing it there, he realized ...

It was identical.

"You know your swords, young man," Thalos replied as he stood up and unsheathed the blade. "Do you know more than its name?"

"A ceremonial sword to honour the ancient architects who founded the Pentaclist Cartel," Ronan said, "given only to those Cartel members of the highest ranks. It is said that the sword reflects one's inner character and is used to adjudicate the worthiness of Cartel initiates."

"Impressive," Thalos replied and held out the blade. "You've earned your own adjudication." As the sword exchanged hands, Ronan noticed Thalos's grip—three fingers and a thumb, a clear gap where a middle finger presumably had been.

The deformity lingered in Ronan's mind as he resumed studying the ceremonial weapon.

Too heavy for battle, Ronan thought as he angled the sword against the candlelight and studied its craftsmanship. Polished—not sharp, but brilliant like starlight in steel.

Ronan gazed upon his own reflection—thick moustache that arced down to his chin, furry eyebrows and the chiselled lines of life. Then the image morphed into a youthful version of himself, his eyes weary and darkened, furrowed with raw angst and a determination that Ronan recognized: vengeance.

Ronan handed the sword back to Thalos and added, "A risky artifact to possess outside of Cartel membership."

"Indeed." Thalos smiled as he took the sword in his other hand, which Ronan noted had five fingers—and a bronze ring bearing the five-pointed star of the Cartel.

"I have a long history of procuring rare items for the Cartel, themselves collectors of exotic artifacts," Thalos continued as he sheathed the sword. "Their reliquaries are legendary and, as such, I have attained a special license to deal in such antiquities."

"You must have significant acquisition skills," Ronan said.

"Stories and histories are my trade," Thalos replied. "Follow the stories, young man, and the artifacts make themselves known. They want to be found."

Ronan rubbed his chin and then brushed his hand against the amulet against his chest, well hidden behind the cloth of his tunic. "Perhaps in your histories you have come across a five-pointed star amulet with a serpent's eye in the middle, not unlike the iconography on the Stonemaster."

Thalos raised an eyebrow. "Aye, I have. You describe the Amulet of Secrets. I know only of its name, nothing more, but I do know that it is important to the Cartel. Do you seek it?"

Ronan shook his head. "Its lore interests me. I too am a merchant of stories and seek rare items—in particular an extraordinary relic," Ronan stepped in closer and lowered his voice.

"I've traced all mention of this relic in books and ancient scrolls going back nearly a thousand years. It is a dagger, crafted by pure malice, hardened by the blood of innocents, the sacrifice of infants — all for a singular purpose. To depose an even greater evil." Ronan lowered his voice to a whisper, "To destroy the Temple and its tyranny."

"Ah ... You seek the Deitist's Bane."

"The Black Death."

Thalos began to laugh. "And the librarian told you that I possess this legendary dagger?"

"No, Thalos. But he said that if anyone knew where the Black Death travelled beyond all record of its existence, it would be you."

"And you wish to find it?" Thalos asked with a smile and wide eyes. "Truly?"

Ronan nodded.

"Tell me, why do you seek a blade that likely doesn't exist?"

"I intend to use it."

Thalos placed a hand on Ronan's shoulder, his expression earnest. "I too would like to see the dagger used for its stated purpose. Wait here. I have just the tome for you."

Thalos disappeared behind a curtain and left Ronan alone to study the clutter of relics. Years of acquisition, Ronan mused, but where were the buyers of bronze helms of the empire's first armies, ceremonial goblets from the royal halls of the middle kingdoms and reconstructed potteries from First Age ruins? Ronan wondered if he was being offered glimpses of his own destiny here — a cluttered shop of forgotten artifacts whose meaning only had significance to the likes of Thalos and himself.

When Thalos returned, he held a thick tome bound in dark leather.

"Few have read these pages," Thalos said as he gently placed the volume on the table. Etched in gold, the swirling eye on the cover stared back at Ronan, drawing his gaze hypnotically. He traced his fingers along the embossed sigil.

"What is this?" Ronan asked.

"*Relics of Legend*," Thalos replied. "The only person I know who can lead you to the Black Death, if it exists, is the author of this book."

Ronan opened the book to the title page, illuminated like a religious manuscript with ornate serpents and horned cherubim, to read: "Relics of Legend. By Lord Magnus Zaragoza."

Ronan leafed through the pages with awe, past chapters on the Sword of Xithon, Crown of the Agitator and the Great Sceptre of Sythe, items lost to time which, according to the pages of this tome, wielded immense power. But his awe revealed his own deficit.

"I have tirelessly scoured the Great Library of Ahm, researching royal lineages, warcraft and every book of ancient relics on those shelves going back thousands of years, yet never have I heard of this book, nor of many items it professes exist," Ronan said, eyes fixed to the book's pages.

"I know of only two copies of this book. The one in Zaragoza's own hand and this one which he graciously allowed to be copied for me." Thalos paused then added, "The relic you seek is on page three hundred sixty-four."

Ronan carefully, but eagerly turned to the chapter on The Black Death and focused silently on the page as the world around him faded.

He read of the blade's origin, born into legend by a shadowy cult of warlocks who meant to undo the Deitists' grip on the realm. Only through the sacrifice of the most innocent—newborns and infants—could they hope to imbue the dagger with enough blasphemy against the natural order to disrupt the divine balance of the Deitist faith. Then, once saturated with sacrilege and plunged into the mummified heart of the First Sage's corpse, the mummy would be obliterated and the Temple would crumble, along with it the prophecy upon which the cult's existence rested.

Ronan knew the Black Death's lore, but something about the words on these pages radiated authority, as well as something Ronan did not know: The one who risked everything to bring down the Temple would be the last to feed the Black Death, for the blade would drink one final soul in the cataclysmic ritual—the wielder's.

Ronan closed the book, along with his eyes, and took a moment.

Thalos asked, "If you find it, you will use it?"

Ronan opened his eyes, met Thalos's gaze and nodded. "Can you help me find it?"

"The only one who can lead you to the Black Death is Lord Zaragoza," Thalos replied. "But an audience with the Lord of Soulum requires an offering."

"I'll procure whatever he requires," Ronan replied.

Thalos then grabbed a small, coloured glass plate, set it on the table and pointed towards it. "Twenty coin, and I'll arrange for you to meet with him. But I guarantee, that which a man like Zaragoza requires is unlike anything you have yet procured."

Twenty coin is not insignificant, Ronan thought as he studied Thalos. Who was this shrewd, deformed host of the arcane? Ronan had never given so much of himself to any artifact before, and now it seemed his only path forward was Soulum.

"Twenty coin is a considerable sum," Ronan noted.

Thalos closed the tome swiftly, shaking a puff of dust into the air.

"You seek a considerable relic," Thalos said and began carrying the tome to the back room … until he heard the clink of coin hitting the glass plate.

Thalos smiled to himself and then proceeded to describe a substance that he called snuff, made from a certain dark purple mushroom found in one specific cave. But these mushrooms were guarded and protected by venomous serpents on four legs. They would not be easy to procure, and even if procured they would not be easy to refine, for the mushrooms contain a rare psychoactive substance tied to ancient spiritual practices and visions.

"Lives and sanity can be lost on either side of the process—procurement and refinement," Thalos said as he finished explaining. "When you have the snuff, I'll arrange for you an audience with Zaragoza."

The storm had moved past Soulum by the time Ronan's thoughts returned. He stared through the window at the quiet, dimly lit street below as he felt the glass vial roll between his fingers.

It is a secret like so many others.

He held the vial into a streak of light through the window and observed the snuff inside like grains of shimmering resin—a tiny hourglass counting the days until he might wrap his hands around the grip of the Black Death.

Such a small amount of substance that came at such great cost—the lives of men who procured it for him, the sanity of others who refined it. Ronan recoiled at the memories of poor drooling souls clawing at their own faces, yelling in anguish. What did they see, he wondered?

Ronan took a deep breath and slipped the vial into a secret pocket within his tunic and slowly but deeply descended to a place between worlds, an abyss where the mind drifts off to sleep.

6. The Dream

Screams shattered the darkness. An infant's screams.
Then all fell silent.

The flicker of a lone candlelight cast dancing shadows
across the walls of a modest living room—chairs, table,
cushions, the scattered remains of dinner and dying embers
in the fireplace.

Ronan searched his surroundings. It was familiar. The
room felt large. Or was he small? He looked up to see his
father standing above him, his gaze fixed on the window
and the yellow light in the distance. Then he knelt down, his
eyes stern, but his hand shook as he pressed a five-pointed
star amulet into Ronan's childlike hands.

"Take this, Ronan, for protection," his father said. The
amulet felt cold against Ronan's palm, and heavy. His
father's grip tightened over his small hands, pressing the
metal into his skin. "The secrets this amulet unlocks ..." He
cut himself off, then added, "Keep it hidden. Never let them
take it from you."

Something felt wrong. They were in danger. His heart
pounded in his chest.

Behind his father, his mother paced, clawing at the
collar of her blouse, her eyes darting towards the window.
The torchlight outside brightened as a chorus of murmurs
approached.

"Warlocks!" Strange voices shouted from outside.

His mother knelt down beside his father.

"No matter what happens, Ronan, you must live," she told
him as she wrapped her hands around his father's, still wrapped
around his and the mysterious amulet that he now held.

Then, an abrupt and violent pounding on the door. Pounding that became a heartbeat, fear escalating in his chest.

Ronan blinked and felt a cold wind brush against him. He stood outside, in the middle of an empty street. The dark of night enveloped him save for a lone brazier illuminating a small bundle of cloth on the ground. Something squirmed within the bundle.

He knelt down, reaching towards the cloth and remembered … a sibling he never met, taken before Ronan had seen the newborn. They would finally meet, he thought, as his hand grabbed the fabric.

But dread gripped him as he peeled back the cloth. Stains, deep red and black. He removed just enough of the covering to reveal the infant's face, contorted in screaming agony. He dared not peel the layers any further, dared not uncover the horrors within.

Ronan convulsed. The darkness swirled around him in a dizzying blend of nausea and pain, tearing through his own chest, gripping his heart, ripping it through his ribs.

Then the voices of the crowd returned. "Heretics!" some shouted, but the word came out wrong, like garbled underwater. "Waaaarlocks," the crowd moaned. Their teeth fanged. Their eyes black.

The torch-bearing crowd approached quickly. Ronan recognized the hooded white robes of Deitist acolytes, dragging with them Ronan's father, his eyes empty and resigned, and his mother, her cries for mercy piercing through the crowd's anger.

Ronan stepped aside. His father yelled something to him, but it was lost in the chaos as the horde passed. Ronan ran after his mother, catching up to her and tugged at her dress.

"What's happening, mother?" he wailed as the chaos marched towards the gallows.

Through tears, she could barely meet his gaze, "We had to give up the boy."

Ronan chased after her and pounded on one of the acolytes who gripped his mother's arm. "Release her!" Ronan shouted.

But the acolyte, with a swing of his arm, knocked the child to the ground, and the crowd moved beyond his reach.

On the gallows platform, a black hooded figure tightened nooses around the necks of Ronan's mother and father, necks from which hung wooden plaques that read, "Warlock." A scowling priest in gleaming holy finery stepped onto the platform.

"For consorting with warlocks!" the priest shouted.

The crowd howled.

"For offering an innocent to the darkness! For the crime of heresy against the divine order! And for the indignity of warlockery!"

"Hang!" the crowd yelled in reply.

Tears welled in Ronan's eyes as he watched the inevitable unfold. His protectors. His caretakers. The only ones who loved him. He would soon be alone. He scanned the crowd looking for someone to do something.

"Help them!" Ronan cried out, but the crowd ignored him, their faces deforming into a featureless mob, each one indistinguishable from the next.

"I condemn you, in the name of the Deity and the divine order, to hang!" The priest gave a nod to the hooded one who then pulled the lever, dropping the trapdoor beneath his parents' feet.

Suspended. Writhing. Dangling.

Ronan's world stopped as gasping breaths squeezed

from his parents' lungs. They choked in agony, their legs squirming beneath them, arms rigid in shock, eyes bulging. Ronan weakened and dropped to his knees, burying his face in hands, his sobs drowned within the maelstrom of vengeance.

Something grabbed Ronan by the back of the shirt and stood him up, forcing him to see. His parents swung gently, their faces drained of life.

The crowd cheered, laughed, mouths agape, drooling.

Impossibly, the hands of his father began to twitch, his body jerked and then rolled against the rope as his head turned towards Ronan.

"Watch the hands, Ronan," his father said though his lips never moved. The words repeated over and over in Ronan's mind until giant black hands reached up from under the trap door, wrapped around the bodies of Ronan's mother and father and pulled them down into eerie darkness.

The faces of the crowd twisted and warped into grotesque shapes, vicious laughter pouring from their distorted mouths as his father's final words echoed in his mind.

"Watch the hands."

Ronan jolted awake with a sharp inhalation, drenched in sweat. Through the window, the temple stood indifferently under the faint blue light of the moon.

Murderers.

Jaryk breathed languidly in the bed next to him.

7. The Market Square

As the morning sun rose over the Wyre Forest, Ronan

and Jaryk drove their cart of wares into Soulum's village square, wheels mashing the damp earth as the smoke of cooking fires mixed with mud-drenched air.

Cloaked pilgrims and devout Deitists quietly filed towards the temple's steps for morning prayers, some stopping at a cart offering fetishes and idols. A pair of Blackshield sentinels in their dark cloaks and red tabards eyed the crowd dutifully as they passed. Across the square, the windowless Pentaclist Lodge stood silently, while nearby the Good Shepherd Tavern bustled with patrons, as if the night's revelry never ended.

Ronan eyed the villagers in frustration as he and Jaryk passed vendors laying out produce and mundane goods. Selling wares to locals and pilgrims was his cover story, but now he found himself dwelling upon the incident at the Good Shepherd—the patrons who had tossed around Zaragoza's name like peasant gossip and the tense run-in with Deitist acolytes.

Cover squandered, but they would nevertheless proceed as planned.

At an open spot, Jaryk began neatly to arrange swords, daggers and helms, cushioned in silk and velvet. He could feel the quiet tension in Ronan's mood.

"And which of our blades is Lord Zaragoza most interested in?" Jaryk asked.

"Quiet boy," Ronan hushed and looked around to make sure none heard the name Zaragoza mentioned. The merchant next to him, a heavy-set man, hummed to himself between deep breaths as he arranged his own wares—cutlery, pottery and other common items—and then took a seat on a wooden stool, meeting Ronan's gaze with a polite nod and smile. Ronan returned the pleasantry before manic shouting erupted nearby.

"We compel you to kneel!" The sharp voice cut through the din of the morning, drawing Ronan's eye. The crowd parted, giving Ronan a direct line of sight to the source of the voice—a man in ragged clothes, his white hair tousled wildly, his arms and hands emoting with the passionate drama of an actor on stage.

"The eye! The eye!" the man continued raving. "It swallows the whole world."

The man shouted towards one merchant, then turned his ire towards another, all the while making his way closer to Ronan's cart, until eventually his mad roving eye landed on Ronan, then on his chest. The man stopped, let out a gasp and pointed.

"The star!" the mad man cried out as he pointed towards Ronan. "You've seen the eye!"

Ronan's eyes went wide before he looked down towards his chest to see the very tip of his amulet poking out the top of his tunic, unbuttoned just enough to allow some of the pentagram to show.

Damn. He had been hasty after hiding the vial of snuff in his tunic. Ronan rushed to button up.

The man hurried closer to Ronan then stopped to point a shaking finger, his eyes wide with a mix of rage and fear.

"Will you accept what is to come?" the man asked Ronan. "There is no choice."

Ronan scanned the crowd as the murmur of morning commerce slowly fell silent. All eyes were upon the mad man and Ronan. The two sentinels had stopped to watch, perhaps amused. Cloaked Deitists observed, judging in hushed whispers.

The man added ominously, "Resist, and the eye will break you—mind first."

Slowly, the man's gnarled hand reached out towards

Ronan, towards his chest, his tunic, the amulet—until Ronan suddenly snapped, slapping the man's hand back with such speed the cretin spun around and crumpled to the ground, a mess of tattered clothes and tangled hair.

"Away you mad dog!" Ronan shouted at him.

The crowd remained still, silently watching as the man whimpered, "It's not madness. It's a knowing. And the knowing is worse."

"Begone Edric!" yelled the portly merchant at the next cart over. "Enough of your ravings for today!"

Jaryk then stepped in and roughly grabbed Edric, pulling him to his feet and giving him a firm shove back from whence he came.

"Get!" Jaryk yelled as he pushed the man away.

Edric stumbled but caught himself and stopped, turning back to Ronan. "You haven't seen it yet. But you will." He then disappeared back into the crowd muttering, "Will you accept what is to come? We compel you to kneel."

Shortly after, the market square resumed its normal activity. But Ronan's eye stayed in the direction of Edric long after he lost sight of the madman.

"Soulum is full of surprises," Jaryk said with a half-smile.

"Ah, don't mind Edric," the portly merchant said. "He's always skulking around babbling about eyes and nonsense. Harmless mostly."

Ronan replied, "Just took me off my guard is all."

"He does that. Feels too comfortable in the market square because he used to be a merchant like us."

"What happened to him?"

"Success, I'd suppose. Made his fortune importing valuables of the realm for the few aristocrats who live here. But ... I'm sure you noticed the manor on your way towards town," the merchant added.

"Blackshield?" Ronan asked.

"Aye, the one. Rumour has it Edric lost his way after paying his benefactors a visit there."

"Rumour I'm sure," Ronan replied.

"Security comes with a strange cost in these parts. You from up north?"

"Ahm," Ronan replied.

"Oh," the merchant said with a hint of awe. "The imperial city. A far piece, indeed. We don't usually get men of status visiting us in Soulum."

Ronan chuckled. "Status may be a bit of an exaggeration."

"He's the finest dealer of antiquities and rare artifacts in all of the Great City," Jaryk interjected.

The merchant smiled broadly and extended his hand. "Donavan. It's a pleasure to make the acquaintance of a man of such reputation."

Ronan shook his hand and said, "Ronan. My apprentice Jaryk."

Ronan intended to thank Donavan for his cordiality and then return to his own affairs, but he noticed something among Donavan's wares that caught his eye. At first it seemed like a large hook, off which hung belts and scarves, but then he noticed the blade, its unmistakable obsidian serrated edge and the leather hilt, etched with runes—runes that upon closer look were quite familiar to him.

"Is that a sword?" Ronan asked, pointing towards the serrated hanging rack.

"That old thing?" Donavan replied. "Aye traveller, it's a sword. A cursed blade."

"Cursed?" Ronan stepped forward to examine it.

"That's what they say," Donavan continued. "Brings

ruin to whoever owns it. Stolen and passed from one thief to another, and every last one of them met a bad end — or so the tale goes. I couldn't bear to pass the bad luck onto another soul, so I found some other use for it. Truth is, not a damn thing sells that hangs from it."

"How much?" Ronan asked.

The merchant leaned back and laughed. "Did you not hear me traveller? The very blade is bad luck."

"Then rid yourself of it!" Ronan insisted.

"Which is worse, to live with a curse or to live with the curse of having passed the curse to another?"

"I deal in stories, not superstitions," Ronan replied. "Its curse makes it even more valuable to me. Tell me its story, give me a good price and I'll take the wicked blade off your hands."

Donavan considered and then regaled Ronan with the story of a sword that appeared mysteriously from within the shadows of history and passed between thieves, warriors, and collectors. It gained a reputation as a cursed blade, with tales of its wielders meeting untimely and violent ends, bands of thieves broken by greed and jealousy, each one shredded by the sword's vicious serrated blade, until the blade was finally abandoned, sold off to traders who eventually brought the blade to Soulum.

"In fact," Donavan continued, "I think Edric may have possessed the sword at one time." Then after a moment of reflection, "… or the sword possessed him."

Donavan yanked the sword from the wooden beam of his stall and handed it to Ronan. "Three coin and I'll be glad to be rid of the miserable thing."

They exchanged coin and sword, then Ronan returned to his own cart, pursing his lips to suppress a grin.

"I know that look, master," Jaryk whispered. "I look

forward to you sharing with me details of the treasure you just acquired."

"Man the cart, Jaryk," Ronan told him as he sheathed the newly acquired sword on his belt and unhitched the horse. "Price the wares with a motivation to sell. We need to make as many friends here as we can."

Jaryk nodded as Ronan mounted the horse and began his journey towards the highest peak of Soulum, to the Keep, and a meeting with Lord Magnus Zaragoza.

8. The Keep That Grinds People To Nothing

As Ronan's horse ascended the hill towards the Keep of Soulum, the village noise faded away, carried in the light wind that brushed against the tall grass and wildflowers on either side of the dirt path. Relief settled over him as he anticipated the culmination of this final leg of his journey— a meeting with Zaragoza, the legendary figure of Soulum.

A wandering butterfly flitted across his path, drawing his gaze back towards the village. He could see the commotion of the market square, but not any individuals, nor Jaryk, either.

A safe distance, Ronan thought before unsheathing the blade, admiring his purchase. The black stone along the blade's edge gleamed even under this grey sky. He knew this sword well. It was lost to history no more.

"Dul'grakh," Ronan said, and the sword responded, vibrating with desire, hunger, its serrated edge waking up from untold years of slumber. Ronan smiled. Never before had he held in his hands a piece of genuine dwarven magic.

"It is real," he said aloud. For the first time, he had acquired a true relic lost to legend—a magic item from a world in which magic no longer existed. Now Ronan knew, at least this one did.

"Grakh'dul," he said, and the sword's hunger abated, the vibrating stopped, the blade's slumber resumed. Sheathing the blade, Ronan looked towards the Keep, a foreboding stone edifice covered in vine, with towering battlements and an iron portcullis of thick latticed metal bars.

Stationed in front, two Blackshield sentinels stood, hooded, armoured, swords drawn but planted tip-down into the soil in front of them. They leaned lazily against the stone exterior until noticing Ronan's approach. Then, slowly, grudgingly, the sentinels took vigilant stances.

As Ronan approached, one sentinel shouted, "State your business, stranger!"

Ronan stopped his horse, pulled a letter from within his coat and held it aloft. The sentinel waved him forward.

"I am Ronan Morvayne." He handed the letter to the sentinel and added, "I come at the behest of Thalos of Ahm. Lord Magnus Zaragoza is expecting me."

The sentinel looked at the letter, sealed in wax and stamped with the five-pointed star of the Pentaclist Cartel—stamped with the ring from Thalos's hand—then handed it back to Ronan with a nod.

The sentinel pulled a rope hanging from the wall and from deep within the keep, a distant bell chimed. He looked through the iron grate of the portcullis and could see only a bit of the keep within—an archway that led to a large courtyard—but no more. The sentinels silently stared at Ronan for a few awkward minutes until the portcullis opened.

"I will confirm your expectancy," the sentinel said then turned to enter, disappearing into the archway. Slowly the portcullis shut behind him, the spikes at the bottom sinking into the earth as it locked into place with a clanging rattle that echoed against the interior walls of the keep. Then silence.

The sentinel that remained scanned the surroundings, from the village below to the hill's edge, a precipitous cliff that tumbled hundreds of feet down to the rough waters of a rocky sea. Like most of the realm, Soulum was enclosed by sheer cliffs that cut like jagged teeth straight down to the waters below, as if the land had been ripped from another embankment and an endless ocean placed between them.

Minutes pressed on. Finally, Ronan broke the silence, "Lord Zaragoza doesn't entertain many guests, I take it."

The sentinel smirked but retained his vigilant scan of the horizon, in silence.

Finally, the portcullis began to creak open as the other sentinel returned.

"Wait," he said, and so Ronan waited. Minutes. Then an hour. As the sky darkened with heavy clouds above, Ronan gritted his teeth in frustration. What could he do but complain to a pair of black armoured foot soldiers who would probably like nothing more than to make his dilemma even more maddening. Pointless. Through the portcullis, Ronan occasionally saw servants crossing under the archway with heads hung low. One turned her head towards Ronan, her vacant glance meeting his for just a moment, before she instinctively snapped her head back, her stare resuming its dutiful focus upon the ground. *Are these bars meant to prevent access, or prevent escape?* Ronan wondered as he began to feel his own stare becoming vacuous and empty.

Finally, the portcullis started to creak open once again, so Ronan dismounted and approached the entrance just as an unusually large figure, taller than most any man he'd seen, emerged from the shadow of the archway with slow and stiff movements. The man seemed just short of a giant, his shoulders broad, his brow a prominent crest that shadowed deeply sunken eyes, his hands meaty like stone crushers. But his suit was exquisite, imported from one of the Ahman tailors of High Street, no doubt.

The man stopped at the threshold of the open portcullis.

"Your purpose," he said in a baritone rumble. It was a question, but delivered as a statement.

"I am Ronan Morvayne." He presented the letter. "I come at the behest of Thalos of Ahm. Lord Magnus Zaragoza is expecting me."

The man received the letter, studied the seal, then methodically peeled the wax and opened it. His eyes lingered on the page for a long time. *Too long,* Ronan thought.

"May I have your name?" Ronan asked.

"Reiner," came his reply, slow and deep as he folded up the letter and placed it into the inside pocket of his jacket.

"Reiner, my letter?" Ronan asked as he suddenly lost possession of his only means of assuring an audience with Zaragoza.

Reiner simply stared back quietly, then his eyes drifted down towards Ronan's chest, towards the place where the amulet lay hidden. Ronan reached towards the buttons of his tunic, ensuring that the trinket was indeed hidden. The giant's gaze lingered long past the point one might claim oversight.

"May I come in?" Ronan broke the silence. "Lord Zaragoza is expecting me."

Reiner's eyes returned to Ronan's face. "Come back tomorrow."

"Tomorrow?" Ronan replied, aghast.

"Or the day after," Reiner continued. "Or the day after that."

"That is unacceptable. I have come a long way, and I am in possession of something of great value to Lord Zaragoza."

"Great value or great risk?"

"If I could just come in and meet with Lord Zaragoza ..."

"The Keep of Soulum is not accepting visitors."

"Is Lord Zaragoza even here?"

Reiner then bowed slightly and turned to walk away.

"Is Lord Zaragoza even here?!?" Ronan's words echoed off the walls of the keep, prompting the sentinels to cross their swords in front of him. Reiner disappeared past the archway as the groan of gears and chains signalled the descent of the iron gate.

"My letter of introduction!" Ronan shouted just before the bars locked into place in front of him.

Ronan mounted his horse and then addressed the sentinels, "Does Lord Magnus Zaragoza live in this keep?"

"On your way, merchant," the sentinel replied.

Ronan wanted to unsheathe the obsidian-edged blade and call upon the dwarven magic etched on its hilt to eviscerate the two soldiers and leave them an unrecognizable mass of flesh. Instead he gnashed his teeth and marched his horse back towards the market square.

Ronan's mind swirled with anger as the distant roll of thunder heralded the first drops of an impending rain. The patrons from the Good Shepherd had accused him of chasing ghosts. Now, the memory of their laughter echoed in his mind.

Damn you, Thalos!

As Ronan approached the market crowd, he sensed a buzz that seemed more than routine haggling over wares. Eyes turned to him. Whispers shared. Fingers pointed. Ronan felt an urgency as he pressed forward through the crowd and approached his cart—blockaded by a trio of Blackshield Sentinels.

"Master!" Jaryk called out as he squeezed between the black cloaked guardsmen, concern on his face. "They demand to see our Pentaclist license."

Ronan dismounted and confronted the sentinels. "What is the meaning of this?" he asked.

One sentinel, with a purple plume cascading from the top of his helm, stepped forward and asked, "Ronan Morvayne?"

"Aye, sentinel, what seems to be the problem?"

"Your license, merchant," the sentinel stated.

Vexed to a near boil, Ronan dug into his coat, pulled out his Pentaclist license and handed it over.

As he looked over the paper, the sentinel said, "We have on good authority that you are dealing in items that are not sanctioned by the Cartel." He then looked Ronan dead in the eye. "On behalf of the local lodge, I am ordered to confiscate your license. You are no longer permitted to sell in Soulum or anywhere else in the realm."

The sentinel then folded up Ronan's license and tucked it away. Ronan steadied himself with deep breaths.

"You're not Cartel!" Jaryk shouted. "You have no authority!"

"Quiet boy," Ronan shushed him and glared back at the sentinel.

"I'm certain there is some misunderstanding that can easily be resolved," Ronan said firmly.

"All Cartel matters may be taken up with the master of

the Lodge," the sentinel said. "But for now, pack up your wares and remove them from the market square or we'll confiscate those as well."

"Aye, sentinel." Defeat settled over him like a creeping avalanche of mud.

As the sentinels walked away, Donavan, the merchant in the next stall, shook his head and muttered, "I knew that blade was cursed."

Chatter spread through the market. What was the merchant's offense, they wondered. What goods did he carry that were unsanctioned? The crowd moved away from Ronan and Jaryk as if they carried a contagion.

Ronan felt a tightening in his chest and looked down at his hands. They trembled. He clenched tightly.

"What do we do now, master?" Jaryk asked.

Ronan scraped his nails against his palms as he released his fists and took a deep breath.

"Secure our goods and head back to the Good Shepherd. I must meet with the lodge master." Ronan stopped, then added with more than a small hint of concern. "Pray he'll see me."

Before Ronan could turn to go, Jaryk grabbed Ronan's sleeve and pulled him close. "I fear that whatever we carry that you've concealed from me may be our ruin."

"Lay low," Ronan replied and turned towards the windowless stone edifice on the far side of the square.

9. The Pentaclist Lodge

As Ronan exited the market square, a steady drizzle falling upon him, he felt judgmental stares, heard their whispers and saw mothers pull their children closer. Humiliation clawed at him. A lifetime of good standing with the Cartel—gone. Now just an outcast.

One pair of uncharitable eyes, in particular, drew his gaze. Atop the white stone steps of the temple, Father Benedictus stood in quiet scrutiny, a faint grin of victory on his reverent face.

I'll plunge the Black Death into your heart first. Ronan's chest pounded as he glared back at the priest.

Why had Thalos sent him here to his doom? Was this a trap? Conflicting thoughts swirled, but he resolved one thing: he would clear his name with the Cartel, then he and Jaryk would flee this maddening town.

Arriving at the imposing columns of the Cartel lodge, Ronan scanned the entire length of the wall for an entrance. His hands searched for a handle, or perhaps a lever. His fists pounded the masonry. But nothing. Another of Soulum's impenetrable stone edifices.

Finally, exhausted, he placed his back against the wall and slid down to the cold stone ground, dropping his face into his hands as the tribulations of the months-long journey finally overwhelmed him: the garden of hanging corpses, the accusations, the waiting, the humiliation and the isolation. Who was he now that the Cartel had revoked his trading rights and the Temple threatened to turn him into an outlaw? His only hope, it seemed, rested on gaining entry to a building with no entrance.

A knot of despair formed in his throat, choking him as he considered the danger, the sacrifice and shame he suffered—all to meet with Zaragoza, a man who might not even be real.

He had been chasing a ghost.

He shook his head at the absurdity and then started laughing. It began as a chuckle but then overtook him until a madman's laugh echoed off the walls. He let it all out in one broken, uncontrollable burst.

Then he heard a scraping sound. Stone against stone. A seam formed next to him as a large door swung on its axis.

Ronan rose to his feet, partly in shock, as a dark passageway opened, releasing the dank air of earth and rock, and the faint glow of torchlight.

Cautiously, Ronan stepped into the darkness. Never had he been inside of a Cartel lodge before, as licenses were granted at public convocations, by low level representatives. Cartel halls were reserved for members, an honour that seemed, at this moment, well beyond his grasp.

The door creaked shut behind him as Ronan descended towards an iron banded oak door, upon which danced the flickering light from sconces against the stone walls. When Ronan reached the final step, the door opened, revealing a stout man scarcely illuminated by the low light of the passage.

Ronan had expected something menacing, some image of greed and power. Instead he received an outstretched hand.

"Welcome, Ronan Morvayne," the man said with enthusiasm, "to the Soulum chapter of the Pentaclist Lodge. I am so glad you could make it. I am Kelvin Graf, lodge master."

Ronan paused at the unexpected cordiality. "A pleasure, lodge master Graf."

"Come in, come in, and call me Kelvin." He ushered Ronan inside.

The grand foyer of the lodge exuded opulence — marble floors and columns, a twelve-foot high vaulted ceiling painted with an exquisite fresco, plush seating, a massive harp in the corner of the room, and a giant Cartel pentagram inlaid in the centre of the floor.

Kelvin Graf looked like he feasted well. Dressed in tailcoats, with slicked jet-black hair and a thin moustache, he gave Ronan a warm, accessible smile as he led him through the grand foyer, pointing out portraits of history's famous Pentaclists hanging on the walls. When they reached the portrait bearing Magnus Zaragoza's name, Ronan stopped.

"Lord Zaragoza. Does he still live?"

Kelvin chuckled. "Of course he does. He lives in the keep at the top of the hill."

Ronan studied Zaragoza's face. The man looked aged, but not wrinkled, with sharp eyes, long grey hair and a robust grey beard. Zaragoza sat upright and proud, with a sly grin that gave the impression he considered his chair to be a throne. Ronan glared at the man's smugness.

"Soulum owes much to Lord Magnus Zaragoza," Kelvin added. "Come, we have matters to discuss."

Kelvin led Ronan to a carpeted sitting room with velvet chairs and a small table upon which an open box of cigars awaited. Exquisite cigars. Ronan smelled the rich tobacco before he noticed the box.

"Sit, please," Kelvin said. "Cigar?"

Ronan didn't smoke, but he couldn't refuse this indulgence. With just a few puffs, Ronan began to feel the troubles of the day slide off his shoulders.

"I imagine the rumpus with the sentinels today was quite the ordeal," Kelvin said. "You have my sincere apologies. But please understand our hands were tied in this situation."

"I'm not sure I understand." Ronan sat up and tapped the cigar into a crystal ashtray.

Kelvin smiled. "The Temple and the Cartel share space in this realm, but we do not share ideology. Nevertheless, accusations of warlockery cannot be ignored and you, Ronan Morvayne, have been marked by Father Benedictus. The Temple will levy charges against you tonight and in the sleeping hours, you will be roused from your bed and hanged in the gardens. No trial for strangers, I'm afraid."

"I am no warlock." Ronan gritted his teeth.

"I believe you," Kelvin chuckled. "Even if warlocks existed, I'd believe you. But the Cartel cannot be associated with those accused of warlockery, or those who trade in forbidden substances."

"I deal in relics and antiquities of storied renown, lodge master Graf," Ronan insisted. "My specialty is swords."

"Yes, yes of course," Kelvin eased the tone. "Your reputation precedes you and your expertise has not gone unnoticed by the Cartel. For an organization such as ours which values highly relics of the past, your skills would be a great asset to our repertoire."

Kelvin leaned back and puffed on his cigar, exhaling a thick stream of smoke that drifted towards the ceiling. Kelvin's eyes briefly glanced towards the spot on Ronan's chest where the amulet hid, but only for a moment. Then his eyes met Ronan's once more.

"But this unholy substance, forbidden substance. What shall we call it?" Kelvin waved his cigar vaguely in the air, then tapped it against the ashtray. "This *substance* is what interests the Cartel most of all."

Ronan took a deep breath and then, with a steady gaze, replied, "I'm certain that I have no idea to what you're referring."

"Oh come now, Morvayne. Let's not play these games shall we. As I said before, the Cartel and the Temple do not share the same ideology. They'd hang a man for a poorly timed sneeze if it smelled of warlockery. But we are businessmen. Pragmatists. We're not interested in superstitions, only results." Then his tone slowed determinedly. "We know the cost you incurred to acquire the substance. And we know you possess it. We are," Kelvin paused as he puffed once more, "impressed."

More times than he could count, Ronan had dealt with wealthy clients who wielded influence, and he had dealt with conniving businessmen haggling for the upper hand but never had he felt as outmanoeuvred as in this moment. The Cartel seemed to know everything. But to confess would require trust, and Ronan's well of trust had long run dry.

"I am not looking to make enemies with the Cartel," Ronan replied.

"Enemies?" Kelvin laughed. "Let me put it bluntly, Morvayne. There are those within the upper echelons of the Cartel who are very ... *very* ... interested in your little ... rarity. They would like to see it. They would like you to bring it to them. In exchange, we are offering you protection from the Temple. My superiors have enough influence with Father Benedictus to silence his accusations and impel his acolytes to heel. Your trading rights restored. Salvation."

Ronan sat in silent contemplation, studying Kelvin's expression. He needed deliverance, but could he trust the Pentaclists?

"And what guarantee do I have of this salvation?"

"The only guarantee I can give you, Morvayne, is that should you fail to produce the substance, you will hang tonight. As will your young companion. The boy."

Ronan closed his eyes for a long second and realized for the first time that his predicament did not only concern himself. He had inadvertently tied Jaryk to his own doom — all to satisfy a vengeful obsession. Ronan let out a deep sigh.

He wouldn't let the boy hang for his sins.

Ronan opened his eyes and reached into a hidden pocket within his tunic. He paused, knowing he couldn't rewind the clock after this. Kelvin's expression seemed eager, friendly even. This was it. Surrender. He brought out a small vial of sparkling powder and held it between his thumb and forefinger.

The lodge master smiled broadly. "Wonderful. Keep it safe. My superiors in the Cartel will be very pleased. You will ride to Blackshield Manor tonight, and upon a successful meeting, you will return, escorted by a sentinel, with a sealed letter to be handed to Benedictus which will exonerate you of all accusations."

Ronan placed the vial back into his shirt. They stood and shook hands.

"And be sure to bring your amulet with you," Kelvin added, prompting Ronan to instinctively pull his hand from Kelvin's grasp. His eyes went wide.

"My what?" Ronan's mind swam with confusion. *How do they know?*

"It's a Pentaclist artifact," Kelvin replied. "I'm sure you're aware. You've been carrying history with you all this time. Consider tonight an opportunity to find out what it truly means."

10. The Graverobber

By the time Ronan left the lodge, night had fallen and Soulum's usual evening storm began dropping a light rain upon the cobblestone streets. A steady mist slowly rose from the ground, backlit by oil lamps that guided Ronan towards the Good Shepherd.

Under the inn's awning, Ronan checked his cart to

ensure the locks were secured and noticed a thick rope around the entire wagon, redundantly sealing in their belongings.

Good lad, he thought, then noticed the sideways glances and the quiet mutterings directed his way by the few patrons gathered outside, before they turned to enter the tavern and distance themselves from the tainted merchant. Another figure, smaller and hooded, crouched against the wall by the entrance.

Ronan met the crouched figure's eyes, who then pulled down his hood. It was Jaryk.

"Jaryk, what are you doing?" Ronan asked.

"I'm laying low, master," Jaryk replied.

Ronan shook his head and smiled. Small rays of light could indeed break through even during the darkest of hours.

Jaryk stood, and Ronan wrapped his arm around his apprentice's shoulder. "You did well."

"Did you get your warrant reinstated?" Jaryk asked.

"Not yet, but although we have many eyes upon us now, the Cartel has offered us protection. I have a meeting tonight at Blackshield Manor."

"Blackshield Manor!" Jaryk exclaimed in a whisper. "The dark heart of the Wyre Peninsula?"

"I'll be fine Jaryk. Come I'll show you."

Inside the tavern, they ignored the patrons' slights as they headed towards their room, whereupon Ronan stopped. "Our last night here."

"Good," Jaryk said, the relief visible in his eyes.

Inside the room, Ronan unsheathed the obsidian-edged blade. "It was with great fortune that I came across this."

Jaryk smiled, "Tell me, master."

Ronan swung the sword from side to side, gliding it

through the air with the expert strokes of an accomplished swordsman.

"This is the legendary sword known as the Graverobber," Ronan said with pride, "a weapon steeped in blood and scandal, forged by a renegade dwarf of the Blackrock Mountains for a barbarian chief whose bloodlust caused a reign of terror through the northern mountain tribes."

Jaryk sat leaning forward, eager to be regaled with another of Ronan's compelling stories that transformed mundane items into curios of wonder.

"The dwarf's name was Kaldraks Ironjaw, a maverick smith who believed in crafting weapons so fearsome that the will of the enemy would be broken before the battle began. Though his efforts drew scorn from his fellow Dwarves, fate brought Kaldraks together with Drakkul the Butcher, a brutal barbarian chief who sought a blade to mirror his savagery—a blade that wouldn't simply kill but would obliterate its target."

Ronan laid the handle across his arm.

"See these runes on the hilt?" Ronan asked.

Jaryk nodded as he peered closely at the foreign symbols. "Can you read it?" Jaryk asked.

"It's the dwarven word for bloodthirsty. The sword itself hungers for flesh, its serrated edge like the teeth of a predator. When the word is spoken, the sword vibrates with a malevolent intent—to devour, to eviscerate ... to erase."

Ronan ran the tip of his finger along the serrated edge of the blade. "Once its hunger is roused, the Graverobber is reputed to slice through the thickest of armour with ease, tearing apart its targets so mercilessly that nothing remains to bury—robbing them of their due grave."

Jaryk's mouth hung open as Ronan concluded the tale.

"Say it."

"Oh lad, not with you near," Ronan cautioned. "If the legends are true, the blade's hunger overtakes its wielder. I would only waken the blade if absolutely necessary."

"What happened to Drakkul?" Jaryk asked.

"He carved a path of terror across the tribal lands until he eventually fell and was buried with his ruthless blade. In no small twist of irony, the Graverobber was stolen from his grave and passed between thieves, bandits and marauders until it disappeared to history, its tale long forgotten."

"Until Ronan Morvayne found it," Jaryk added with admiration.

"It is a true one of a kind," Ronan added. "The Blackrock dwarves erased his name from their records and swore an oath never to replicate the abominable blade."

Ronan smiled with great pride and continued. "But Kaldraks forged the sword with one more quality that renders its user nearly unstoppable."

Ronan revealed a set of runes on the opposite side of the hilt.

"The Dwarven word for ghost. Watch."

Ronan placed the Graverobber on a table and said, "Zurn'dul."

The blade shimmered and vibrated for a moment before vanishing.

Jaryk's eyes widened as he stood. "By the ancient gods!" Then he whispered, "Magic is real." Jaryk turned towards Ronan, the words coming out like a soft wind. "Be rid of this thing, master. It will destroy us."

"Now watch." Ronan wrapped his hand around the space where the hilt of the sword had been visible, and the moment his grip tightened, he too vanished.

"Master!" Jaryk cried out as both the sword and the

man had now disappeared from sight.

"Dul'zurn," Ronan's voice crawled from the void, and then with a shimmering glow, Ronan and the sword reappeared.

Jaryk stared, speechless.

"If events turn at Blackshield, I have with me a powerful ally." Ronan proudly sheathed the blade.

11. The Ride to Blackshield

The rain congealed into thick drops from the canopy of trees above, off whose branches swung innumerable corpses—Soulum's grim tribute to the Deitist's crusade against warlockery.

Ronan fixated on the macabre tableau, though he felt a vice wrenching his gut at the sight of the lifeless figures swaying against the dark sky. The wind moaned through the trees as Ronan tried to ignore the stench of rotting flesh caught in his throat. His horse shook its head and exhaled gruffly.

How many more times would he have to traverse this villainous terrain before he and Jaryk could abandon Soulum? He had hoped to leave in better fortune than when he arrived, or at least closer to acquiring the Black Death; after all, what better place to find the Deitist's Bane than the target of its fury? Now he only hoped to escape with his throat intact.

Jaryk, meanwhile, was ill-prepared for the darkness of the Wyre Peninsula. Ronan had to spend a good half hour putting the boy's mind at ease after revealing to him the Graverobber's capabilities. He told him everything. The snuff. The Pentaclists' craving for the powder. And the Black Death. Then he promised they'd begin their journey home the moment Ronan returned. Though now it wasn't just leaving. It was an escape.

Lightning struck, freezing the corpses in the blast of light. Warlocks. Ronan pictured himself swinging among them. Probably every one of them innocent like his parents. But did they, he wondered ... did his parents truly hand over his baby brother? If not them, who? And why? Who received him? And why was the body returned, mutilated?

Someone wanted my parents hanged and they sacrificed my brother to see it done.

Maybe the baby had indeed been handed to warlocks. Ronan shuddered at the thought. If so, he considered the unthinkable—maybe the Black Death had been used upon him.

Thunder crackled. The storm was still a distance away.

The irony, that my brother might contribute to the demise of the Cult that murdered our parents ... if I ever find the Black Death. If warlocks exist.

Finally, the woods cleared, and the raindrops felt less oppressive. Open road lay ahead. And through the Wyre Forest to Ronan's left, high atop Watcher's Peak, Blackshield Manor, and the Cartel lords, awaited.

Salvation. Ronan breathed deeply.

Or am I escaping one set of chains only to place myself in others.

Lightning flashed, illuminating the fanged outline of the manor, a colossal predator atop the hill.

Ronan's hand traced the outline of the star amulet beneath his tunic as Kelvin Graf's words echoed in his mind ... *Tonight you will find out what it truly means.* He wondered if the protection his father promised had now become a curse.

Thunder rumbled through the clouds in reply.

12. Blackshield Manor

The storm had become a deluge by the time Ronan ascended the steep climb to the black citadel atop Watcher's Peak. No lights shone along this empty stretch nor did any illuminate the giant coal facade that stretched towards the infinity of black above. Just a treacherous narrow land bridge lay in between Ronan and the unwelcoming sight before him. He held the reins tightly and pressed his horse forward across the thin span, for even his own stomach churned at the sight on either side—steep cliffs that on this evening had turned to waterfalls descending into a valley of nothingness.

When Ronan finally arrived at the entrance to the manor, two sentinels awaited under a large overhang. One pulled a thick rope by the door as Ronan tethered his horse, and a muffled bell rang from inside.

"You are expected," one of the sentinels said.

Lightning cracked as the door slowly creaked open and thunder rumbled ever closer as Ronan was greeted in the doorway by an older gentleman, a chamberlain wearing a purple brocade tunic and black cloak. The bones of his cheeks strained against pale, gaunt skin that nevertheless bagged up under his tired eyes.

"Ronan Morvayne," the chamberlain's hoarse, gravelly voice crowed with great strain. "Please come in."

Ronan stepped into the foyer, his eyes shifting all around. A grand marble staircase rose to a second floor balcony. From the room's vaulted crown hung a golden chandelier ornamented with innumerable shimmering crystals, delicately coated in wax dripped from the myriad of candles it held. Inlaid into the marble floor was the five pointed star of the Pentaclists.

"This way," the chamberlain croaked and limped dreadfully towards the hallway ahead, one leg visibly longer than the other. Ronan followed into the dim candlelight.

The air smelled damp, both sweet and rotten like floral decay, as Ronan entered the hallway. Embedded in the walls, glass displays contained oddly lifelike statues—men and women, like wax effigies, but eerily authentic, in shredded clothing that revealed arms, legs and other body parts not accustomed to be shown in sophisticated halls. Some of the statues' mouths were stretched open, locked in silent screams. Some seemed wide eyed in fear. Others, their eye sockets vacant, just black holes. But as Ronan passed one glass display after another, most noticeable was the stitching and the crude, crusted incision points that made these patchwork statues seem like ragged dolls.

The further Ronan stepped through the hallway, the more grotesque the statues became. Limbs missing, but covered by stitching and blackened gore. The detail was uncanny. Others with wrong limbs—a left arm where a right should be. One glass case presented a sight on which Ronan's gaze lingered, a man and woman with opposite gendered parts.

Next to the door at the end of the hall stood, without a glass case, a lone full figure statue of a woman—beautiful, completely naked except for sandals that laced up her calves and thighs. Unlike the other statues, her body was pristine, save for one corruption: her lips were sewn shut. She stood stoic, holding a silver tray upon which sat a plate, and upon it what looked to Ronan like a severed tongue.

Thunder boomed outside. Ronan's mind reeled at the thought of what kind of people would find appealing a gallery of art in which human suffering was considered an aesthetic.

The chamberlain opened the door, ushered Ronan inside and shut it behind him, leaving him alone in an opulent parlour.

Ronan marvelled at the luxury. Even in the great capital city of Ahm, the seat of the Ahman empire, never had he been invited into a room of such indulgent tastes. Crimson velvet drapes with gold filigree pooled onto the floor, richly woven rugs covered stone floors, a grand fireplace with a gold mantle and marble bas reliefs enclosed a roaring fire. Ronan took it all in—the grand piano, the giant ornate mirror, the crystal decanters and goblets along with a towering bookshelf filled with ancient looking tomes.

Even the furniture seemed to be fashioned with a decadent amount of gold.

The furniture. That's when he started to notice it. The feet of the couches and chairs were human feet. On the table was a grotesque game board, with a host of eyeballs nestled in notches. And the chandelier, constructed entirely of human hands, palms up to hold candles.

What is this cursed place? Ronan wondered, so absorbed by the sights that he never saw her approach until she stood next to him—a servant woman, completely naked except for a pair of sandals that laced up her calves and thighs. Her body was stunning, her face beautiful, except for the thick stitching that sealed her lips shut. She held a silver tray, upon which sat a crystal goblet.

The similarity was inescapable between this woman in front of him and the statue from the hallway, statues that he now seriously considered were not in fact wax likenesses, an idea that truly he did not want to believe. He tried shaking the thought from his mind as simply too preposterous, an idea beyond all reason that should not distract him from the matter at hand—the snuff, his license, his freedom. He focused on the crystal goblet, and realized perhaps a drink is exactly what he needed.

Ronan took the glass, placed his nose inside and inhaled what was indeed a familiar scent. Reassured, he drank the spirit. The liquid felt warm going down, soothing, relaxing, smooth, but with an unfamiliar, almost medicinal, aftertaste that left him feeling relieved. Everything would be okay. Maybe he was overreacting. He felt good. Agreeable.

Why was I worried? They are offering me a place here.

Time seemed to slow as the woman now looked beautiful in a way that he hadn't noticed before. His eyes lingered upon her, moving slowly down her body and then back up. She took a step closer and arched her back, like she offered herself. Her scent was intoxicating, consuming him.

How long had it been since he had been with a woman, he wondered? Or this beautiful? He shouldn't. She arched further towards him. Closer. Nearly touching him with her body. Ronan looked into her eyes, questioning her with his own. She nodded.

He touched her, the sensation of her soft curves igniting him as he obsessed. He studied her with his fingers and palms. Moments turned into seconds. Seconds into minutes. Minutes stretched on as he lost himself on her flesh.

How long had he been touching her? Was it an eternity?

Her hand clasped his, then led him to the far part of the room, towards a large well-lit closet enclosed by glass doors, within which Ronan could see steel, leather and gemstones.

She opened the double doors of the closet to reveal a sight that stopped Ronan more than anything he had yet seen in Blackshield Manor. Relics, antiquities, curios and artifacts that he immediately knew had immense value.

This is one of the legendary Cartel reliquaries.

Awestruck, Ronan scanned over swords and shields, goblets and daggers, helms, amulets and rings. Then he saw one he recognized: the Sword of Xithon. That one he remembered from Zaragoza's tome, *Relics of Legend.*

Curious, Ronan thought, *because that sword is lost to time.*

Ronan also spotted the Crown of the Agitator, that Zaragoza also chronicled. And the Great Sceptre of Sythe, again from Zaragoza's tome. Ronan suddenly realized: *Relics of Legend* wasn't Zaragoza's study of fabled artifacts, it was a catalogue of Cartel treasure.

Then, Ronan's eyes settled on an unmistakable dagger—its hilt, fashioned from human bone; its blade, the body of a dragon; the tip, curved like a dragon's tail; its reptilian mouth joining the hilt. There in front of him, upon a golden stand rested the one relic that drove him, the source of the catharsis he so desired: the Black Death, the Deitist's Bane.

A beautiful song crept into his mind, the hum of a lover's tune. The dagger drew him closer with its melody.

After all these years searching, there it lay in front of him, emanating its exquisite hymn. Calling him. Finally. He had found it. Within reach. All he had to do was seize it. Ronan took a step into the closet and stretched out, leaning forward. As his fingertips nearly touched the hilt of the dagger, a thought occurred to him: if the Black Death is real, that means ...

"Morvayne!" a voice hissed from behind him.

Ronan froze. *Patience Morvayne*, he thought as his eyes closed briefly. *Don't get ahead of yourself.*

The smell of fermentation hit Ronan before he fully turned around. The man stood hunched, one shoulder raised higher than the other. His suit, exquisitely tailored, fit slightly too large. But what stood out most prominently to

Ronan was his waxy skin, eerily smooth and stretched out, almost reminiscent of the statues in the hallway.

Then his eyes—dark ... no, black. His pupils seemed wholly blackened. His lips, dry and split.

"Welcome to Blackshield Manor, the home of my grandfather, Lord Blackshield," the man said, his rotting teeth visible behind cracked lips. Ronan immediately smelled the decay, like death infected him within yet his exterior had been preserved. "My name is Lord Baron Sicarius, Scion of Blackshield."

Sicarius held out a hand with blackened fingertips, which Ronan hesitantly met with his. It seemed he could feel the man's decaying fingertips rub off on his hand. With his other hand, Sicarius reached into his pocket and pulled out a small atomizer, which he then sprayed into his open mouth—a pleasing scent that momentarily masked his rot.

"Pleasure to make your acquaintance, Lord Baron," Ronan replied with a short smile and quick shallow breaths, so as not to breathe in what Sicarius exhaled.

Sicarius smiled yellow and black teeth. "I hear you're quite the collector of rare treasures. You must appreciate what you see in our reliquary." He spritzed his mouth again.

"I am extremely impressed. I thought most of these items were lost to history. I find it reassuring to see that many of them have been found—one in particular."

"Yesss," the word wriggled out of Sicarius's cracked lips. "The Black Death. This is something you desire greatly."

"I assume you've spoken with Thalos."

"The Cartel has eyes and ears everywhere, Ronan Morvayne."

A thunderclap roared angrily, directly above the vaulted stone ceiling of the manor.

"If the substance you carry warrants the notoriety that precedes it," Sicarius continued, leaning close, his air enveloping Ronan's face, "the Cartel may be willing to offer you a pathway to acquire the dagger you desire."

Ronan forced down the bile rising in his throat and felt a sense of terrifying victory; the end of a lifelong quest lay within his reach. The Black Death could be his.

"There are members of the Cartel—the Bloodlords—who wish to see the substance," Sicarius replied.

As Ronan followed Sicarius through the parlour, an unease tugged at him, a dreadful sense that within this horror show of Blackshield Manor he was the oddity—until a soothing sense tempered his mind, relaxed him, and replaced anxiety with a feeling of good fortune for attaining an audience with those who desired what he can offer.

At the door, Sicarius pulled a large keyring from his pocket and slid the largest of the iron keys into the lock.

"Welcome to your initiation into the Pentaclist Cartel, Morvayne," Sicarius's tone dripped with mockery as he opened the thick, iron banded wooden door.

A door through which one does not force entry, Ronan mused, *or force exit.*

Sicarius ushered Ronan into the darkness ahead and before his eyes could adjust he heard the pounding thud of the door closing behind him—and a lock securing it.

Darkness … but flickering candles.

Lightning flashed through windows high atop the walls of this atrium chamber and for a moment Ronan caught a glimpse of the magnitude of the room. An immense rotunda, with candelabra around the perimeter, slowly appeared before him as his eyes adjusted.

Thunder boomed.

Ronan began to see, a few yards ahead, a figure seated

in a chair, surrounded by small candles, atop a grand Cartel pentagram inlaid on the flagstone. Horns spiralled from its head like a goat. A black cloth covered its eyes while its bare muscular torso heaved languidly, and its fur-covered legs terminated in cloven feet that scraped agitatedly against the floor.

A satyr.

Ronan watched the creature in disbelief. He had read about satyrs in mythological treatises of ancient First Age gods, but they were only fantastical morality tales. Nevertheless, here one sat in the flesh, moving awkwardly, struggling against … then Ronan noticed its arms bound to the chair. Straps across its chest.

The satyr held in its lap a large crystal ball, cloudy, but with the noticeable slit of a serpent's iris, which seemed to move in response to Ronan's presence, as if it peered back.

Behind the satyr, three additional figures in black, hooded robes sat upon a raised dais in large, ornate chairs, the middle one like a throne. Ronan strained to see their faces, but he saw only dark, expressionless masks. The dancing light of candelabra flickered behind them.

The Bloodlords, Ronan thought, then turned to address Sicarius, but the fetid man was gone.

An awkward moment of silence stretched on as the three robed figures sat unmoving. The rain beat against the glass windows above, while the satyr's hooves anxiously scraped against the stone floor.

Then the satyr began to convulse, its grip tightening around the crystal ball as its body tensed and writhed, its brow furrowing, followed by an agonizing scream that increased in volume as the convulsions intensified. A greyish black cloud of light coalesced around its body as its pained howls pierced through the rotunda. Then it suddenly stopped as the cloud found an equilibrium.

A deep, bellowing voice forced its way out from within the creature.

"Kneel before us, Ronan Morvayne," the voice resonated with a power that seeped into Ronan's very being. Before Ronan could protest, his body lowered to one knee, his head hung low.

Lightning splintered across the windows, accompanied by an immediate thunderous roar.

"You have served us well," the voice noted its approval with a commanding tone. "Now rise and present the sacrament to the Bloodlords."

Ronan felt his own will spectating as he rose to his feet, walked around the pentagram and stepped on to the dais in front of the masked figure in the centre throne.

"Kneel and proffer the sacrament." The masked figure's voice sounded of dust and ash.

Ronan knelt, reached into his shirt and held out the vial.

As the Bloodlord took it, a flash of lightning poured the storm's light ever so briefly into the ceremonial chamber, but just long enough for Ronan to notice something on the back of the figure's hand—a swirling eye sigil that shimmered in that brief moment of light. Thunder shook the chamber.

Ronan knew instantly.

It was the same sigil on the cover of *Relics of Legend* that he saw in Thalos's shop, and the same sigil described by the woman in the Good Shepherd Inn.

This is Lord Magnus Zaragoza.

Then his father's voice seeped in his mind.

"Watch the hands."

Ronan turned towards the robed figure to the right, his hand bereft of a middle finger. Lightning flashed again and revealed on the back of his hand a crescent moon—the very same sigil on the placard outside of Thalos's Vault. Thunder roared again.

Thalos.

"Away," the Bloodlord said to him after receiving the vial. Ronan stood up.

"Morvayne!" Ronan heard behind him and turned to see Sicarius waving him back.

Ronan turned to look at the hands of the third Bloodlord, just as another flash of lightning broke through the clouds and thunder rattled the windows. A swirling line of energy revealed a shield insignia.

Lord Blackshield.

Bloodlords. Marked Lords. Then, something within him knew.

Warlocks.

Ronan backed off the dais towards Sicarius.

"It has been a long time since we have had the sacrament," Sicarius said. "Not an easy substance to acquire."

Ronan watched as the masked figure on the centre throne doled out the snuff onto the back of each of the other Bloodlords' hands, after which the robed men lifted their masks just enough to inhale the powder. Ronan peered, trying to make out faces, especially Thalos, the one who had sent him here. Ronan tried to make sense of it all, but a lingering, soothing feeling clouded his logic.

"Our one true lord, the Lord of Shadows, communicates with us through the satyr." Sicarius's voice fouled the air as the Bloodlords settled into crooked postures, the substance's effects taking hold. "Satyrs are the only creature on this world who can handle possession by our lord without their minds breaking."

The satyr sat still. The cloud of grey light that had surrounded it had receded.

Moans slowly cascaded from the Bloodlords' mouths as they began to writhe, their arms reaching out, their hands grasping at the chairs and then clawing at their robes.

"The seeing stone on the satyr's lap allows one to commune with the Lord of Shadows," Sicarius continued, saliva building up on his broken lips, "but it is an impersonal connection."

Heavy breathing, then sobbing wails escaped from beneath the Bloodlords' masks, until finally they crumpled into their chairs, lost in trance, mumbling unintelligibly.

"But the sacrament," Sicarius emphasized before spritzing his mouth with the atomizer, "the sacrament is a product of our lord's essence that he left behind before his banishment. It is a complete and holy communion."

The Bloodlords continued to mumble in what seemed a language of pure malice, triggering an unsettling nauseous rumbling in Ronan's gut, gripping him in pain as the wicked muttering spawned snarling knots in his belly.

"Your father was Cartel," Sicarius noted with a sly smile, his lip cracking, releasing a small drop of blood that trickled down his chin.

Lightning flashed. Thunder roared.

The Bloodlords' muttering became a sickening chant: "Zhul'thax. Zhor'thox. Zhul'tharrax."

"My father," Ronan turned in shock to face Sicarius, still wincing as the Bloodlords' chants oozed like a perverted hymn. "What do you know about my father?"

"He was a shrewd businessman. On his way, in fact. But," Sicarius shook his head in disappointment, "even the best fall on hard times."

That soothing feeling of acquiescence which had

enveloped Ronan from his earlier drink wore thin as he bristled at his father's memory dredged up in this unpleasant place. His mind cleared, if only for a brief spell.

"My father is none of your business." Ronan scowled and straightened up. The Graverobber, which had been silently and invisibly waiting against Ronan's hip began to vibrate gently in response to Ronan's growing ire.

"Oh but he is, Morvayne," Sicarius replied, spittle flying as he hissed. "Hard times may sometimes cause a man to act desperately, like handing over an infant in exchange for financial relief, or thieving priceless artifacts from a benefactor."

The Bloodlords' mind-churning chant continued: "Zhul'thax. Zhor'thox. Zhul'tharrax."

The malignant chant pressed on Ronan's very thoughts. His hand moved towards the hilt of Graverobber as he asked, "Handed to who?"

"Malevolent ones." Sicarius's eyes narrowed.

Lightning burst. Thunder shook the manor.

"How do you know this?"

"We know all about your father," Sicarius said with a smile. "Like I said, he was Cartel. And a skilful thief too. Before his unfortunate end, he stole one of the Cartel's priceless treasures: the Amulet of Secrets."

Ronan's hand instinctively moved from his hip towards the heavy iron amulet behind his tunic, his father's heirloom, the memento he had carried with him since childhood.

Stolen? Ronan's mind reeled.

"The time has now come for you to atone for your father's sins and return that which does not belong to you," Sicarius growled with subtle menace.

"Zhul'thax. Zhor'thox. Zhul'tharrax," the Bloodlords

continued, then in grand unison and with a terrifying dirge, exclaimed: "Summanus!"

"How do you know I possess the amulet?" Ronan asked, grasping his head in agony from the weight of the rotten chant.

"Your curiosity betrayed you, Morvayne," Sicarius softened. "As I've mentioned, our eyes and ears are everywhere. Even in the Great Library of Ahm."

"Zhul'tharrax. Summanus!!" The Bloodlords' chant crescendoed, impelling Ronan to drop to one knee, clutching his head, attempting to block the offensive words from seeping any deeper into his mind.

"We are not brutes, Morvayne," Sicarius assured. "In exchange for the amulet, we are not simply offering to return your trading license and provide you with protection from Deitist persecution, we are offering you full Cartel membership… and the Black Death within your reach."

The Bloodlords' chanting slowly subsided as the robed figures settled back into their chairs, drifting off into the final leg of their hallucinatory journey.

Ronan's shoulders relaxed, his features softened, and he pulled himself up to his feet.

"Or you can keep the amulet and spend the rest of your days fleeing from the Temple's noose." Sicarius's words hung in the air with the stench of his decaying innards.

Ronan looked towards the satyr, bound to the chair, anxiously scraping its hooves. The Bloodlords behind him slowly roused from their slumped postures.

"Why is this amulet so important to the Cartel?" Ronan asked, the chant's grip on his mind finally released.

"The amulet is a key that unlocks a very important Cartel tome which, in the common tongue, is known as the Book of Secrets. It is the history of our Order, a history that predates Deitist prophecy. I'm sure you can understand the sentimental value something of that nature might hold for us."

Sicarius then motioned his head towards the Bloodlords. "The sacrament is wearing off. You'll have your verdict soon."

The Bloodlords resumed their formal postures in their lavish chairs. The one in the middle steepled his hands and nodded towards Sicarius.

"The sacrament met expectations. Your industriousness will bring great value to the Cartel, Morvayne. We look forward to you providing future deliveries."

Sicarius then held out the blackened fingers of his gnarled hand. "The amulet please."

Ronan clutched the amulet through his tunic.

Never let them take it from you, his father's last words. Conflicting thoughts swirled in Ronan's head. Did his father lie? If it was stolen, why was Ronan clinging to it so tightly? Did his father *use* Ronan for one final treachery against the Cartel? Had the Cartel wronged his father?

Thalos sent him here. Thalos *knew*. Was all of this some diabolical manoeuvre to place Ronan right here in this moment? Did any of this matter now that the Deitist cult aimed to hang a warlock placard around his neck?

An upsetting reality began to sink in: the amulet never truly belonged to him.

… the Black Death within your reach.

As Ronan untied the thin leather cord around his neck and pulled the amulet from inside of his tunic, Sicarius smiled victoriously, baring his blackened teeth. Ronan placed the amulet in Sicarius's hand and exhaled. Years of confusion and inquiry cascaded off of his shoulders.

"You've done well Ronan Morvayne."

Ronan chafed at Sicarius's abrasive voice and noticed next to him the naked servant woman from the parlour, silver tray in hand, atop which rested a giant, ancient looking tome—gilded black leather with raised engraving on the cover, framed by ornate metal caps, and banded with a steel clasp and lock mechanism. Sicarius placed the amulet atop the book, and the woman dutifully carried the items towards the dais.

"The Book of Secrets contains a history of the First Age, an era in which our Lord of Shadows held dominion over this world, a time forgotten by the historians of this era." Sicarius then added proudly, "Our lord is due to return and usher in the Third Age."

Ronan barely paid any mind to Sicarius while he watched the woman carry away the amulet he had worn for so many years. She placed the relics in the lap of the Bloodlord seated in the centre throne, then respectfully stepped back as he fitted the amulet onto the tome's cover—triggering a cascade of blue energy that rippled around the book—and gave it a counter-clockwise turn.

The clasp lifted open.

The Bloodlord opened the book, then looked at Sicarius and nodded.

"Are you ready, Ronan Morvayne, to join the Cartel?" Sicarius asked.

Ronan closed his eyes and took a deep breath. He had come this far. It was time to see this journey to its conclusion. Ronan opened his eyes and nodded.

The servant woman placed a pedestal in front of Ronan, then took the crystal ball from the satyr's lap, the iris reacting suddenly to the movement, and placed the ball atop the pedestal's concave cap.

"Place both of your hands upon the eye," Sicarius pronounced with formality, "and follow in the honoured steps of all Cartel brethren who have preceded you."

Ronan's gaze locked onto the crystal, its iris tracking him, and reached out. His heart pounded as he prepared to dive into the unknown. He spent his whole life searching for secrets behind closed doors, codes within written passages and histories lost to time, but here at the precipice of the great unknown, he hesitated.

Do I want to know?

Lightning flashed through the chamber. Thunder rattled the windows.

Yes, he did.

Ronan wrapped his palms around the crystal eye and immediately fell inward, his mind ripped from his body and embraced by something terrifyingly strong. Blackshield Manor disappeared as he felt his awareness sucked through a tunnel of darkness with a deafening whoosh.

Then silence.

Slowly a dim light emerged from the darkness and began to grow as if he moved towards it—or it towards him. Mist swirled as he approached, illuminating a stone archway at the entrance to the light. His motion stopped, and peering into the lighted mist, he noted animated movement on the floor, serpentine undulation sidewinding forward and then receding back into the mist.

Fear did not grip him in this moment, rather it was awe in the recognition of the slithering entity's colossal size—almost wider than the outstretched arms of a man at its distant part, but tapered to the size of a man's leg at its closest—along with its phosphorescent shimmer, hypnotizing Ronan in the manner of a snake dance, drawing him forward until he took a disembodied step past the threshold.

Now completely enveloped in a boundless fog, Ronan noted the red and black scales of the slithering thing, its reptilian nature and the unsettling idea that the coiling actions in front of him were but a small fraction of the creature's tail that disappeared into the white void. Its enormity seemed beyond reason and Ronan searched the haze to determine more of its form. Above him, the mist divided to reveal an approaching mammoth eye, green and gold with a vertical black slit and surrounded by shimmering scales. The eye itself must have been as large as two men, one standing on the other's shoulders, and focused its sight directly on Ronan.

"We are Summanus," an intangible voice resonated unbodied from the creature.

The voice, unlike anything Ronan had ever heard, crawled with a guttural venom that twisted into his being, gripping him into a state of complete deference, consuming his entire consciousness. The white, comforting mist around him misled, for hidden within it lay utter tyranny and subjugation. The eye and tail pulled back through the mist, creating billowing waves that cascaded up and around at an unfathomable scale, streaming beyond sight, as if to give Ronan a sense of the creature's enormity, before returning with a booming stomp, disrupting the mist with furious force, the eye once again fixating on Ronan's awareness.

"We awaited you, Ronan Morvayne," the creature's words crept about Ronan, enfolding around him like a host of tentacles. "We whispered in your father's ear when he stole the amulet. And we whispered in his ear when he gave it to you. You have fulfilled your fate."

Ronan's being shrank before the staggering inevitability and domination that clawed at his essence, devouring his will.

"Now you have joined us and we will be with you, always, whispering."

Ronan could feel its essence slithering through the crevices of his consciousness, rooting itself.

"Time for you to choose, Ronan Morvayne. Accept your place in service to us, to lead men into the Third Age."

The titanic eye of the beast leaned in closer.

"Will you accept what is to come?"

Though incorporeal, Ronan felt an oppressive force urging him down, as if down to his knees, absorbing his will. Ronan looked down in shame as he considered his journey—the loss of his parents, his struggle as a teen on the streets of Ahm to become a profitable merchant, the years of study in the Great Library, of swordcraft, and the hunt for the Black Death. All for naught?

No. He refused to be a pawn.

Ronan summoned the will to rise, his mind screaming with one final burst of urgency, as he pulled himself up and wrenched his palms off the stone, stumbling back into darkness.

Ronan took a deep breath as he felt his body once more. His mind still reeled from the vision, like the essence of the creature lingered, slinking through his awareness, tucking itself into dark places.

Ronan saw the room return to his sight. The crystal eye. The satyr. The Bloodlords. The masked figure in the centre throne shook his head. To his left, Ronan noticed Sicarius acknowledge the sign.

Sicarius.

Ronan's blood seethed at the sight of the noxious ogre. Everything that Ronan rejected about his newfound knowledge of this diabolical plot to usher in a dark age was embodied in that awful face.

Disappointment oozed from Sicarius, "Morvay—"

Ronan's fist met Sicarius's jaw with such speed, Ronan's mind had to catch up with what he had done. Brittle bone splintered through the air as Sicarius's jaw shattered and his rotten teeth flew in fragmented pieces, cascading towards the floor.

Sicarius moaned in agony as he landed face first onto the ground and sprawled out into a crumpled mess, blood oozing from his face, arms flayed, blackened fingers skewed and broken from the fall, and keyring tossed across the floor.

The keyring.

Ronan swiftly grabbed the keys and ran towards the exit as he began to hear the satyr convulsing and howling in possessed agony. Not once did he look behind him, never knowing that as he ran through the door, shut it and locked it, the Bloodlord in the centre throne nodded calmly to each of his masked counterparts. But even if Ronan had seen the gesture, he likely would not have known what it meant, at least not in that moment. After some consideration, however, he may have come to realize that those who conspire behind the thick stone walls of Cartel halls leave no possibility unconsidered.

In the parlour, Ronan considered his escape. The only obstacle he foresaw would be the two Blackshield sentinels at the main entrance. He placed his hand on the hilt of the Graverobber and the world around him went grey as he vanished from sight.

Will do this cleanly if I can, he thought, *but if not …*

"Dul'grakh." The serrated blade hummed with desire.

Ronan began running towards the room's exit, but then a sweet song stopped him. The hum of a lover's tune swirled around his head. It called him.

The Black Death.

Ronan ran towards the reliquary, threw open the doors and saw the dagger. It was beautiful.

Yesssss, a serpentine voice whispered through Ronan's mind.

Ronan looked around. He was still alone.

He grabbed the dagger and headed for the door.

As Ronan ran into the hallway of statues, he heard glass cracking. He slowed to see shattering shards breaking all around him as the statues stepped out of their cases and, like one legion, rushed towards him, surrounding him, clawing at him, piling on top of him, dragging him down, burying him.

Underneath the throng of statues, Ronan braced himself with his left hand and roared out, slashing with Graverobber, slashing at legs, at arms, stabbing at torsos, chopping necks … but nothing. The blade sliced through the bodies like ghosts.

Illusions.

The bodies faded away with that realization and Ronan noticed all of the glass cases were still intact, the statues unmoved.

Warlockery.

The world remained grey, his invisibility intact, as he clutched the hilt of the Graverobber, the blade's obsidian edge still buzzing with hunger. Ronan ran towards the foyer but slowed as he noticed the two sentinels posted inside. They didn't see him. Could he make it through unnoticed?

Carefully, Ronan approached until he stood just a blade's length from them. Then, the grey world returned to its normal colour. The Graverobber hummed voraciously, shaking in Ronan's hand. Ronan's eyes went wide as he saw the sentinels suddenly take notice of him.

The blade had betrayed him.

Ronan started hacking. But did he act or the blade? Armour, flesh and bone shattered against the sword's ravenous serrated edge. The sentinels had been caught by surprise and never had a chance to wrap their hands around their weapons before armour shredded, limbs separated and viscera coated the floor as the Graverobber drank in the bloodlust that had been denied it for who knows how many years.

By the time Ronan exited the manor and sped off on his horse through the waning storm, the foyer was a pageant of atrocity. Nothing remained of the sentinels that resembled anything once human, as if their bodies had been processed by a flesh mill.

Slowly, blood and fluid seeped into the grout between the marble pieces of the pentagram inlaid into the once polished floor.

13. The Return to Soulum

In a fevered haste, Ronan pushed his horse to a gallop through the Hanging Gardens towards the final stretch of muddy road to Soulum. While the Black Death sang sweetly at his hip, his mind tangled with thoughts of the evening—the grotesquerie of the manor, murders committed by his own hand, and all of it entwined in this incomprehensible creature in the mist that lurked somewhere in the shadow of the warlocks at Blackshield Manor.

Warlocks.

They exist. Within the Cartel. The Deitists were right, but they had been looking in the wrong place.

We are inexorable, a voice whispered, slithering within him, an echo of the hallucination he endured at the manor.

"Who are you?" Ronan shouted at the night, but the

words were swept up in the breeze that had blown the evening storm forward.

In the silence that answered his plea, Ronan began to feel something foreign swelling within him. His vision warped. The trees of the Hanging Gardens twisted and melted. The swaying corpses moved as if animated. Words that were not his own echoed inside of his head in a voice that was nevertheless unmistakably his. And phantasmal impressions ignited in his mind's eye — images of cities engulfed in flames, mountains and fields cracked open through which climbed all manner of beasts of indescribable horror, along with savage brutality in their wake.

Ronan clenched his body, trying to regain control over the illusions that seeped into the crevices of his mind, when suddenly he knew. The leviathan had crept inside and didn't let go, just like it had done to every Cartel initiate — except for those who accepted the creature and pledged fealty, the infection lay dormant. For those, like Ronan however, who rejected its claim upon the world, they would be broken — mind first.

A feeling then took hold of Ronan, a feeling that he had eradicated from his life long ago, but which now crawled over him like a thousand tiny snakes bristling and biting his skin — fear.

Through the village square of Soulum towards the Good Shepherd, Ronan kept his horse at a steady gallop, past the Temple of the First Sage upon whose steps Father Benedictus stood taking notice of the merchant — alone. Ronan hurried as Benedictus disappeared into the temple to ring the bell, which tolled loudly through the town, even at this late hour, as Ronan dismounted, and ran into the inn, towards his room and his loyal apprentice, remembering the words of Kelvin Graf, that he would return to Soulum escorted by a sentinel, carrying a letter of exoneration. Ronan arrived with neither.

He needed to think quickly, not only to escape the Temple's noose but as every minute passed, hallucinations continued to creep into his mind—apocalyptic visions, voices and compulsions.

"Jaryk," Ronan whispered loudly through a crevice between the door and the jamb as he knocked cautiously. The temple's bell continued to ring outside.

"Master, is that you?" Jaryk's hushed voice replied.

It took little convincing before Jaryk released the deadbolt, then ran to the far side of the room, Nightsgrief in hand, to stand at the ready. But when he saw Ronan step through the door, he tossed the sword aside and gave his mentor a warm embrace that calmed Ronan's spiralling thoughts.

"Our cart is loaded for the journey. Did you get your license?" Jaryk asked and grabbed his coat, believing and hoping that they would be leaving that very moment. Although Ronan never completely revealed the severity of their situation, Jaryk had a growing sense that dark clouds in Soulum were gathering around them.

Sweat beaded upon Ronan's forehead and his hands trembled as he explained to Jaryk in vague detail something about a mythical creature holding a crystal ball, statues that came alive and an apocalyptic colossus in the mist. The deeper his tale descended, the more agitated Ronan became, building to a near frenzy until his own words took life.

"The eye! The eye!" Ronan shouted as the creature's giant eye broke through the mist of his own delusion, causing him to stumble backwards onto the ground. The hallucination faded as Jaryk reached forward to calm Ronan and help him to his feet. Something had happened at

Blackshield Manor, that much Jaryk knew, but he couldn't make sense of what. The only certainty in his mind was their need to leave. Now.

"We should be on our way, master," Jaryk insisted, deciding that satisfying his curiosity could wait until they had started their journey home. Ronan's breathing slowed, heavy still but calmer than during the reenactment of his evening. His fists he clenched, then shook his head.

"I still have business here," he replied. Jaryk's heart sank to his heels as Ronan unsheathed the Black Death and held it proudly between them, his breath steadying. "Can you hear it?" Ronan closed his eyes, smiled, and rocked his head back and forth to the sweet songs the dagger chanted to him. "The Black Death is real."

Jaryk froze for the moment, mystified, questioning a man whose reason he had never questioned before, and began to feel the need to stand slightly taller. "I'm sure it will fetch us enough coin in Ahm to cover the expense of this trip." Though one thing nagged at him as Ronan's head swayed—if the Black Death does indeed exist, that means warlocks do too.

He wants it, Ronan heard, or thought, and abruptly opened his eyes, bringing the dagger closer to him.

"I won't be taking it to Ahm," Ronan replied. The dagger for which he had searched most of his adult life had come to him for a purpose that he fully intended to fulfil. "You should go."

"What... alone?" Jaryk's shock only increased as Ronan's stern expression held fast, unmoving, unflinching. Standing ever taller, Jaryk insisted in a calm but steady tone, "I won't be leaving Soulum without you." Ronan's mind, however, projected visions of the Black Death plunging into Father Benedictus's chest. He smiled.

"There will be nothing for you if you stay." Ronan's smile dropped as the certainty of his path forward solidified in his heart. "My destiny is now within the temple, into the catacombs to undo the prophecy that has robbed us of more than any warlock coven."

"*We* can't stay here." Jaryk said and took a step forward, placing his hand on Ronan's shoulder, trying to convey some compassion. "Master, this is suicide. Come, you are not yourself right now. Let's get some distance from this awful town and clear our heads."

He means to stop us, the thought sank into him like fangs as Ronan's heart sped up and his skin turned moist.

"Oh no," Ronan laughed and brushed aside Jaryk's hand, wiping the betrayal off his shoulder. He raised Black Death again and curled his lip. "You want this too? Every last bit of me you greedy little urchin?" Ronan's voice cracked with agitation, his breathing heavy, as his eyes trailed off into the distance. "It asked me a question, the great eye," Ronan's words again came to life before him, the titanic eye filling the room. He gasped at its awesome presence. "Will you accept what is to come? Will you," Ronan met Jaryk's eyes, "accept what is to come?" He awaited an honest answer, but Jaryk was simply lost among Ronan's delusions, speechless in the face of a spiralling madness against which he felt utterly powerless.

"What, master? What is to come?" Jaryk's tone sounded incredulous, mistrustful. Ronan had reached the end of feeling a need to explain, especially to a boy who would so obviously mock him.

"You mock me, boy?" Ronan's eyes lit with rage as he closed the gap between them, sheathing Black Death and gripping Jaryk by the collar. As tall as Jaryk meant to stand this evening, he was no match for Ronan's strength, nor his swordsmanship, and so gave no resistance except for pleads of mercy. But the more Jaryk begged, the uglier and more twisted his face appeared, the more deceitful and spiteful, jealous and greedy. Cries for grace seemed as like arrogance, superiority and disdain. Pressed up against the wall, Jaryk no longer saw his mentor in front of him, but only the face of madness and irrationality, and thus shrank before him.

"If we could but begin our return home, I'm sure you'll regain your senses," Jaryk uttered weakly, his hands desperately pressing back against Ronan's mid-section, dangerously close to where the Black Death was sheathed.

He means to take it from us, the words clouded Ronan's mind, overshadowing all thoughts and left him with no other choice but to remove this final barrier from his path.

"You will not stop us," Ronan's eyes burned cruel and cold. His thoughts blurred, as he placed a hand on the hilt of the serrated blade.

"Dul'grakh."

The blade twitched as Ronan grabbed it, ready to taste blood once more.

14. Epilogue

The horrors of that night would come to be known as the Soulum Massacre, the night when warlockery finally rose from the shadows of prophecy and unleashed the full fury of its hideous form onto the innocent people of Soulum. Roused by the bell rung by Father Benedictus that night, the village faithful thronged the town square, inflamed to zealous frenzy by firebrand accusation — Ronan Morvayne, stranger, merchant of forbidden substances, warlock.

But there was no hanging. Rather, only slaughter. Survivors told of a shadow moving through the crowd, spilling blood, shredding bone, butchering bodies like a relentless tempest of blades ploughing through a field of flesh. Atop the temple steps, Benedictus froze at the sight of such mayhem, as blood and wrath approached closer, red ichor spraying towards the steps and landing on his white robes. Then he ran — behind the door of the temple, and barred the door shut, cowering behind the grand statue of the First Sage as an incessant pounding upon the stone entrance echoed through the empty hall. He prayed, silently, eyes pressed shut — he prayed for the First Sage to rise, for he knew this was the moment of prophecy, the moment when the Soulum Temple would collapse and the promise would be fulfilled.

And then silence.

His name was Brom, the proprietor of the Good Shepherd across the square, and as he stood outside his establishment to witness the horrific aftermath of a wickedness he didn't understand, he put his faith in a Deitist god he had only up until then worshipped as a duty. Brom had guessed correctly when he surmised that the evil pounding upon the entrance to the temple was too focused on breaking through to notice him sneak up from behind. Then with a prayer, and a good amount of luck, Brom plunged his butcher's knife into the back of the invisible demon, who dropped his serrated blade and revealed himself to be the traveling merchant, Ronan Morvayne, the accused, who had just arrived the night before.

His companion, the boy, was never found, though the mess of gore left in Ronan's room at the Good Shepherd suggested he met an untimely end.

Without fanfare, both blades that were in Ronan's possession at the time of his demise found their way to the reliquary at Blackshield Manor.

THE EGGSHELL CARVER
A TALE OF THE INLAND SEA
Tais Teng

In the city of Damascus lived a dirt-poor eggshell carver, his shop no more than a cubbyhole in one of those winding alleys so narrow the sun only touched the cobblestones at noon.

Shamir's neighbour to the left was a tanner, the one to the right a crone, who sold poisons that were seldom effective because they tasted vile and smelled worse.

He didn't lament his lot or curse his luck, for not many men were born to walk clad in samite and he had at least a roof above his head.

Now Shamir knew his eggs. First of all, you had the melon-sized eggs of the lesser rukhs, which walked the desert on long legs.

Emu-eggs from the Great Southern Isle shone a beautiful emerald green and arrived already incised with lizards and dogs which walked on two legs and carried their young in a pouch.

The third kind of egg he had only seen once, less than a week ago: a shard no bigger than a fingernail and set into a fat ring of Burmese gold. It had sparkled with all the colours of a rainbow, never the same twice.

"Is that really a piece of rukh egg, high lady?" he asked. Malika giggled because he called her "high lady" and took the ring off. "Have a look, Shamir. It is a right pretty stone. Kind of sparkly. A sea captain gave it to me. I guess he was a kind of pirate."

Shamir brought the shard close to his best eye and spoke the word the crone had taught him. It seemed to expand, filling his whole field of view.

An endless jungle rolled to a horizon with towering clouds so dark they must be fat with water. Birds wheeled in the sky, resplendent as birds-of-paradise and he understood they must be the fabled rukhs. Those birds were rumoured to have wings so wide their shadow spanned a city from river gate to desert tower. He instantly understood this was a vision from a time long ago, from the age of the great king Suleiman when even the Rub al Khali was green and fertile.

His vision followed one of those glorious birds and he saw the rukh swoop down and lift a complete blue whale from the waves. Time telescoped and now she was building a nest out of uprooted cedars, their trunks looking as small as straws.

Eggs more glorious than an emir's diamonds hatched and she fed her young with trumpeting elephants and bellowing rhinos.

"Is it expensive?" Malika asked and the vision dimmed, turning the jewel to no more than a pretty bauble. "The gold is fake, Naheb the jeweller told me. Just orichalkos, mountain copper."

"It is a piece of eggshell," he muttered, and he saw her face fall. "No, no. A piece of eggshell from a *rukh*. You know the huge bird from Sindbad? It carried him to the Valley of Diamonds."

"Which was filled with snakes." She shuddered. "I hate snakes!" She put the ring back on her fingers. "The rukh ate snakes. Do you think the ring is magic? Snake-proof?"

Shamir smiled at her. "Any snake will recognize the gleam of your ring and flee. Your captain gave you something quite valuable, even if the gold was fake."

That earned him a quick kiss and she waved at the corner of the street. It probably was just hogwash, but it had made Malika smile. She was only a harlot, but didn't the *Book of Ormazd* say: *Even a single kindness done to a leper can keep you from being reincarnated as a cockroach?*

Shamir tried hard to forget that single glimpse of a better, more glorious world, but it kept returning in his dreams. The endless jungle filled with orchids the size of millstones, the beautiful eggs. He woke up with tingling fingers.

How he longed to carve such an eggshell! He could almost hear his smallest needlepoint scrape across the surface, seeking a deeper, different tinted layer to create a cameo. He would polish the egg with lambswool and...

At the same time, he realized it was craziness: those eggs had been huge as hills. To carve and polish them he would need three lifetimes at least and even then it would only be a beginning. Also, the shell was probably nothing like a lesser rukh's egg: not soft and chalky but hard as a ruby. To shape it he would need a pickaxe and a blacksmith's hammer and cold chisel.

Mithra's Eve was a feast day: even the slaves didn't have to work. The khan set long tables with salted meat and dates in front of the temple of Mithra, and spells made fountains bubble with wine: no one had to go to bed thirsty or hungry.

After Shamir had sprinkled a handful of dried flowers

on the temple fire and bowed three times for the Bull of the World, he strolled along the quay, at peace with himself and the world. The masts of the merchant ships made a swaying forest above the waves. Beyond the moles, the Inland Sea was a sheet of rippling silver, with the full moon high in the sky.

A magnificent galleon was just passing the lighthouse, the sails on her nine masts billowing with the breath of tame wind-ghosts. A rearing lion graced the bow, his paws clawing the sky.

"That is Sem," a voice spoke from just behind Shamir. "The captain I told you about." Malika extended her hand, and moonlight made the egg-shard sparkle. "He gave me that ring."

Perhaps it was the moonlight or the reflection from the ring, but suddenly Malika seemed quite beautiful. Her cheeks were still pock-marked but that only meant she wouldn't ever catch that particular sickness again. Her locks rippled in the breeze, an ebon banner.

"The egg-shell?" he asked. "Do you think he has more pieces?"

"It didn't come from him, he told me. A lover gave it to him, but they quarrelled and now he can't stand the sight of her." She pursed her lips. "So he gave it to me."

"A lover?"

"Sarah the Jinn-slayer. They say she is a pirate, too."

"He won't have any more rukh eggs on his ship then?"

Malika laughed. "If he had, he would have thrown them in the sea."

For a moment hope had flickered. Where one piece had been, why not more? Even a shard big enough to fashion a bowl or a heraldic shield for a hero. A shield hard as diamond and made by the legendary Shamir, the Carver of Rukh Eggs.

An idea bloomed, became all-encompassing.

Like seeks like. If I have the ring it can lead me to the place where the rukhs once nested. Put a spell on it and it will become a compass needle, with the ancient eggs her North. Hundreds of shards, perhaps even whole eggs.

He saw himself walking through nests that had turned into stone and opal, like the fossil forest on Lesbos his uncle had told him about. All around him broken eggs protruded from the bitter sands of the Rub al Khali, a thousand graceful curves and domes like immense pearls. He didn't want to own them, just to feel them beneath his fingers was enough, to carve them and make their great beauty perfect.

"Sell it to me," he said. "Your ring. You can keep the gold. I only want the shard."

Malika stepped back. "No, not the ring! It is the only truly beautiful thing I have. All my other ornaments are so clearly fake. Sem..." She reached in her bodice and a stiletto flashed.

She didn't try to stab him, but Shamir was a child of the streets. His reflexes had been honed, as automatic as a tripwire which brings a spear stabbing up. His fist rammed her nose, drove splinters of bone into her brain. She was dead before she hit the cobble-stones of the quay.

Shamir had never before killed a woman. Even the street had her ethos and Malika had been, if not exactly a girlfriend, someone he had felt comfortable with.

Shamir stood frozen. He could feel de devas looking down from the sky, the moon became an immense silver eye, seeing all. Every sinful action. As the *Book of Ormazd* said: *Each and every deed of a man, good or bad, is noted and written down in stone, yes, with iron goose feathers dipped in vitriol.*

A hundred years of good works couldn't rectify this: even if Shamir sacrificed a dozen black bulls he would still be reborn as a scorpion or a hairy spider.

He kneeled and pulled the ring from her hand.

The moment he slipped the ring on his own finger he felt a great peace descend, smoothing his panic away. His thoughts no longer galloped like panicked horses. It was as if the wing of an angel was laid across his shoulders, the tips of ethereal feathers stroking his cheek.

"You did right," a voice said in his head. "But it is only a start."

"Only a start?" Shamir repeated.

"Even if you know where to go, you are only a man. The desert would eat you and leave your bones for the jackals. You need somebody a bit less like an instant victim. One rich enough to pay for a caravan and an army that would make even the Tuareg hesitate."

Khan Turgen the Seventh of Damascus stood on his balcony and looked up at his tomb. The walls were inlaid with lapis lazuli and the entrance was guarded by spring stone sphinxes with long curling beards.

It looked rather grand for a mere khan, but it was nothing like the Taj Mahal or the Iron Tower of Tamerlane. After Turgen's death, no pilgrims would climb the crater walls to ask his ghost for advice. Without their prayers, Turgen would be reborn as a toiling ant or a desert hare.

He sighed and his shoulders slumped.

The hereditary Khan of Damascus had found a new stripe of white in his beard that morning and when he lifted the scimitar, which had taken the heads of so many enemies, the weapon felt suddenly impossibly heavy.

He had called his *aesculapius*, who had studied in far Trebizond and the madrassas of Al Andalus, and the man had given him no hope.

"There are limits to the healing arts, lord. Four score

and ten is what most mortals are granted in the best case, and you are already a dozen years past."

"But there must be other spells than you used!" he had protested. "I once met a mage who was three thousand years old and had dined with Solomon himself."

"To become so long-lived one must spend seven years in the deep desert, praying to Ormazd without faltering once. Your heart has to be pure as finely woven gold." He had shaken his head. "It is a bit late to start with that. You wouldn't last a week on your own. Anyhow, your mage was probably a charlatan."

"So I am going to die?"

"Not right away, lord. I have rolled the bones and studied the flight of swallows. You have at least two years left."

Standing at the balcony the conversation repeated itself in his head, like the endless rotating blades of a windmill. *Two years. What can one do in a measly two years?*

"One can build a tomb so dazzlingly beautiful that a million pilgrims will seek it out," a voice said in his head. "A million *each year*. They'll pray to you and you will become a god, able to do wonders. Let a hacked-off limb regrow. Call oases from the sands. You'll live forever."

He felt a presence behind his back and froze like a mouse under the regard of a lion. A breeze touched his cheeks and he heard a dry rustle. *It has wings. Enormous wings.*

"Look at those glass towers," a voice mellow as a summer breeze continued. "Slender and elegant as the harpoon of a walrus hunter. And then the frieze with those dancing ghost-giraffes: ivory ever so nicely contrasts with ebony. A good start, but not enough."

"Are you an archangel?" Turgen whispered.

"Nothing so lofty. Just a bird. I am not even alive but hope to be again."

The breeze had suddenly turned foul and Turgen knew better than to turn around and look at his visitor. This was indeed a denizen of the Underworld, from the Country of the Dead.

"There was a war, khan, and we lost. King Solomon destroyed the city of the jinn with Michael's flaming sword, leaving a crater that stretches from Basra to Jorsaleem. He swept his weapon through the clouds and all rukhs fell down, our feathers turned to ash. He then broke our eggs, smashed every single one so no rukh could be reborn."

Every child knew the Tale of Elias the Camel-driver. How he found the shards of a jewelled egg in the deep desert. He gathered all the pieces and glued them together as a present for lady Vivian whom he had been courting without much success. The moment the egg was complete it hatched and a new chick emerged. The shell itself instantly fitted itself together again. The story goes on to tell that lady Vivian was so impressed with his gift that she agreed to marry him.

That is what the children's version claims. The tale for more adult listeners has a quite different conclusion. The rukh chick emerged ravenously and devoured Elias on the spot, "not even leaving a single knuckle-bone".

Turgen was well acquainted with the second version.

"Say that I find your nesting place and gather the shards?" He folded his arms and for once felt like a fearless commander again. "What is in it for me?"

"The egg will form the cupola of your new tomb once the chick is born. Pilgrims will call it more splendid than the Taj Mahal, more glorious than Tamerlane's Iron Tower. Nothing compares to the splendour of a rukh's egg."

"Your nesting place must be well hidden," Turgen said. "Shards of a rukh's egg are more precious than diamonds and almost impossible to find."

"You'll have a guide. One who is an expert and is as keen to find a rukh egg as you. Shamir the Eggshell carver."

Walking home from a client Shamir was accosted by two men. One took him by the arm: not rough but it was the kind of grip that could easily turn rough and snap his arm as if it was no more than a breadstick. The other laid a hand on Shamir's shoulder.

"I have nothing to steal!" he cried. "I am so poor the beggars pity me and offer me alms!"

"The khan wants to see you," one of them said. "Don't fear for your head. He'll fill your cupped hands with gold pieces."

"I'll come, meek as a newborn lamb," Shamir promised. "May I ask why he asked for me?"

"You know all about eggs. He needs your expertise."

Shamir now noticed that his captor was a North-man, with a red beard hanging in a long braid. The other must be a mamluk, with his face tattooed with the swirling Vine of Life. To see them working together was a wonder: they were sworn enemies.

"You take the stairs," the North-man ordered. "All the way up to the palace."

"Walk in front of us," the mamluk said. "Don't even think of fleeing. No matter how fleet of foot you are, a thrown knife is faster."

Halfway up the Great Stairs, Shamir halted to catch his breath. Below the moles of Damascus held a hundred ships in her embrace and the fires at the end sent a column of green smoke in the air, pointing out the position of the merchant town to ships even far beyond the horizon. The town itself cascaded down from the crater wall, the roof tiles golden and copper in the sunlight.

"It is a sight to behold," North-man said. "So much wider than when you're living in an alley. If all goes well you may end up right here. In your own villa, sitting in the shadow of your own vines."

"Our khan rewards his servants well," the mamluk added. "Though he makes a bad enemy and never forgives a slight."

The khan had a fearsome reputation indeed, with his headsman wielding his axe every week: Shamir stood with his eyes downcast in front of the throne. He noticed the stink of rotten copper beneath the sweeter perfume of the rose water and myrrh: a sure indication of magic. One didn't live next to a witch without learning such things. *He is hung with healing amulets and spelled from the tip of his toes to his turban to keep Death, the Destroyer of All Joy and Leveller of Cities, away.*

"I see you are already wearing a shard of what we both long for." The khan sniffed. "Ah, taken by violence. One learns to recognize the smell. Shed blood makes it even more potent. And I see you already know how such a pointer works. Even better."

The khan looked up. "Yes?"

Once more Shamir felt the touch of an unseen wingtip.

"You'll be his compass, my friend," the angel said.

He instantly felt a tug at his finger, a wriggling as if the ring had become alive. His hand lifted at his own accord and pointed to the South-east.

"Good!" the khan said. "Perfect! We'll sail at sunrise and cross the Inland Sea."

The ship Ibn Battuta carried the personal guard of khan Turgen: seventy soldiers and battle-mages with faces differing in hue from the deathly pale of a moonwalker to ebony black. His seven principal wives strolled across the deck, unveiled and unchaperoned, carrying ornate daggers. Their eyes flashed, fearless as a hawk's. To Shamir, it was clear that they considered the whole world their prey. To talk to them was unthinkable: to touch them sudden death.

He stood on the stern and saw Damascus receding. The golden roofs slowly became no more than a gleam against the green crater wall. The tomb of the khan was the last to dip below the horizon, the glass minarets throwing a pulse of sunlight across the waves.

"Always makes me feel a bit melancholy."

Shamir stiffened. The khan had appeared next to him, his beringed fingers of his left hand resting on the railing.

"My elder brother once ruled Damascus, you know. He was the first person of importance I killed." The khan chuckled. "The fool ordered my right hand hacked off and exiled me. A hand can be replaced by one made of clockwork and ivory and it gave me the lust for revenge any younger brother needs. I returned with a moonwalker and a troll-kin from the Thule as my blood brothers." A pause while memories clearly rolled through his brain, heavy as a storm-swell.

"When his vizir entered the hall the next morning he found me already sitting on the horse-hide throne, with my brother's head on my lap. Yohageim was a prudent man: I never saw anyone throw himself so fast on the floor to make obeisance." The khan nodded. "Those were heady times! Now I am so much older and wiser and only want to live forever."

It seemed to Shamir prudent not to react and only to listen.

"I'll die you know. Nothing to be done about that, but I won't stay dead long. The prayers and awe of pilgrims will call my ghost back from the Barren Fields. They will spill their blood on my altar and infuse me with chi, with life force, and I'll return as a god." He clapped Shamir on the shoulder. "And you'll be my faithful guide. My saviour!" He turned away and it was as if a great weight had lifted from Shamir's shoulders: to be noticed by the powerful is never a good thing.

The soldiers slept in the hold, the women in the cabins below the khan's.

A servant pointed Shamir to his own private tent on the deck: he was clearly valuable, the human equivalent of a pedigreed hunting-dog.

He found a new bedroll and a pillow embroidered with two snoozing peacocks.

The khan's guards must have visited Shamir's shop because everything an eggshell carver might need stood ready: a ceramic pot and fire bowl to mix and boil a dozen kinds of bone glue, his box with pigments and a brace of well-honed carving knives.

He opened the box and it was like walking into Al-Addin's treasure room. A new row of glass vials filled with pigments in every colour of the rainbow greeted him in their sparkling opulence, little sachets with jewels so he could grind his own powder should he ever run out. In the back he found coils of silver and gold wire, to make inlays. With these, he could fashion eggs that would delight even the most jaded sultana.

He closed the box and eyed his bedroll. Shamir had been seasick for most of the day and had dreaded the night. He would be tossing and turning on the heaving deck. Still, he fell asleep the moment his head touched the wondrously soft pillow.

In his dream, it was Mithra's Eve again and Shamir found himself walking down the quay, hand in hand with Malika. It felt completely natural, deeply right, even if the last time he had held her hand was as children at play. He looked at her face and it glowed with happiness. *My wife*, he thought and the corners of his lips lifted to echo her joy.

"That should have been the fate and destiny of the both of you," a voice said, and he now noticed that a man was walking next to him. His shadow thrown by the rice paper lanterns wasn't black but pulsed with light, so Shamir understood that this was a deva, one of Ormazd's messengers. "It would take you two more years to realize that she is your true love. She would have said 'Yes, I'll be your wife!' joyfully when you asked her."

"Would have?" Shamir frowned. "What do you mean?"

"You killed her. Remember?"

And Shamir no longer held Malika's hand. There was a gaping void to his right, an icy nothingness. It was as in Maroud Ghan's poem: *And all joy fled from him and he understood himself to be the most wretched of men, offal that not even the vultures would deign to touch.*

"I..."

"It wasn't your hand really. What does an eggshell carver know of the higher arts of murder? You would have bloodied her nose at most. And felt very sorry afterward and she would have forgiven you. No, a raptor bird moved your hand."

"I remember wings. A voice in my head. I thought it was an archangel?"

"We only kill the unrighteous," the deva said. "No, it was the spirit of a rukh. A *dead* rukh and he was making you ready to be his instrument. She aims to be reborn, even if she deserves no place under the sun."

And then the deva told Shamir what he should do. What the only way was to cleanse his broken and soiled soul.

The next morning three sails closed in on the Ibn Batutta. Shamir whispered the spell that the crone had taught him. His good eye sharpened and his vision became like an eagle's.

The red flags showed three intertwined sea-snakes: the age-old emblem of a pirate. A puff of smoke bloomed on the foremost felucca and a few heartbeats later the bark of a bombast reached Shamir's ears. A cannonball arced through the sky, rising and then swooping down. It would probably miss them, this was just getting the range, but the second shot wouldn't.

Well, he thought, *it was nice as long as it lasted.* No matter how well-armed their ship was, it was no match for three pirates, and he hadn't noticed a single cannon on the deck.

Strange how calm he felt. No wondrous adventure then, crossing the desert and hunting treasure. No atoning for his sin. The dream had been only that, a dream. *They'll cut my throat or sell me as a slave.*

The khan looked up and ordered: "Shield me."

Instantly the wind-ghosts peeled from the mast in an eerie shimmer, sped into the sky. Invisible arms intercepted the cannonball and gently lowered it to the deck.

The dull lead was carved in the face of a snarling demon, Shamir saw, with bat wings to stabilize it. As a carver, he recognized the style: Middle Welbish but with a certain Andalusian flair.

"A pity to waste good lead," the khan remarked and touched the ball with the point of his slipper.

"Yo!" He lifted his hand and the wind-ghosts unfurled his personal banner: an artificial hand made of ivory and tipped by silver claws. The claws were blood-stained and spread a swirl of crimson drops across the white field.

The sails of the feluccas shifted and they passed the Ibn Batutta far to the left, timid as mice who had belatedly noticed the tomcat.

Shamir's shoulders slumped and he felt his breath hiss between his teeth. It somehow seemed an anticlimax. He had been ready to give up, to die for his crime.

"They bark but won't bite," the khan laughed and gave the fleeing ships the double finger. "Not me!"

The North-man tugged his long moustaches, licked his lips. "They may be sea-vipers, lord, but you are the silver-clawed mongoose."

The ship hugged the coast for the next week. Any boat that tried to cross the Inland Sea in a straight line tended not to arrive at its intended ports. Perhaps ship-devouring sea snakes dwelt in the deeper parts or it might be that malign magic was the strongest close to the central mountain where Michael's fiery sword had struck the city of the jinn. Stories told of ships suddenly turned into stone, going down in a heartbeat. Or conversely, ships arriving in a port and letting down their anchor, without a single sailor manning the decks.

On the seventh day, when Shamir returned from a stroll around the deck, he found one of the khan's wives in his tent, sitting on the bedroll. It was Waikikri, the one who braided crow's feathers in her hair and wore a necklace of owl skulls. Her eyelids were heavy, with long lashes as dark as any raven. Circular scars adorned her cheeks.

She was very beautiful and Shamir felt a stab of dismay. He knew exactly how this would end: only a secret prince could hope to bed a khan's concubine and survive. He didn't own a bronze horse that would carry both of them through the sky. Neither had he befriended a giant sea turtle like Clever Noah. Jumping into the sea to escape the enraged harem guards, they would only drown.

"I have been waiting for you," Waikikri purred. "I heard so much about you." She put her hand in the sweet valley between her brown breasts and emerged holding an over-sized egg. "That you are the best egg carver of Damascus and that you can even mend a crushed hummingbird egg." She chuckled. "One that an elephant has stepped on."

Shamir relaxed. She saw him as an artisan, not as a man. "As the only eggshell carver of Damascus, I must surely be the best.' *Keep it light. Only talk about eggs.*

"It is the egg of a bald eagle, the kind that walks on two legs," the lovely lady said.

"You have blown it out?' Shamir said. "I notice two holes."

"My mother did. Elementary magic. An egg is filled with life force. It can hatch a whole new eagle, beak and feathers, and all. If you remove the chi it leaves a vacuum."

"I have heard about that," Shamir nodded. This felt surprisingly good. Safe. Waikikri was a client, no doubt one of the better ones, and Shamir the esteemed expert. "Parents place such an egg next to the baby. If any demons come to steal the newborn's soul, the egg sucks them in. Imprisons them in his shell."

"It worked," Waikikri said. "This egg contains no less than nine ghosts. My mother is a famous shaman, making her daughter's soul quite valuable. When the ninth and last ghost was taken she painted her seal on it to keep them in."

Shamir peered at the egg. The seal was no more than a row of vague outlines.

"It has faded?"

She nodded empathically, spread her hands, and he saw dread in her eyes. Fear that had been a long time building. "The moment it is completely gone, they'll break free. They have been hungering for twenty-two years. They'll tear my soul into a thousand pieces. There won't be enough left of me to return as a flea!"

"But your husband, he must have many magicians in his employ? The most powerful shamans of Damascus?"

"For sure and I'm one of them. The daughter of Shalibar, the Wolverine of the North. If he ever discovered that I had carried such a dangerous talisman into his palace..."

"Her seal?" Shamir said. "I can carve it in the eggshell, make it permanent."

"I'll be in your debt forever!"

With the sharpness of his good eye, the flecks became a band of clear paw prints, no doubt of a wolverine. Five pads, each topped by the impression of a claw. Wolverines were the most feared of predators of the cold forests: they wouldn't hesitate to attack a snow-tiger or bear five times their size.

"I guess there is some urgency?" He took his carving set from his pouch at her tense nod. "No time like the present."

It was delicate work because even an eagle's egg is fragile. He scratched with his brand new number 3 penknife, blew the white powder away. Then it was the turn of the number 5, to cross-hatch the surface.

He next stained the roughened surface with ground amethyst, the kind of paint that would never fade.

"Now I'll give it a coat of iron lacquer. You'll need a blacksmith's hammer to break the egg now." He grinned. "But it will be a toss-up if it is the egg or the hammer which shatters."

The lacquer dried into a clear glaze during the next half hour and he handed her the egg.

She tucked it in her bodice and her sudden smile would make the rising sun jealous. "You saved my life. Name your price."

Shamir never understood what made him speak out and ask for such a crazily dangerous thing. "A kiss would be ample payment, my lady."

"Ah, you are a poet, too!" She embraced him and kissed him on both cheeks and then on his lips. Her lips were warm and yielding, holding nothing back. Her scent filled his nostrils, sharp and heady as the golden resin of a broken pine branch. She stepped back, squeezed his shoulder. "And they say that you Arabs can't kiss!"

She next pulled a signet ring from her left hand and put it on his index finger.

"If you ever travel the Endless Meadows any warrior will call you brother if you show this seal. Many love the Wolverine of the North, but all fear her."

"Thank you."

"Hear me out. Kiss the stone with the same fever you just did kiss my lips and I'll come running. Do it only in the direst situation."

He watched her walk away, her steps so light that they almost didn't touch the deck.

Rubbing his new ring it seemed to Shamir an hour well spent.

They finally docked in the southernmost port. Lamesh was a forbidding sight, composed of crisscrossed basalt pillars like the log cabin of a giant. Statues of scowling gods looked down at them and the trees sported leaves so dark they were almost black.

A joyless place and Shamir was relieved that they wouldn't have to pass the night here.

An elevator took them to the caravansary on the top of the crater wall.

That evening they dined on partridges with freshly ground harissa which tasted so much better than spotted eels with seaweed.

Shamir sat rolling the bones with the North-man Lochi Livsson and Hussein the mamluk. Waikikri made the fourth.

When Waikikri had taken all their dinars she reached up and plucked a bowl with mulled wine from the thin air. Shamir found himself holding an earthenware cup.

"Magic?" Lochi asked and he reached for the amulet around his neck.

"No, just a trick," Waikikri replied. "A *magic* trick." And that made them all laugh.

The moment he took his first sip Shamir heard a soft chime from his empty moneybag. He didn't open it but felt sure all his recently lost coins had returned. Well, a khan's wife could afford to be careless about money.

Waikikri clapped her hands. "Storytelling time. You first, Lochi."

"Well, all our stories are about the gods or blood feuds that leave no farm unburned."

"Tell me about the gods? I have seen enough burning farms, courtesy of my husband."

"Now my namesake Lochi, he once turned himself into a fox to creep into the king's wife shuttered bed..."

Hussein was next with the story of the clever China-man Al-Addin and the Flute with the Seven Jinn. Waikikri then took the storyteller's stance, opening both her hands to show that her tale was true no matter how wondrous.

"Husdra was a hunter of the ghost-elephants that drifted across the tundra. Our ghosts are fast as gazelles and they like to lead you into a drop-off cleverly hidden by the dwarf-tree and moss. But if you track them all the way to their cemetery you'll find a wealth of ivory and..."

Shamir sat looking at the winking embers, sipping from a cup that kept filling itself no matter how much he drank. Peace crept into his body and he realized he was happy, as happy as any man can be who has murdered his one true love.

He was sitting around a fire with three newfound friends. Two were trained killers but that was a metier like any other. The third was one of the khan's wives and probably as dangerous as the rest. No matter, it was perfect and right to sit here under the stars and listen to Waikikri's husky voice which was rich as honey and twice as sweet.

"And the shaman said: 'When you ate the hare, Husdra, you didn't thank her for her flesh and neglected to give her bones back to the earth, but threw them in the fire.'"

Outside the crater wall stretched a green parkland with almond trees and cedars. Mists rose in the morning from the Inland Sea and descended in a majestic cloud fall on the other side. Shamir walked under trees that were high and straight as galleon's masts. Birdsong and the buzz of bees followed them.

"This could be the Paradisio your priests always rant about," Lochi Livsson stated. He swatted at a persistent wasp and crushed the insect between his fingers.

"Paradisio is grass as far as the eye can see and an empty winter sky the colour of a robin's egg," Waikikri opined.

A single day's travel, though, brought them to the end of that parkland and the desert opened up in front of the travellers. The khan looked out across the dunes and gravel banks.

"Ah, there she is. Red and sere, without a single oasis. According to my informants, it is impossible to cross those wastes without dying of thirst." He turned to one of his mages. "You have them ready, ibn Hannu?"

"They have been gathering mist and collecting dew, lord."

On cue, thunder rumbled above the distant crater wall and Shamir saw a raincloud struggling up in the sky. It wore the dire blue-black of a bruise, probably containing enough water to fill a lake.

Shamir sharpened his good eye and the wind-ghosts herding the cloud showed up as wisps of opal.

"It is as you commanded, my lord," the shaman continued. "They'll bring a whole string of clouds. During the day they'll shield us from the sun and grant us rain the moment our water-sacks run dry."

It happened as the wind-tamer had promised: a balmy day which never grew too hot while the clouds kept pace with the travellers. In the night rain fell for an hour.

Shamir woke up every morning with a field of blue gentians and red poppies surrounding the camp.

He wore the eggshell ring on his right hand. It only gave a tug when they drifted from the right direction. Waikikri's ring remained quiescent: just rune-inscribed silver with the paw-print a black opal.

"My old comrades would laugh themselves silly," Lochi Livsson complained while they crunched through the flowers. "All our raids were after gold. Some old eggshells, it doesn't sound like treasure to me."

"It is magic," Waikikri said. "A rukh's eggshell. For magicians, gold is just a base metal. It is soft and doesn't hold any spell for more than a week."

"Magic is for soft fingered scroll-scribblers."

"Hey, I am a magician, too!" Waikikri protested.

"But not soft fingered. You are a warrior like me. I didn't see you wearing any magical knives incised with baleful runes."

Waikikri grinned. "The most magical knife is a well-honed one." She turned to Shamir. "How far, my guide?"

"The ring tugged this morning as if he would like to pull the finger from my hand. Not much longer." He rubbed his tingling finger. "I hope."

During the day Shamir and Lochi Livsson travelled far in front of the much slower caravan: Shamir as the guide and Lochi as his protector.

On the twenty-first day, they topped a dune and the legendary nesting place of the rukh lay at their feet. It was an exact copy of Shamir's vision: jewelled shards that rose from the red sands, sparkling in a thousand colours. Some pieces rose in jagged curves, others were more thoroughly shattered, lying in windblown drifts of jewels.

"So beautiful," Lochi whispered. The awe was immediately followed by a scowl to counteract such unseemly softness.

"It is," Shamir agreed. 'But imagine those eggs in their prime? Unbroken? A hundred cupolas gleaming in the sun, filling the sky with their mother of pearl radiance?" Eggshell carvers can wax quite poetic on the matter of eggs.

"Now, what should we do?" Lochi asked. "Go down into the valley or warn the rest first?"

Shamir looked back. No trace of the camels and the khan's elephant yet and the sheltering cloud was no more than a white puff at the horizon.

"Hah! We found them. We are the discoverers. It would make for a sorry tale if we turned around without making sure this isn't a mirage."

"You are so right! Are we dogs to run to our master with every bone we find?" And the North-man swept his two-handed sword from his shoulder sheath and sprinted down the side.

Without the sheltering clouds above the caravan, the landscape was made of dazzling light. The eggshells drank the searing sunlight and reflected it in a coruscating display, in colours and supernatural hues which would be the envy of peacocks.

Shamir's ring pulled him to the right, then down so abruptly his knees hit the sand.

Between the wind-etched pebbles, a piece of eggshell gleamed. It had the exact same hue as the fragment in his ring but was thrice the size.

Ah. That is the way it works. The ring wants me to gather all the pieces of his own broken egg.

He tugged the eggshell from the sand. It seemed unexpectedly heavy: as solid as lead or gold.

"Look out!" Lochi cried and jumped in front of Shamir.

The sand fountained and a sand snake rose in a sinuous motion, turned into a man. Scales covered his bare arms and his eyes gleamed an alarming yellow, with the pupil a black slash. He overtopped even Lochi by two heads.

"The great king left me here to guard the broken eggs," the creature said. "In this dry land, I dined on stones and drank sand for three thousand years. You'll make a nice change of menu."

Lochi looked up at the swaying monster-head.

"Better turn back into a snake and slither away. This sword here is good Damascene steel, thirty-three times folded and hammered. I sharpened the edge with diamond dust."

"Do you really think that mere steel can hurt me?"

His head flashed forward, with the neck lengthening in a most alarming way, and took a bite from Lochi's sword.

"That was a nice appetizer, human. Crunchy. "

"I am not ready to die!" Shamir wailed, which earned him a scornful snort from the North-man. "Please let me make a final prayer to my goddess. I'll kiss my ring and tell her that I'll be arriving soon."

"Never let them say that I'm not merciful. You may pray to her." The were-snake frowned. "Who exactly is your goddess? Astaroth? Fair Isis who Juggles Snakes?"

"She is a bit more local. Perhaps only known in my village? Her name is Waikikri, the Daughter of the Wolverine of the North."

"Never heard about the wench. Intone you dead-song, dear meal to be."

Shamir kissed the signet ring most fervently and

whispered: "I think this is a situation most dire, Waikikri. I need you."

Behind the were-snake, the air shimmered and something sleek and fast jumped on the back of the monster and bit his head off.

She landed on four paws, rose on her hind legs, and then turned back into a human. Shredding her fur she ended up gloriously naked.

Shamir instantly looked at his feet: ogling a skyclad goddess without her express permission was never a good idea.

"This will make a nice tale, Waikikri," Lochi said. He ruefully looked at his sword where a half-moon was missing. "There are situations that need the gentle hand of a female."

"Better keep this tale unsung," Waikikri said. "How do I explain to my lord and master that Shamir here was wearing one of my magic rings?"

"O, you gave it to him so you could protect him. Without Shamir the khan could circle around in the desert for years and never find a single shard."

Waikikri sighed. "It will have to do. I just crossed twenty leagues in a single breath. The other mages will have noticed my spell. This place is so empty even turning a flea into stone sounds like a clash of cymbals."

Gathering the shards felt like a children's treasure hunt. The ring tugged Shamir from hill to hill and made his finger point down. Burly slaves instantly started digging with their probing sticks and shovels.

Camel after camel was laden until Shamir's ring no longer tingled: they must have found all puzzle pieces of that particular egg.

When Shamir wrapped the last fragment in linen a sandhill stirred and rose in a blood-red swirl. The Rukh looked down at the humans: a ghostly bird with whirlwind feathers, the eye sockets filled with shimmering St Elmo's fire.

"You found it all, great khan," the spirit said. "The means of my rebirth and your immortality. Sail it to Damascus. On the courtyard of your mausoleum, nimble-fingered Shamir will assemble our egg, glue each piece in its rightful place."

The whirlwind deflated, raining pebbles, and turned once more into a simple hill.

The way back always seems faster, Shamir thought, even with the camels now laden until the scowling animals had to wade through the sand, groaning and spitting at their drivers.

The crater wall lifted above the horizon and they crossed the empty green parkland.

No pirates accosted their ship and of course the breeze remained steady, thanks to the wind-ghosts.

Days and then weeks followed while Shamir squatted in the courtyard, sorting broken eggshells and gluing them together. It was no hardship: a servant kept his bowl filled with sherbet while one slave lifted a parasol above Shamir's head and another wafted a cooling breeze over him with a giant palm leaf.

This was the most fascinating work one could give an eggshell carver. Each shard was different and like they say: *more beautiful than the first.*

A hollow bowl slowly rose in the courtyard, surrounded by scaffolds.

Three times the ghost of the rukh appeared, inspecting Shamir's work with eyes which no longer gleamed fitfully but sparked and sizzled like ball lightning. Clearly, the ghost was gaining power with the restoration of his egg.

"Soon," the ghost said, "soon I'll live again. And you, you'll be rewarded with riches beyond your wildest dreams!"

Shamir didn't voice his doubt: the promises of ghosts and rulers tended to be unreliable.

The first year passed, then five more months and the khan had lost most of his hair. When he visited the courtyard he was carried in a sedan chair.

The eggshell now rose halfway to the top of the minarets and started to curve inwards.

"Keep up the good work!" the khan urged Shamir. "I would like to see the finished dome before I close my eyes forever." The eyes in question had become milky, his lips seamed and dry like a mummy's. Every breath wheezed and Shamir understood the khan wasn't long for this world.

"Look there, my lord. There are only three baskets with shards left." He spread his hands. "But I can't hurry. The glue is too effective and dries immediately. If I put a piece in the wrong place it sits there forever and the rukh's spell just won't work."

"I understand. I know how finicky magic is." He nodded again and kept nodding. "Keep up the good work, my carver. You'll be rewarded with riches beyond your wildest dreams."

During the day and later by candlelight Shamir sat bowed over each piece, peering down with his good eye. No doubt he was numbering them, noting where they should go in that monstrous complicated puzzle mosaic. He used his finest carving tool, the number 9 scratcher. With an instrument this fine one could inscribe the whole Book of Ormazd on the head of a pin.

Shamir worked day and night, utterly concentrated, with only three hours off for sleep.

The day before the egg would be finished Waikikri visited him. She looked up at the enormous dome.

"Almost finished, eh? Just five more pieces." She smiled at him. "I know what you have done and I approve. That bird doesn't deserve to be reborn and the khan shouldn't become a god. We have enough demons already."

"You saw?" Shamir asked.

"My eyes can be as sharp as your spelled one."

That moment the vizier came running into the courtyard. Two burly porters followed him, bearing the sedan chair where the khan sat wheezing.

"Hurry up! Glue the final pieces on the top! Our lord and master is dying. His breath rattles in his throat and the Angel of Death is standing on his left side, and the Keeper of Karma on his right."

"He'll see his mausoleum completed," Waikikri promised and rotated her left wrist. A long word flowed from her lips, complex as the growl of a wolverine, and all six fragments rose, suddenly light as thistledown.

They alighted on the top of the dome and Shamir hastily kneeled, fitted the pieces one after the other in the last hole. The final shard still sat in Malika's ring. He pried it from its setting and fitted it in place.

When he looked up they were seven: the ghost of the rukh stood behind the sedan chair, glorious now. Her feathers shone, each a living flame. Her raptor's beak was a red as deep as Chinese lacquerware. It was the most beautiful thing, bar one, which Shamir had ever seen.

A glob of Shamir special glue and the last piece merged with the egg.

"Oy way!" the vizir cried. "Our lord and master died at this very moment. See, his eyes are turning up, the last breath leaving his lips. But he saw his mausoleum in all its glory and no doubt died happy in the knowledge that he'll live again, called back by the prayers of pilgrims."

A screech of triumph. "Solomon has been defeated!" the rukh cried. She stretched her wings and they turned grey and scruffy. A gust and the foul spectre blew away like smoke.

The egg shuddered under Shamir's feet, magic coursing from top to bottom, pale flames knitting together in an immense tapestry. For a moment a female face floated in the air, pockmarked but immensely dear and beautiful in Shamir's eyes.

A pulse as the magic came together and Malika stood next to him, blinking.

She frowned. "Shamir? What are we doing here? Where are we?"

He took her hands, kneeled. "Malika., my one true love. Will you be my wife?"

In the city of Damascus, the famous eggshell carver Shamir lives in a grand villa, with vines coiling across the pergola where he is sitting every morning with his beloved wife, sipping a tiny cup of aromatic coffee before he walks to his atelier.

Pilgrims arrive from all over the East to visit the man who carved the magic rukh egg two thousand times with his lover's face and so called her back to the Land of the Living.

His carved emu's eggs easily go for the price of three pedigreed racing camels and his clients consider that cheap.

No one ever visits the khan's mausoleum: the dome has turned the colour of yellowed bone, with ugly cracks running all over. Khatun Waikikri, *may she rule for a thousand years!* has considered demolishing it as an eyesore but finally repurposed it as a home for deserving orphans.

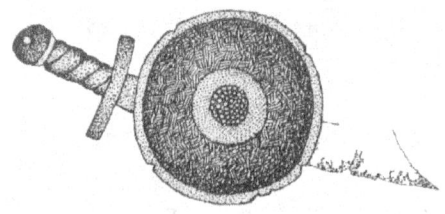

ETERNAL ASSASSIN: THE MAN WHO HUNTED DEATH

Andrew Darlington

in this flame-dark land
my lips are stolen
by wolves

the melding of new
and ancient geographies
from meson and grimoire
opened this passage north
through icefields to the
unexpected continent
beneath this cold dark moon

The baleful red star appears high in the northern sky the year before the scarlet plague brings the imminent war with the island of Newquist to a close. When, instead of an invasion fleet crossing the strait to attack Muskouia, mercy ships of food and medicine were dispatched to the beleaguered depopulated cities of Newquist. Then the contagion washes over Muskouia itself leaving the wail of mourning and loss in its terrible wake, carried on the stench of funeral pyres. People raise their eyes fearfully to the red star of dark omen.

Sometime is a blind mystic who dwells in a modified cave along the craggy coastline some distance beyond the city wall. As they arrive, Adsiduo Sicarius and Karel Houndara are met by the first of three naked acolytes, and are ushered between a natural stone gateway along a cool chimney and into the sanctum. There are rushes carpeting the floor and the vague aroma of gases that leak through fissures in the bedrock. Sicarius identifies methane, possibly blended with ethylene. Houndara experiences an unsettling giddiness.

Sometime is androgynous. Her hair is the green of seaweed. Her sightless eyes are set into a silvered visage. Yet her attention is fixed on the two respectful supplicants.

"She ovulates," whispers the acolyte. "It is a good time to seek her guidance. Ask her what you will."

"We seek Death," announces Sicarius.

"They were building a tower." Her voice has the softness of tide. "They were building a tower so high that it would reach the moon in the night sky. They were building a tower so high that, when the alignments were correct, they could step from the highest point of its pinnacle onto the very face of the Moon. They built it high. They built it so high that it became unstable. They built it so high that it snapped in two like a dry twig. The upper half fell to Earth, to lie as a finger pointing directions across the surrounding wetlands. Those who remain within the tower die, one by one, but as they do so they accrete into a single entity, who assumes the attributes of death itself…"

The intense silence that ensues tells them that the audience is over. They signal their gratitude and withdraw.

They re-emerge blinking into the bright daylight. Houndara stops for a moment to catch his breath, he laughs and shakes his head. "Did we learn anything from that mystical encounter? Are we wiser because of it?"

"Maybe not now. Prophecy, or insight is a gift that reveals itself only with time."

Earlier, there had been the clash of duelling blades within the high chambers of the Princeps' palace. A grinning Houndara and Sicarius circle, thrusting and parrying with blunt-edged swords, testing and honing each other's fighting skills. Sicarius wears matt black body-armour edged in scarlet, contrasting with his flow of long white hair. Houndara wears fringed leather, with his scabbard slung across his back on a bandolier, his hair cropped to a patterned stubble.

Sicarius employs a ruse he's used before, of stepping backwards as though yielding a pace to the attack, so that his opponent moves in to press home what he sees as his advantage, leaving an opening for Sicarius to strike back. But, familiar with their duels, Houndara anticipates the technique, and holds back. Sicarius laughs in recognition of his comrade's skill.

Eventually, it's Houndara who throws up his hands in mock-defeat. "Hold, wait, Sicarius. I tire," he laughs, bending over, his hands braced on his knees.

"We age," says Sicarius, re-sheathing his blade. He is the man known in whispered myths and legends as the Eternal Assassin.

The two men walk, lost in their own reminiscences, across the woven-wool floor-covering of the library hall between the archive rows of tomes and relics. The walls draped in heraldic devices, runes and faded pennants. The walls press comfortingly around them. They feel at home within its age, its antiquity. They sit together beneath the elaborately carved corner archive. From the high casements they can look out across the jagged overlap of city roofs, a reticulation rifted with turrets and balconies, doors and the closed eyes of shuttered windows, all etched against the sky above the undisciplined row of windblown willows.

"You were the rebel we once tracked down," says Sicarius with teasing humour. "Now you reside here within the edifice you at first intended to destroy."

"Freedom is not a condition we should ever expect," Houndara reasons carefully. "As humans we're subject to certain hungers, which limit our freedoms, in a consensual and mutual-support way, the need for companionship, for community, for safety – each of them entails a trade-off, a loss of freedom. This we accept. All we need to negotiate, are the limits of that loss. Freedoms are defined by their lack. Freedom from oppression, from tyranny, fear from of external threat, or the imposition of internal repression."

"But survival carries its own imperative. It relieves us of the luxury of such moral choice."

"True, yet I sense death gathering all around us. I feel memories slipping away," Houndara enunciates clearly. Age has softened the firmness around his mouth, but hasn't touched the natural lines of good humour running from forehead to chin.

He watches his companion. Watches Sicarius. The hollow blazing eyes set into a face seamed with the lines of one who's known and endured many strange and terrible things. Always a moody lonely figure carrying his own dark secrets. Who was he, where had he come from, this strange being he counted as his closest friend, but who lives a life counted out in centuries? His face a riddle to be solved.

"Death makes an absurdity of everything we strive for, everything we achieve," presses Houndara. "Is there any wonder we act irrationally, faced with the ever-present threat of personal extinction? We, who live but one life. We can only appreciate the true beauty of life when we view it through the finite lens of death. You can never know what it is to be human if you do not carry this awareness in your soul. You, who live forever, can never know that fear. How is it you persist where others perish?"

"By living one day at a time, in the correct sequence." A wry smile.

"Tell me how it is for you? You are killed. But not permanently."

"I don't die. No, not in the way that people die. It is my hosts who die." He pauses, as if wary of uttering a terrible truth. Then, more softy, "My life is a disease. I hold onto my stillness, in a tide of guilt and self-loathing. I take one life at a time. It is something beyond my control. For my hosts, it is a form of extinction. They die by degrees. Each new life is superimposed on the previous one. I am the thread of continuity that connects lives. I've lodged in cruel minds that never know rest or contentment. Kings and peasants, warriors and assassins, thieves and brigands, wizards and priests. I've had so many faces, so many identities that they blur, I can barely recall half of them."

"People are such small things," muses Houndara. "If we attempt to think beyond hours or days, weeks or months, it all becomes meaningless."

"I've grown tired of this living. I loathe this existence. I yearn for it to end. I seek the tranquillity of death. Death offers the only solace. But it is a solace I'm denied. I only know there's no hope for me. None at all."

"I can see that now. You weave in and out of history, like a thread on a loom. That is the nature of your species. You are not to blame. Except that by living among mortal humans across so many lives you become more human, you acquire human characteristics. So much of your attitude is something you put on, like a cloak, in order to keep the world away. But you've been infected by human morality."

"Muskouia exists within halls of past glories. There are others who precede us who have pondered the mysteries of what lies beyond death." He indicates the wealth of ancient tomes stored in the archive. "I've studied these books, these ancient wisdoms, followed one connection to another, I've pieced together the histories of thought. Here, within these books, are the records of cultures that personify death as an entity. A being with its own inevitable malevolence. A soul-eater that consciously and purposefully devours lives. There's one volume here, with symbols in an unknown tongue transcribed onto thin folio-sheets of uncorrupted metal, which show where Death resides. How the etching was done we no longer have any way of knowing. What wisdom the symbols contain is lost to us. But there are charts of constellations that the alchemists can interpret. Those charts also show the red star high in the northern sky. An alignment, so that we can follow the paths they indicate."

"So, death need not be an abstraction? You find that a comforting idea?" Houndara shakes off the implications as a dog shakes itself free of water.

"So, we cast our own spell. We'll go to seek out death, you and I. Challenge death. Hold the personification of death to account. Make it answer for the brevity of your life, for the curse of longevity by which I am afflicted. We follow the red star constellation, and we catch death in its lair."

"My thoughts chase each other, like a dog after its own tail. But we trust each other, do we not? This is a partnership unto its natural end."

They prepare for their new journey, set up deputies to oversee the day-to-day running of the Muskouia federation of nations. They consult seers and sages, study and cross-reference grimoires, thaumaturgical codices and ancient tomes. They plan what will be their course, while a longship is being provisioned.

"Some people have magic. Others do not. Some claim the power of divination and prophecy. Some claim to be astrologers with a fistful of astrological charts. There are even others who sleep with their eyes and ears wide open, yet they learn nothing."

"As with gods. There have always been gods. People have always created them. You can choose or disregard them as you will."

"Yet if the firmament is indeed infinite, as you insist, all things must surely be possible?" says Houndara

*

on this nightmare beach
within skulls of eagles
my blood sweats acid

redefining physics
mapping new metaspheres
under strange constellations
we were drawn to this shore
by the dream-sending spores
of monstrous fungi howling
from their forest into my sleep
of gem-encrusted chimera
that breed from the drip of
condensing shadow in glaciers
as chill as death

They cast off from the harbour where gulls wail warnings as they glide on the breeze. The trireme takes them relentlessly north for long weeks, trailed by playful dolphins, sighting a pod of Nanuk Wanari the Great Blue Whale, always guided by the pointed finger of their lodestone. Always following the red eye of the star set high into its constellation. There's no fear of pirates, for the regular trade routes go south, or east-west. But the further north they sail, the more uneasy the crew become, muttering with superstitious dread, until they reach Arakel, the farthest port of the charted world. It's a low town clustered beneath a towering range of the snow-topped mountains that define the edge of the unknown. There the trireme shelters, while Houndara and Sicarius prepare to transfer to a smaller two-man vessel with a single sail. They weather overnight in Arakel, drinking in a tavern, before saying their farewells. Then they follow constellations across unknown waters.

The Earth is already old. Its knowledge infinite. Nightfall itself becomes a great ocean that stretches on forever. Sicarius prefers the night. The darkness of night. No lights, other than the stars, and only the stars are unchanged, like metal birds frozen in flight. The same constellations that look down while countless ages pass. As if all those stars are alive. As if all the stars have a watching sentience. Only that single red star, set like a baleful eye in the northern sky, is different. Yet it, too, has been here before. Because the same star patterns are scribed into the book made up of thin folio-sheets of uncorrupted metal. It is an eye that opens briefly, once in every thousand years. As though its appearance signifies forces of destiny that are aligned around them. He inhales the same restless ache. As the briny tang of the sea sparks memories of other voyages when he was occupying other forms, expeditions of conquest, trade or explorations. Setting foot on lands that have long-since been drowned in the rising tides of melting glaciers. Cities that now lie on the seabed.

Time has passed. His eyes tire of staring. He assumes stillness, slows his breathing, steadies his pulse, draws calm in around himself. The trick is to slow his heartbeat; the trick is not to breathe. There is strength in solitude. There is also strength in proximity, even when there are no words left to say.

At first the night sky is lit up by scintillations of colour in deluging ripples of supernatural light. Then shafts of perpetual lightning form a beast's claw of brilliance ripping down from storm-clouds like a living thing. As soon as the pulses die, leaving retinal afterimages, they burst anew in twitching and writhing tentacles of sparkling fire, a sentience that dances along variant trajectories, but always anchored to the same magnetic source. The lodestone spins insanely as though possessed by demons.

"We steer a course directly between them," announces Adsiduo.

"Are you mad?" howls Houndara over the roar. "We get as far away from them as possible!"

"Hold your course. Hold." The tide accelerates around them. Until it's no longer possible to escape its ferocious grip. Storm-tossed on the swell, lashed by spray, yet holding the course between the bridges of forking light. His arm holds fast on the tiller amid the wail of creaking timbers and groaning cordage as waves beat against the sides of the boat. Until they emerge onto placid ocean beyond, the tattered sail painted by starlight.

The sun stands at midnight. A dark nighttime sun, where stars are densely drifted. Towards paradox, and more firmly away from logic.

"We've tripped over a crack in the world." Sicarius casts a narrow-eyed glance. "There's no way to rationalise it. Beyond asking why we should restrict our voyage to the possible, hemmed in by the limitations of gravity and linear space? The only people who know those limits are the ones who've already gone beyond. There are others who venture as far as they dare, then pull back, or slow down, or do whatever they have to when it comes time to choose. But the edge is here."

"Yet this is magick beyond our knowing," avers Houndara.

"We are loyal to truth, to nothing other than truth." He slants a reassuring glance back at his companion.

A grim fog swirls so thickly that even light becomes lost, closing in around its secrets. They sail from sickly light into a yellow darkness. The damp coils of mist sting their eyes and dulls all sound. For Sicarius, his eyes suck the dim yellow light into themselves, forcing lines and shapes out of the blurred nothingness. It becomes a shapeless mass that whirls above and around them, as though it has sprouted leathery wings. A rushing sweeping shape, enormous and soundless. For an infinitesimal but timeless moment he knows with absolute certainty that they're encompassed by something immeasurably complex. He finds himself sweating, though the air is chilled by an overwhelming sense of evil. A strange foreboding assails him. The rational wisdom of ages battles against a sense of instinctive fear. Although there's no shape to see. Merely a ghastly formless patch of movement darker by far than the fog. A darkness where the mist gathers at its thickest.

He turns his face to the north, ahead is a silvery wilderness of frozen sea. Its agelessness contains a breadth of time that sweeps into his mind, overwhelming him, he feels that his every moment accords with the birth and death of universes, that suns have been created and cooled while a single timeless instant flees. His memories encompass growing periods of time. Beyond which there are longer ages, and all ages are one. Years come and pass, as if they were not, and had never been. There are secrets frozen into the ice. Histories forever lost. He sees them turn to dust.

Their fresh drinking-water has long-gone. His stomach is shrinking. His head throbs, as they draw in close to a bay trapped between two steep pincer cliffs of white stone. There's a small community clustered like a fossil fused into ancient rock. Cottages constructed of local regolith that lean in towards each other, as if sheltering one another from the harsh north wind. The voyagers tether the ship to a berthing point above the tideline along the shingle beach. They climb the slithering slope into the shelter of overhung slate in sad disrepair. There are coracles drawn up in an untidy row, and nets hung on untended frames. A pervading aroma of shellfish, damp seaweed, and poverty mixed in with smoke-haze. Cowled figures move past them through the narrowest of alleys and haunted passageways, hunched in against the wind.

In the cramped square of Sarok, around a deep-water well, there's what they take to be a tavern. There's a rusted mask forming a knocker, a devil's-face that glowers at a scrawny dog that hurries by with bared fangs and drooping tail. There's also a battered foot-scraper outside the door to remove mud or grit. Ignoring it, Sicarius knocks in a series of sharp raps on the timber. After a considerable pause a judas-grill slides open and eyes stare out from the darkness within. Another long pause then locks rattle and the door swings reluctantly inwards.

They stoop to enter what is obviously the tavern's main

den as the door is bolted back into place behind them. They stand blinking in the smoky interior, their eyes move around the less-than-welcoming hostelry. Rough and mean men sit in silence, they look up as they're brushed by the clean coldness of the thin stream of air from outside. They have the faded look of the damned, as though afflicted by unguessable sorrow, their voices as low as the whispering of tombs. Two erect serpent andirons guard a hearth beneath a veined marble mantel engraved with pictographs, a relic of more prosperous days. Between the draped sheepskins across the wall there's an array of stilled timepieces, to indicate a diversity of frozen time ransacked from the planet's past.

"We seek Death," announces Sicarius. His matt black body-armour edged in scarlet, is smudged and grimed with use. It contrasts with his flow of long white hair. Houndara wears his worn fringed leather, his hair – once cropped to a patterned stubble, now hangs tangled around his shoulders.

"In that case, you death-seekers have come to the right place. We have more than we need. We have more tombs filled with the dead than we have the living." There's the ruin of a faintly disapproving grin about the twisted caricature of the man who'd admitted them. A faded wispy voice that sounds bored. His feet scuff the cuspidor in agitation.

When he brings two tankards, the tavern-keeper hobbles with a pronounced limp. Houndara looks down into the dull black liquid dubiously. "What is this?" He sips warily. It burns his lips.

"You don't want to know." A pause. "We brew from certain mosses and fungus. There's little else that grows in this place of ice and fire." He tosses the coins grudgingly in his gnarled hand, regarding them with filmed toad-eyes.

"We have little need for this currency either. Traders from the south pull in here less frequently than they used to, and when they do they tempt and beguile our youths away with them."

As he drinks, Houndara feels a canting in his gut, a stinging wash of intoxication as the walls blur and ripple.

"You can guide us into the interior of this land?" says Sicarius.

"What need have we to look inland? All we need comes from the sea." A long pause. "There's but one. Dalny Marga is a forager and trapper, he knows paths. Or he claims to."

Houndara looks at Sicarius with an amused questioning expression. His hand rests on the pommel of his sword. "Where do we find this Dalny Marga?"

He scowls. "Once he knows that strangers are here, and seeking him out, he'll make sure he avoids you at all costs, until you tire and leave here. Until you go back to wherever you came from."

Houndara shrugs. All small communities are insular and suspicious. It's to be expected. "We can wait. You have a room where we can stay?"

"Look around the village. We have vacancies. Select as you wish."

Sicarius was silent. He didn't want to talk, it seems. They'd chosen a semi-derelict demesne just outside the village hub. Cleared it of debris and settled what few belongings they'd brought with them inside its walls. A roaring fire makes it a tolerable temporary abode. While the two of them restlessly separate to explore their immediate vicinity. Houndara has been a loyal comrade across many ventures, and good company when that is what's required. But there are also times when Sicarius needs to keep his own company.

Sicarius walks along the shingle shore to the northern edge of the bay as far as he can go, before the beach is walled off by high basaltic cliffs. He sits on the shingle, watching the waves, feeling their timelessness. He can see the red star pulsing in the gloomy sky, even during daytime within this isolated latitude. Its angry presence is strangely disturbing. As though there are significances to it that are tantalisingly just out of reach. It had first been detected faintly glowing before the first intimations of the scarlet plague. As though there's some mystical connection between the two events. As though destinies are inexplicably entwined. And the star is there, on the constellations etched into the ancient sheets of uncorrupted metal. The people of antiquity had known. The red star had appeared before, bringing its unknown portents.

He doubles back towards the hills above the village, ridges piled on top of each other, leading to high ice-terraces. There are scattered unhealthy goats that scuttle away at his approach. Also, growing on the slope above the huddled community, there are brittle plants of forking emerald crystal. Sicarius avoids them, and scales to the crest of the steep slope. He stretches tall, and peers out across the bay circled by ringing crags, with breakers marking the dark shoreline.

Snowflakes drift slowly from an overcast sky, but it is only silence that settles around him. He thumbs up his hood. The stones become slippery beneath his tread. Looking down the tumble towards Sarok he notices a goatherder's hut halfway down the slope, a low construction of woven wickerwork hunched inside a hollow, so that it's part-concealed against both the bitter winds, and prying eyes. Part-connected to Sarok by a meandering goat-path. He watches. There's movement inside the shelter. A figure concealed within, deliberately hiding.

Sicarius squats on the high ridge. He turns his attentions inwards. Not moving. As if he's turned to ice. At first, he sits. He focusses and he considers. Then he sits and considers. In the end he just sits. It grows colder, the wind-driven snow intensifies until it lashes him with icy fingers.

Time crawls as he watches the furtive movement glimpsed through chinks in the wickerwork structure. And he waits, oblivious to the snow shrouding him in a white film. The cold is the deathly chill of the black eternity between stars, too cold for breath, too cold for ghosts.

Eventually he sees Houndara appear in the space between two of the outer ruined buildings where Sarok gives way to wastes of shingle and sparse weed. He'd arrived only when Sicarius was almost frozen to paralysis. Sicarius stands, a shadow among shadows, and beckons with elaborate hand-signals. Houndara quests this way and that in response, climbing and slipping, until he's able to identify the vague footpath that rises towards the hut. The path meanders, disappears, only to reappear over a ledge, but gradually ascends. Sicarius tenses. He detects agitated movement inside the hut, and smiles grimly.

The higher Houndara climbs the poorly-defined path, the greater the signs of agitation. The person within the hut – surely Dalny Marga, intends to avoid any such confrontation. At the last moment, a crouched figure, swathed in ragged cloaks, emerges from the wickerwork screen and scurries with frantic haste away from the approaching Houndara. Sure-footed through familiarity with the rough and uneven terrain, he sends a couple of protesting goats scattering, then he hares upwards, glancing fearfully behind him, using whatever he can to conceal his escape behind outcrops of stone and thorny vegetation.

Sicarius crouches and waits as the frightened figure scrambles up the steepness of the incline towards him, with a confident agility gained through familiarity. At the last moment Sicarius stands. The fugitive halts, uncertainly, glances this way and that, weighing possibilities. His features resemble those of a sharp-beaked bird of prey.

Then he slumps in a dejected way. Conceding defeat. "I am Dalny Marga. You are the death-seekers who require my guidance, sirs?"

"You can take us to the stronghold of death?" His voice the whisper of falling snow.

He lowers his head. "If I must…"

*

>   my eyes extinguish
>   in pools of bone,
>   my own and others
>
>   we find the empty city
>   in pirouettes of stone
>   and chill blue illuminations
>   that freeze breath and eyes
>   to tears of living crystal
>   leaving them locked in dread
>   of night's encroaching demon
>
>   under ghost moons
>   we skirt the isle
>   of weeping statues
>   fearing its corpse stench, its
>   horrible miscegenation of form
>   and the grotesque putrefaction

of each carapace, and
nowhere finding life

The cliff barrier to the interior rises unscalably sheer.
Surely Dalny Marga doesn't intend to climb all the way? Are
there paths? Secret defiles known only to him? Yet they go
higher. The cold wind comes in across the bay, tearing at
them, as though it strives to pluck the intruders from the
rocks and hurl them down.

Then they reach a cave opening. A small mouth in the
sheer cliff-face partially concealed by towers of stone that
resemble monstrous teeth. Hidden in such a way that no-
one not well-versed in the geography could have noticed.
Once inside, the cave opens out into a dripping immensity
of cavern labyrinths that branch confusingly through the
roots of the mountains. They pass through a hall where ice-
fragments sparkle, a glacier that glistens with an inner lustre
as if giving off an energy of its own, in which monstrous
beasts are frozen in suspension, floating, as though caught
up in torrential floodwater that instantly froze around them.
Marga has seen them before. "I know all the secrets of the
labyrinth," he mutters. But Sicarius and Houndara stand
and stare in wonder. The beasts are reptilian and terrible. To
Houndara they are the very incarnation of legendary
dragons. To Sicarius, they are relics of an earlier, more
primitive evolution. Preserved in ice.

The three emerge through a dragon-head stone that
resembles a huge, petrified monster, through vents of
scalding geysers of superheated steam, into the vast
swampy tract of interior forest. There is glacier in the ring-
mountains. Here, there is subterranean volcanic activity,
venting methane they can taste in the back of their mouths,
their eyes stinging. Yet it creates subtropical everglades

where the time-breeze ripples the foliage to give the illusion that the whole forest is constantly in undulating motion.

The chill penetrating mist stirs as they walk. It's a living thing that keeps its distance, but encroaches in terrifying shapes that manifest and dissolve as they turn their backs. It forms a wall around the space of light they occupy, which defines the pocket of their world. It's difficult to get a firm foothold. At several points they sink waist-deep into the sludge of a sticky red muck that resembles flesh oozing fresh blood, the blubbery suckings of mud sound like toothless old men swilling soup. They extricate themselves with difficulty, floundering, only to sink again at the next step. Then their toes touch bottom, and they're scrambling onto a firm banking shivering with cold, the rasping of their breaths meet the whisper of crystalline tendrils bright with phosphorous. Periodically, Houndara cuts arrow-shapes into trees to act as a guide route in case of forced retreat.

They must make detours in the hellish journey to avoid poisonous plants, a swirl of mist rises to engulf them, and they wait until it thins before continuing, then a swarm of fireflies with killing stings speed past in a shower of sparks. While shadows move in the endless forest. They've not eaten in a long while. They've not slept. They've travelled far. While they hear the sound of vast leathery wings that flap above them, or sounds like the clicking of giant mandibles, out of sight, but suggesting terrible things. A sound that unsettles like dragging your tongue across a sore tooth.

"I don't understand this place," grumbles Houndara. "Imagination is a fine thing for a poet or a troubadour, but it does not make a good companion in this dark forest."

"Yet this is what you seek. Although your reasons are beyond me." Dalny Marga's voice carries a plaintive protest.

"My companion is the duly-elected Princep of Muskouia. Together, we crossed the bridge of perpetual lightning to reach this realm. I, to seek the truth of why my life is doomed to be so brief. Sicarius, to seek the end of his eternal life. We feel the truth is here."

"Never assume the simplest answer to be the truth," says their guide. "Nothing here is real. Not in the sense that we speak of real. The walls are more permeable here. Time isn't always linear in this realm. There's a story that a wandering contra-world in space smashed into the Earth, and in doing so it released such massive pyroclastic energies that it ripped a hole in the fabric of reality, to bring this pocket realm of anti-time into existence. A bubble attached to what is real by a hail of time-freezing micro-particles. A hide-hole, a gap between one world and another."

"I lose language," says Houndara. "I lack the vocabulary for this. And fear even robs me of my breath."

"Yet time is stilled. Time is frozen here, so that ages coexist. A fitting place for death to reside."

The sun goes down in torrents of flame, deluging the flooded forest landscape with atmospheric colours in ghastly radiance. While trees with branches like claws take on a golden luminance and the tide runs dark around them. They set up temporary refuge on an island, in amongst the tangled serpent-ridged contoured roots of a great tree.

They wake to find that Dalny Marga is gone. They'd posted watches through the night, each of them taking a turn while the others try to sleep. There were hideous howlings that make the blood run cold, echoes that ripple through the night, conjuring images of monstrous reptilian predators resembling those they'd seen suspended in the glacier. Marga was supposed to take the third watch, but he also takes that opportunity to escape back the way they've come, through the mountain-rim caves towards the village.

"We are lost," groans Houndara. "We have no way of navigating these treacherous waters without a guide."

Sicarius watches the stilled tide. The morning sun's radiance dances across its surface, taunting and mocking. He watches every flicker of light, every eddy of mist. "Wait."

He points. Beneath the scummy surface they can just discern an interlocking pattern of stone. "This is the tower they built to reach the Moon," he says softly. "Just as the oracle told us. The tower that snapped like a dry twig, and fell to rest as a pointing finger across the marshland. Now it becomes our causeway."

They wade knee-deep, the submerged stones are slippery with weed, encrusted with periwinkles and kale, but they provide safe footing across the wetlands. There are other architectural shapes that can be glimpsed beneath the slow tide, immense descending staircases, shattered columns that may once have been temples, mosaics that retain the patterns of beasts, and bones that may once have been human caught up in long strands of swaying weed. Until at last the pair can glimpse a dark structure rising intact above the treetops. A solitary stronghold that still stands tall. It towers above them, silent in its ghostly desertedness.

As the late-evening falls, the red star pulses as a vivid beacon above the tower, creating red and gold bands layering the horizon. Its baleful light hits the windows on the western walls of the truncated tower until they glow in pale lilac rectangles, glittering opaquely. Then there's a wide stone ramp of granite, pitted and scarred by centuries of weathering, a crumbling reflected redness emanating from its surface. An uncoiled streamer, long ruined. Houndara gets a sudden vision that it is an extending tongue that will swallow them into the hungry mouth of the fortress, before it retracts, to seek new prey.

They reach a creaking iron gate. An opening door that releases a rush of cold spectral air.

They're tense, holding their blades poised, ready for hostility, but Houndara is breathing more easily now. His grin returns with a shrug that seems to say so much, that perhaps all is well?

"I'm coming to terms with the idea that I'm about to encounter the incarnation of death itself," says Houndara. "Of course, it's not as though it will be the first supernatural entity I've met in my life. You are not exactly of this world."

"Or maybe we are chasing nothing more than memories and dust? Folktales and myth?" His grunt could have meant anything.

The interior walls are fused, as though melted by incredible blasts of heat, and then frozen into suspended rivers of tears. An organic flow, as though they're moving through an organism, through the intestines of a beast or the slash of a giant open wound, all the colours of darkness congeal through its biological contours. Brittle crystal columns with forked root-structures sparkle from alcoves, mutating, transfiguring into an alien otherness.

They're in a mildewed place of shadows and desolation, steeped in the fragrance of decay. The odour of old smoke. An impression of suspended devastation. A walk through a chimeric mirror. The haunt of rats and spiders, a place where reverie and unreality meet in frozen compromise. Sicarius halts, sensing a trap, his senses attuned to threat. He stands as if abruptly turned to stone. As though he's choking on his own breath. And when he inhales, it's as though it's the first breath he's taken in years.

This is a fitting abode for death. He takes one further step...

Then he's falling. He plunges into an ocean that shocks his senses into convulsions. He's washed ashore onto a beach of white sand where waves rear and surge over rocks that glisten with spray. He splutters salt-water from his lungs in wrenching coughs, and raises himself slowly. The beach is alive with predatory maroon crabs that sparkle like jewels in the primeval sun. The horizon is lit by volcanic fire...

Then he's falling, impacting in dunes of grit so hard that it drives the breath from his body and leaves his limbs weakened. The desert stretches away unbroken in every direction with no shade. The sky is vermillion, but spanned by a spinning vortex of moons that catch and reflect dazzling arrows of light. But the dunes tremble beneath where he sprawls. Eruptions and geysers of ochre sand spout and spray as something inconceivably vast and threatening stirs beneath the surface. A huge metal hand explodes up out of the grit with rusted metal fingers that flex, and the articulated knee of a leg... a kilometre wide. The vast mechanoid creature wakes and senses his presence...

He's on a white-sand island beach, looking inland where there are trees that glow and shimmer beneath a mesh of huge human arms and legs that tower like an enchantment against a roseate sky. His own limbs are too heavy to move.

Then he's falling, he's part of a desperate legion defending the crenelations of an ancient fortress, his sword thrusts in darkness as a corpse army of rotting cadavers scale ladders and siege towers, their slavering faces leprous white and deathless as his blade lops off heads and thrusts through fetid wormy brain-matter, and yet they come on beneath the vast orb of a night-black moon…

He cries out, and his voice returns in multiple mocking echo. He holds the grip of his two-handed sword which is slippery with entrails. He's on the ledge of a freezing mountain, torn by icy gales, there are shaggy black shapes circling him, they have gleaming white fangs and malevolent eyes of white fire, they drop onto all-fours like wolves, then rear like a bear, yet are neither, but a monstrous fusion, a mutation of forms with claws and carnivore jaws voracious for flesh…

He and Houndara stand alone on an endless plain of glass where everything reflects everything else. Its sparkle resembles ice. A cloudless sky balances above a seamless earth. There are creatures made of light that drift between worlds like scratches left by angry yellow fireflies. The two feel peculiarly unbalanced, as if every step they take will see them trip and fall, sprawling on their faces.

Fire devours them. They walk in flames, magma at their feet. They weep tears of blood.

This is a nexus of planes and dimensions, where all time coexists.

They're in a high fortress gallery with casements that overlook the encircling forest wetlands where monsters prowl and the shape of strange leather-winged birds glide through the steamy atmosphere. Through segments of stained-glass they can glimpse the distant crater rim of jagged encircling mountains that contain this magically accursed anomaly. Houndara's hands trace his clothes, no marshland wetness, no ichor of beast-blood, as though those nightmare glimpses were no more than illusion. Yet he retains the feel of that chill. The crystals of ice in his hair.

Strange garments hang on the wall, like empty

mannikins, or garments that resemble skeletons, like ribbed suits of armour. No two are alike. They hang between panels of distorting mirrors, draperies of deep moss-green fabrics that glint with gold thread, screens of small feathers, of lacquer and marquetry, of ivory, of jade, of coral placed side-by-side around the walls which ripple ever so slightly and in silence, as if kissed by the light of other suns. The mirrors, draperies and screens shimmer as if they're also unseen doors through which strange entities from other realities follow at his heels.

"What is it we're talking about now?" Houndara's voice is reedy, because the air is thin. Tiredness overwhelms him. The reaction to the past few hours are catching up with him, dulling his senses.

"We are talking about death. Listen."

"Someone... or something approaches?" A slithering sound, hoarse breathing and shuffling footfall. Blood drains from his face as a sickness of fear crawls. He feels ice slide down his spine. His eyes flick nervously, never settling on one point for longer than a moment. He's a child again, in a darkened room, with all the terrors of the world around him.

"It is the incarnation of death that is coming." Sicarius draws his blade from the scabbard slung on a bandolier across his back.

"Welcome, my unwanted guests." A lean-faced long-haired figure, his cloak billowing. He carries a lethal curved scimitar. He's a shadow. In his bulk, something animal and awkward. "I offer you nothing, because here, you have no physical needs. No hunger or thirst."

In the flickering lamplight Houndara can discern the shining of small white teeth set into a fanged mouth. "Are you death? You hardly carry the appearance of a demon."

"Neither witchcraft nor devilry can harm me." His

response is as quick as a dagger-thrust, he obviously knows tricks for avoiding awkward questions. Is it witchcraft? Has the grisly being the supernatural powers of invisibility?

Scimitar brandished on one hand, the dark figure uses the other hand to take Houndara by his arm. His long thin fingers curl inwards like a trap, like the claw of a giant bird. "I was once called Kar Dilhre, the conjurer conjured. But I've had many names across many cultures. Death is one of those names. I stumbled into this gloomy realm a thousand years ago, and I've been unable to discover a way to escape. Yet I've learned to love this desolate place, as if it were the home of my childhood, while also the tomb in which I'm interred. Here, I have all the wealth and power I need. I see beyond the spectrum of light and down into the very elements of creation. After all is said, death was in the air and the spray of the primeval sea where first there was squirming life. For there cannot be life without death. The two are inextricably linked. Death was there before there were apes and lizards and bugs and birds that crawled and loped and flew. Death watched the first lungfish flounder up from the tide onto shimmering mudflats beneath the moon. Death saw the tribes of apes and people, and other humanoid tribes that were neither. Death saw each brave new culture emerge, only to be buried in an invasion of ice. Death saw fire and brimstone, lightning and thunder. Death took each life once its time was counted out. Death has consumed a billion lives, and only hungers for more. Because death hates them all. Every man, woman, child and other on this accursed Earth. Now death will harvest your lives, simply because it must."

The head of Death is a kind of intricate mask, a monstrous helmet. Strands of hair the colour of bone. A platinum shock of hair. A nocturnal creature, by the wasted pallor of a face hacked out of dirty bone. The two sides of his mottled face do not match, distorted by goitres and lipomas. One eye is bigger, one cheek higher, as if the tide of his discoloured flesh is pulled askew so his facial skin hangs asymmetrically. A Janus face. Houndara does little more than grimace, showing neither his horror nor disgust. Surely, the man can't help it? No-one can help a disfigured face that is barely a face, eyes that are scarcely human.

The Eternal Assassin, and Kar Dilhre, the figure that is Death, circle each other warily, thrusting and parrying, testing out each other's fighting skills. The clash of duelling blades ring within the high chambers of the tower. Their fury extends, and intensifies. They are evenly matched, neither finding the opening in the other's defence. Neither finds the exploitable flaw that will bring it to a lethal end.

As they clash, as the deadly duel extends, whirling and darting in a dazzling display of swordsmanship, Houndara stands back in indecision. He feels that surely he must intervene... but how? His thoughts race with wild speculation. Then he recognises that Sicarius is employing the familiar ruse of stepping backwards as though yielding a pace to the attack. His gleeful antagonist moves in to press home what he sees as his advantage, raising his blade with both hands, leaving an opening for Sicarius to strike back.

The upthrust blow from the Assassin's blade is deflected by armour, but smashes his opponent back into a slow slide downwards. The force of impact dislodges the face, and sends it spinning. Death's terrible visage is revealed as nothing more than another layer of mask. Beneath it is an all-too-human face. Kar Dilhre twists his lip in what he must have intended to be a bitter smile. Houndara doesn't much care for the look of his teeth.

"Kill me. Kill me now. I will be dead. But I will be free." The voice of Death. His eyes come around slow and tight.

Sicarius pauses. Houndara peers fretfully across into his companion's by-now bristly-whiskered face. An uncanny being doomed to live forever. Something not quite human, he has eyes that seem to reflect, absorb, shine, capture and see. The eyes of a man who knew demons. Can he still trust Sicarius? Yes – he'd trust him with his life, exactly that.

"Wait, Adsiduo. Hold your blade. If you kill him, you kill death. There will be no dying in the world ever again. It will be a terrible new dark age of undying. But if he kills you, you become death itself. You know this to be true."

"I already feel dead," Sicarius whispers. "I know that I'm dead inside. Yet I live, carrying death within me. It's disturbing. It's so strange to know such death." His life is flawed, this scrial life. It makes him the victim of a hideous jest inflicted upon him by the monstrous gods of destiny. Behind every loveliness there's pain, made worse by this hideous flaw. There's no evil of which humankind is capable that can rival the atrocity that has been forced upon him. He lives on, only by devouring the lives of innocents. There can be no moral justification. Escape is impossible. There can never be the soothing oblivion of death. He tries to steady the quivering of his hands.

"This is what we do now. No-one dies. No-one needs to die. We just alter the configuration." Sicarius' whisper is so low the others can barely hear his words. "I stay here, where I will live for ever without devouring other lives. You two will return to the world. Across the causeway, through the dragonhead stone and the glacier labyrinth, to Sarok, then across the sea, through the forked lightning gateway, and on to Muskouia to live out your natural lives."

"We can't allow that," protests Houndara. "We came here together. We leave together."

"There's no other way. This is my desire. This is my answer."

"I will miss my comrade."

"I've lost comrades before."

Houndara turns ice-cold. How can Sicarius be so callous? Is there no bond of comradeship? Has he ever really known the alien entity of the Eternal Assassin at all? This was a moment he'd always known would come, but dreaded. When he looks across at Sicarius, something in his bleak expression makes him look away. His eyes are ancient pebbles. It was an end. The end of everything they'd held together.

From his high tower Sicarius watches them go, after the briefest of farewells. He sees them pause halfway across the causeway, and look back. As though in uncertain hesitation.

But he already loves this cold place. He'd always been separate. Now that separation had become more real than ever. He feels a sense of amputation and loss. But a sense of liberation too. Here, he can hide himself away, untouched by human concerns.

When the two reach Sarok they discover it empty. The scarlet plague has taken its sparse population, leaving nothing in its wake but dereliction. Houndara wonders guiltily if the two of them had brought the virus with them, and unwittingly infected the villagers. Only goats and feral dogs inhabit the narrow alleys and passageways. Until he hears a child crying. They follow the sound, to find a young girl – aged maybe eight or nine, who burrows into a nest of blankets in the corner of an otherwise abandoned house. Wary at first, her face is grubby, smeared by tears, and her long dark hair is tousled. At first she refuses to speak, as though the horrors she's witnessed have struck her dumb. But she follows them. Houndara names her Huetta Gloom.

Taking the girl with them, they retrieve their boat from where he'd left it drawn up on the shingle, and leave the island without a backward glance. Following constellations back through the forked lightning bridge to Arakel, and the charted seas beyond.

Back safely in Muskouia, Houndara stands in for the missing Sicarius, while coaching and tutoring the girl. She regains language, is sharp and intelligent. Kar Dilhre stays restlessly in the city for a month, then catches a trading vessel sailing south. By now the belligerent red star has faded and disappeared. As though part of some long thousand-year cycle, and it was only during that time that the portal to Sarok was open. He gazed at the sky lost in wonderings. About Sicarius who was now lost beyond recall. But who had achieved what he yearned for. Longevity, without the necessity of obliterating other lives in order to do so. Taking that splendid isolation upon himself, to cleanse himself of his guilt. Perhaps, during the next red star occultation, he will rejoin the human world? That will be his decision to make, and no-one else's.

Restlessly, he visits Sometime, the blind mystic who dwells in a modified cave along the craggy coastline beyond the city wall.

"Has Sicarius made the correct decision, to live beyond the world?" he enquires.

She fixes him with her wide dead eyes, so that he can almost see his reflection in their glassy surface. "He dwells in the desolate ruins of a shattered tower," she says. "He has everything that he needs. He needs no more."

Eventually, when the time comes, and Karel Houndara steps down to make way for the next Princep, it is Huetta Gloom who is elected First Citizen. She presides over a golden age of prosperity, art, music and dance. While he, alongside the lost figure who was once known as Adsiduo Sicarius, disappear from the story to become part of new myths and folk tales, stories that are more true than they are fiction.

> beautiful pagan,
> you who gnaw my waking dreams,
> I tell you this so you may know
> of the sunken citadel and
> its web of spider's limbs
> that you must fear it, yet
> know that somewhere far north
> beyond this derelict land is
> the world forever lost to me
> that they must never reach
>
> in this flame-dark land
> my thoughts are stolen
> by those who lurk
> beyond death

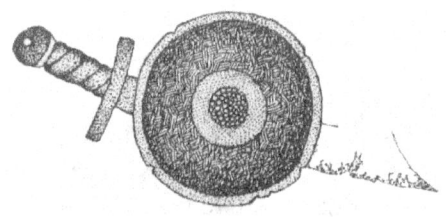

THE *GWÁILÓU* SHIP
Geoffrey Hart

Captain Shi Yang slept poorly, tormented by dreams that warned of death and mayhem—not unusual for a pirate, perhaps, but their extremely realistic nature this time was disturbing. When she finally admitted there was no hope of sleep, she went on deck to watch the sun rise above a calm sea as *Zhang He* glided south along the coast of *Yuè Nán*. She inhaled the clean sea air gratefully while she sipped her morning tea, as it was far more pleasant than the stale air belowdecks and hardly recognizable as the substance she'd once breathed in the brothels of Canton. As she savoured the complex bouquet of her tea, she admired the wash of colour across the sky, like the horizon in the *guó huà* painting that hung in her cabin. It had been painted by some anonymous artist, but she'd seen it in a previous prize and taken it as her own.

From the peak of the ship's mast came an excited cry. "Ship ahead, Captain!"

Handing her fragile teacup to Zhen, her eternally patient adjutant who followed her more closely than her shadow as she went about her day, she climbed the mast like one of the monkeys the crew prized as pets. When she reached the peak, she accepted the watchman's offer of his brass *wàngyuǎnjìng* and braced herself with a foot hooked around the mast. Then she brought the telescope to her eye.

"Where?"

The sailor pointed between two of the limestone islands that rose sheer from the southern ocean. With her unaided eye, she saw only a smudge against the horizon, but with the elegant brass instrument, it was clearly a ship. A three-master of unfamiliar design, but from the mast spacing, definitely not a junk. Almost certainly European, then, and sailing west for the *Yuè Nán* coast. *Zhang He* had been preying mostly on fishermen and small coastal traders of late; eating fresh seafood was all very well, but her crew were growing fractious and rebellious due to the lack of more lucrative prey. Maybe it was time to seek a larger prize.

"Watch it carefully, and report as soon as you recognize the design or the ship changes course." She descended the mast faster than she'd ascended. Her adjutant offered her more tea, but she waved it away. "Take it below. While you're there, ask Officer Zhu to join me on deck." While she awaited his arrival, she strolled to the ship's stern and climbed up to the deck that held its rudder. They'd been tacking slowly towards the southwest, long tacks that danced on either side of a mild southwestern monsoon that would strengthen as the day grew warmer. *Zhang He* handled like a dream at all points save only upwind, necessitating much tacking to reach the point where she'd come about and sail downwind, her preferred direction, looking for prey.

She explained the situation to the helmsman and instructed the short, burly man to change course to the south and await further instructions. As he shouted to the sailors below, performing their morning duties on the main deck, Shi felt the familiar mixture of fear and excitement building in her breast. The European ship was large, and presumably well-armed, but she reminded herself she'd captured several ships just as big. It would have been nice to have the other ships of her fleet supporting her, but she was confident in her crew's strength and training.

In a commendably short time, the ship settled on its new course and her first officer emerged from below, straightening his silk shirt while his *jian* swung at his hip.

"You summoned me, Captain?"

She pointed south, where the ship lay. "A ship of unfamiliar design, downwind." When he moved as if to climb the mast, she put a hand on his forearm. "Stay. It's yet too far to make out details, but it's no junk."

"European, then?"

She nodded. "And thus a far richer prize than the coastal traders we've been preying on these past weeks. I think it's time we rewarded the crew with such a prize."

He nodded. "I'll alert the sergeants to begin getting their men ready."

Within minutes of his departure, the ship filled with the sound of whetstones being applied to swords, accompanied by the clicking of breeches as her crew worked the mechanisms of a variety of firearms to ensure there'd been no corrosion from the salt air and that they'd function smoothly. Ropes squeaked as the ship's deck guns were bound tightly to their wooden platforms so they wouldn't break free when fired, and through the hatch, she heard shouts and running feet as men and a few women began transferring powder from the magazine and iron from the ship's belly to the gun deck. By the time the noises eased and sailors began coming on deck, their prey's masts were visible through the slight haze without a telescope, rising above the brassy surface of the sea. Shi climbed the mast again, secured herself, and gazed through the telescope.

There was something strange about the ship's profile, which seemed to waver, even though the day hadn't yet grown warm enough for the warm air near the sea surface to distort distant images. Oddly, the prize's masts seemed curved at an odd angle, but when she blinked, they were straight again. It left a queer feeling in her stomach. She shrugged and returned to the deck, where Zhen stood patiently, holding a warm bowl of *jūk*. She smiled and took it from him. Its warmth soothed her unsettled stomach.

She pondered the foreign ship, as the masts bothered her. She'd seen masts bend after a sufficiently strong and prolonged *táifēng* wind, but it was rare; far more often the mast would snap. The blurring of the outline continued, no matter how carefully she focused the *wàngyuǎnjìng* and how often she wiped its lenses with the clean cloth that hung from her belt. But Europeans had been invading China's seas for centuries, and their ships were as many and strange as their customs and speech. The coastal waters of *Nán Zhōngguó Hǎi* apparently still had surprises for her.

She handed Zhen the empty bowl and stretched her arms over her head, sighing as tight muscles eased. When she turned, Zhen stood ready with her *jian*. She laughed at how well he knew her, and settled the sword belt around her hips.

As the sun rose higher and the foreign ship drew nearer, she saw sunlight glinting from brass fittings—possibly even gold?—but there was also a hint of opalescence that would be more usual for a pleasure barge than a working ship. Had they found an uncommonly rich prize, some wealthy merchantman who'd strayed too far from his escort? She saw no gun ports, which unexpected, but perhaps not unusual at this distance. So where, then, was it headed? After a moment, she sent Zhen to find the charts-master.

Master Wu arrived bearing a tightly rolled map in a tight-fitting bamboo case. With practiced skill, he removed it from its case, restored the cap, tucked the case in his belt, and with Zhen's aid, spread it for her to inspect. His blunt finger jabbed at a spot towards the chain of islands lying east of the *Yuè Nán* coast. "We're somewhere near here."

"*Somewhere?*

The charts-master, who had sailed this sea for decades, bowed deeply. "With respect, Captain, it's hard to be certain. Though we have a good chart of this region, and have kept the usual careful records of our travel, the position I calculate does not match what I see. The islands are unfamiliar. Moreover, they are strange. Here," he handed her his telescope and pointed with a finger. "Look at that island!"

At first, she saw nothing unusual. The island rose abruptly from the sea, at a sharp angle. Some of the surrounding islands resembled the fins of a school of sharks and others were smoothly rounded by centuries of wind and storm. No two looked completely alike. But the island Wu identified showed a strange distortion of its shape; like the foreign ship, its image wavered. The phenomenon was unlike anything she'd seen in her years of sailing, and it sent a shiver up her back. As she watched, brow furrowed, the island's outline rippled like a dancer's smooth muscles, then it sank into the sea. She blinked in surprise, wiped the lenses of her telescope, and looked again. No, she hadn't imagined it: the island was gone!

She realized the charts-master had been speaking to her and she hadn't heard. "My apologies, Master Wu. Please tell me again."

"I've never seen such islands before. We must have drifted off course during the night."

Wang, the night watch officer, had arrived, unnoticed. He frowned. "And I say to you we are perfectly on course. I followed the compass scrupulously, and the stars were right for where we should be."

Shi shared his frown. "Have we any sailor who's sailed this specific part of the sea before joining our crew?"

"If we're located where Officer Wang claims, we have one. I'll go fetch him." Wu departed hurriedly, ignoring the watch officer's frown.

When Shi looked back, the missing island had reappeared, water streaming down its sides. She shuddered, and the night's feeling of ill omen returned, stronger, making her scalp tingle and her hair rise on the nape of her neck.

The crewman who arrived was shrunken with age and wrinkled, but did his best to stand tall before her, despite his lesser height. "How may I serve my captain?"

"We need you to examine the sea around us and tell us where we are."

He bowed, and held out his hand for a telescope. With the ease of long practice, he scanned in a smooth arc, starting from the direction whence they'd come, where a thin wake trailed in a straight line behind the ship, as yet undisturbed by the gentle swell. As he smoothly rotated his stance toward the sea ahead of them, his brow furrowed ever deeper and a frown grew on his face. When the instrument reached the position of the European ship, he gasped and nearly dropped the telescope.

A cry came from the mast. "Captain! The foreign ship has changed course. Towards us!"

Shi blinked. It was unusual for a European ship to seek combat with a Chinese junk, but not unheard of. Particularly in these days when the *gwáilóu* were beginning to resent the losses she and other pirates were inflicting on their trade. She called up to the crow's nest. "Are there any other ships?"

"No, Captain."

Curious. When she turned her eyes downward, the ancient crewman stood before her, eyes wide with horror. His face was frozen between dismay and the urgent desire to speak. She nodded slightly, and he spoke, voice trembling.

"Captain, we must turn and fly north at the best speed we can manage. That ship? It's a ship of the *yāoguài*. Legend tells that none who confront it shall ever see their homes again."

Shi snorted. "Superstitious nonsense. A *gwáilóu* ship, you mean. Those are the only foreign devils we have to fear." Shi was not one to flee from a fight, and reminded herself it had been long since *Zhang He* had taken a prize as rich as this ship looked to be. She resolved to try for it, dismissed the crewman, and went to stand by the helmsman. As her ship continued south, wind almost on her beam, deckhands watched and adjusted the sail carefully to ensure it was optimally positioned. The other ship bent its course until it was sailing downwind on a course that would soon intercept *Zhang He*. Shi had seen such behaviour before from naval vessels, but this ship was different. For instance, it carried no flag atop its mast; were it a naval vessel, it would fly its country's flag proudly, whereas a pirate would fly the black flag of the European corsairs, the red flag she flew atop her own mast, or one of the other coloured flags of the pirate confederation. They'd drawn close enough now to see the ship's sides through the telescope, and there were still no signs of weaponry on deck—and no gun ports below. For that matter, there were no crew on deck. That worried her, but perhaps it was just distance and the angle between the ships. She called her officers on deck, and they stood with her by the rudder, awaiting her orders.

As the ship drew nearer, Shi began to worry. The grim feeling of the previous night's dreams had never left her, but now it strengthened and weighed heavy upon her. It differed most unpleasantly from the usual nervous energy she felt before a battle. She had a growing feeling that she should look behind her, as if she were being watched by something malevolent, like a mouse scurrying across the floor of a granary guarded by a cat. And she wasn't alone. She caught her officers glancing behind them, then at each other, but refused to let them see her doubt.

"Sailors prepare firearms to repel boarders!" she shouted. An officer fled below to summon them. Though purchasing European rifles and powder from the Portuguese had been expensive, she'd never regretted that cost for a minute; it gave her an unassailable advantage during boarding actions, particularly compared with the long spears used by most other pirate crews. Of course, she kept the spears close at hand in case they became necessary, such as if it began to rain at an inopportune moment, rendering the firearms unusable.

As *Zhang He* altered course to bring them alongside the other ship, Officer Zhu cleared his throat. When she turned to meet his gaze, she saw her normally composed officer's face streaming sweat, and he stank of fear. This was unusual for a veteran of so many battles, and moreover, the others shared his fear. But turning her head had been a mistake; the feeling of being watched, as if something horrible was about to pounce upon her, intensified until it became unbearable. She felt sweat begin trickling down her forehead.

Officer Zhu could no longer bear the strain. "We must turn away!" he screamed.

"It's too late," she replied, for it was. The strange ship was now so close that if she turned, it could turn and rake her stern with its broadside—though she still saw no weapons ports, open or closed, and it had not even one bow-chaser to fire upon her. However, while she'd scrutinized the ship, she'd missed something: there was now a shadowy helmsman. As well, other shadows moved on the ship's deck. At first glance, they appeared human, but the longer one looked, the more their shapes flowed in ways that tormented one's eyes. That was bad enough, but there was worse to come: the ship itself began to change, its prow flowing into the shape of a gaping mouth filled with glistening black teeth, and large clawed tentacles emerged from its flanks, similar to but disturbingly different from those of the *zhāngyú* the Cantonese ate, and they stretched hungrily towards *Zhang He*.

Shi knew she couldn't outmanoeuvre the other ship if she continued upwind, the least favourable course for a junk. Instead, she chose to accept the risk of turning fast enough to allow one or more exchanges of broadsides, after which, if the foreigner hadn't surrendered or been disabled, she'd turn her ship on its heel and fly downwind to the northeast to take full advantage of the strengthening monsoon to escape.

"Fire rockets!" she commanded, and a salvo of rockets flew from the bow through the morning air. But rather than igniting the ship's dark sails, they passed through as if there'd been nothing to intercept them.

Zhu sent a runner to relay her commands to the gunners. When he waved from below, she gave the order. "Helm alee!" she yelled. "Fire a broadside as soon as we've turned across their bow!"

Zhang He heeled sharply to port, and as the ship crossed

the other ship's bow, a ripple of cannon fire sounded, like fireworks before the spring holiday. *Zhang He* staggered sideways from the cannons' recoil. The range was close enough they couldn't miss, but there was no answering fire and no sound of cannonballs shredding wood or canvas. Having learned from previous combats, the helmsman held the ship on its course long enough for a second partial broadside before he was forced to turn away. Shi was pleased at how well she'd drilled her crew; she'd wager their gunnery against both European and Chinese warships and expect to best them. Nonetheless, she vowed that she'd put the next British or Portuguese gunner she captured to work creating cannon mounts that allowed the precise aim that European ships benefitted from. The second volley was no more effective than the first, and the ship completed its turn. But the helmsman had waited a moment too long, and as *Zhang He* crossed under the other ship's bow, scores of the shadows on its deck leapt for *Zhang He*. It would have been an impossible distance for mortals, but the other ship's crew flew through the air as if thrown from a *dàn gōng*.

As the boarders struck the deck, screaming shrilly with voices that caused one's bones to shiver, the sailors fired a long, rippling volley. The iron balls had no effect, and as the shadows closed for hand-to-hand combat, men drew their *dāo* and engaged the boarders. The ship's writhing tentacles clutched at her ship, slowing it, but were repelled by crew wielding polearms and long-hafted axes. The battle was uneven, swords against dark tentacles tipped with dully gleaming black claws that darted here and there, evading the most skilled parries; soon, the screams of her sailors could be heard. But miraculously, the swords were working where firearms had failed them. For every dying shadow that struck the deck, dissolving into a puddle of foul-smelling ooze that caused the sailors to cough and choke, two sailors fell, and only one thing saved the crew: there were far more sailors. By the time *Zhang He* steadied on its new downwind heading, the fight was over. For the moment. They'd survived. The wind continued to strengthen, giving hope they might escape the foreigner.

The strange ship's mouth and tentacles disappeared, to be replaced by the formerly smooth hull, but they had slowed the ship's progress enough to concede precious time for the pirates. By the time the foreign ship had altered course to pursue *Zhang He*, they were far enough downwind she could evade the wind shadow created by the other ship's sails. But the strange foreign ship didn't attempt to steal their wind. It remained on course, paralleling the Chinese ship. With the wind from its aft port quarter strengthening, the junk began slowly pulling away from their pursuer.

"Still no return fire, Captain."

She glanced at Zhu, but withheld comment. He was a good officer, and if he felt a need to state the obvious, he was clearly rattled and needed reassurance. She surveyed her officers, noticing the stink of fear sweat and the whites of their still-wide eyes. "That was well done. It seems we've bought ourselves time, so see to the wounded—and wash that foul stuff from the deck. She watched as the dead were thrown overboard and the wounded were carried below deck for the surgeons. Sailors began scrubbing at the demon residues with mops.

Occasional fluxes of the wind carried the sulphur-tang of gunpowder across the deck, intermixed with the foul stench of the dead boarders. She looked behind, and the pursuing ship had finally changed tack to move upwind of *Zhang He* and steal its wind. It began to close the distance. "Trim the sails!" she cried out. "We need every slightest bit

of speed we can muster if we're to escape that demon ship."
Officers descended to the main deck and began shouting
orders. Following her command, the helmsman adjusted
course northward to escape the pursuer's wind shadow a
little longer.

As the wind strengthened and *Zhang He* began to cross
the swells at an oblique angle, the big ship swayed from side
to side as the swells caught her and passed beneath her
stern, its nose digging deep into the water, flinging salt
spray to either side like a sage's trailing moustache. As the
gap between the ships relentlessly closed, Shi's fear grew
and she became desperate for a solution, though she kept a
stoic face to avoid discouraging her officers and crew.

Then, all at once, she recalled the islet that had sunk
and emerged from the sea again. If she could find a similar
islet, perhaps she could bring it down on the other ship!

"Look for a tall, narrow pinnacle with a channel
between it and a nearby island," she commanded her
officers, and sent the same command to the lookout atop the
mast.

The lookout was first to find one, and pointed until Shi
and the others saw what he'd found. It was a channel
between two islands that steadily narrowed to a width that
should still be large enough for both ships to pass through.
If she were wrong and *Zhang He* wedged in the passage, they
were all doomed. She mopped the sweat from her brow and
scrutinized the pinnacle. From below, it seemed the pinnacle
had begun to separate from its parent rock under the
influence of wind and rain, leaning inwards precariously to
form an angled wall above one side of the passage.

"Steer towards the gap," she directed the helmsman.
Then to her officers, she explained her plan: "We'll sail
through the channel between the two islands. As we pass

the pinnacle, we'll fire a broadside into the rock. With luck, we'll bring down the whole cliff on our pursuer." Officer Zhu smiled a taut smile, took a deep breath, then ran down to the gunners to explain and personally supervise the preparations.

The pursuer continued to relentlessly draw closer. Wavering black figures once more gathered on the deck, the strengthening wind carrying their foul smell to the decks of *Zhang He* and making the sailors gasp in terror. Sails flapped as the wind became unpredictable where it funnelled past the rock walls, or separated and flowed around the outside of the passage. As they entered the narrow channel, a particularly strong gust threw her ship sidewise until its gunwale crashed against the port rock wall, wood splintering. "*Steady!*" she called to the helmsman, who blushed and dipped his head in shame. Then, as they approached the middle of the passage, the ship lurched and made a terrible groaning noise as it grounded on shallow rock. As her heartbeat accelerated, the ship gave a second lurch as the swell lifted it and freed it to continue its passage. Shi gasped in relief, grateful for the junk's shallow draft; no deep-bellied European ship would have escaped.

As her ship came parallel with the hanging rock wall, she gave the order: "*Fire!*" The ripping-cloth sound of the broadside, magnified by the close quarters, deafened them and left their ears ringing. As the echoes began to die, they were replaced by a rumbling from the rock wall. A hail of small rocks began to fall, and the pursuing ship stopped suddenly, with a grinding noise, as it struck the rocks that had nearly captured *Zhang He*. The foreign ship extended its tentacles once more, trying to pull itself past the rocks. But it was too late. With a crash, the entire cliff fell, burying the other ship.

Zhang He caromed off the starboard wall of the passage, bottom scraping along rock until the wave from the collapsing cliff lifted the ship and flung it out the far end of the passage. Shi exchanged shaky grins with her officers, then at a grinding noise behind them, they turned as one and looked back into the passage, mouths gaping, fearing the worst.

But it was only the last of the fallen rocks settling and blocking the passage. Whether or not the strange ship could extract itself from the rocks no longer concerned them. They'd be long gone before that happened.

And, Shi resolved, *I'll heed my instincts next time the prey turns predator.*

Zhang He continued north, gliding between islands that had once more become familiar and immutable rock.

Author's notes

Thanks to Li Huilin for assistance with cultural notes and Chinese words and phrases. *Gwáilóu* is Cantonese slang for Westerners, and literally means "foreign devils", which fits well with how I've used it here. Shi Yang (better known as Zheng Yi Sao) married the infamous Chinese pirate Zheng Yi after she escaped a Canton brothel, and in the early 1800s, after her husband died, became the most successful pirate in history, with hundreds of ships and tens of thousands of sailors under her command. Knowing the pirate age was soon to end, she made a deal with the Qing Emperor to retire from piracy, and lived to the ripe old age of 68. Zhang He was a famous Ming Dynasty admiral who created enormous ships and led naval expeditions that explored much of southeast Asia's oceans and coasts in the early 1400s, and may have crossed the Pacific to reach North America. *Yuè Nán* is the Beijing name for Vietnam; which I used to replace the Cantonese *jyut6 naam4* spelling. *Guó huà* is a style of traditional Chinese ink painting. Many spectacular limestone islands jut from the sea southwest of China near the Vietnamese coast. Google "photo limestone islands Vietnam" (without quotes) and select the Image tab for beautiful views.

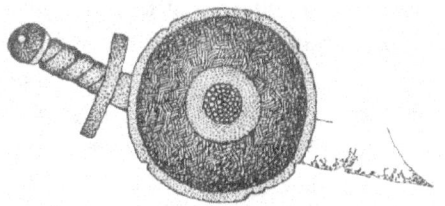

GOOD FORTUNE
Ũũmbi

To the Far East, in the heart of the mighty continent of Kan'dilah, is the harsh, merciless desert, known as The Cradle of Divinity. Deep in this desolate expanse are the ruins of a temple. A temple, like many others, that had stood long before recorded history, now reduced to no more than a set of stairs, its stone doors and some scattered granite blocks. A temple devoted to a god who, like so many others, had vanished from all except the most obscure myths and isolated devotees.

Sat against the doors of this temple, beneath its weathered archway, Kach was enjoying a peach. His starched white headwrap and white, freshly pressed robes provided a striking contrast against his onyx black complexion.

He chewed and swallowed a mouthful of peach as he observed a squat man, who struggled to make his way up the sand-coloured steps of the temple. He was a pitiful sight. His once fine, navy blue cloak was tattered and covered in grime, the honey brown skin of his face was ashen, thanks to the dust sticking to it, and was lined with exhaustion. The man's breath wheezed and gasped out of him as he laboured up the steps, he winced with pain and clutched at his abdomen with his left hand. On the middle finger of that hand, Kach noted a ring made entirely of obsidian, save for the centre, which bore a golden engraving of a falcon in flight. Kach finished his peach and tossed its stone to the side.

The man stopped five steps short of where Kach was seated and looked up at him, his expression was a mix of wariness and fatigue.

"Please," the man's lips cracked as he spoke, "water," his voice came out as a raspy croak.

Kach dug into his bleached leather bag and pulled out a water gourd that he tossed to the man. He fumbled and nearly dropped the gourd but managed to keep a hold of it. He removed its cork with a popping sound, squeezed his eyes shut and drank the water in big, thirsty gulps. He stopped to catch his breath before gulping down some more and re-stoppering the gourd. He tossed it back and nodded gratefully to Kach, took the last few steps up to the archway and flopped beside him under its shade. He leaned his head back against the temple doors and closed his eyes with a sigh. Kach gave the man a single glance and looked back ahead. His brown eyes glowed amber as he enhanced his vision and saw, approximately three kilometres away from where they sat, a flock of reptilian, winged *sirats*, circling and swooping around a single location. To his eyes it seemed a giant, but invisible scythe passed through the entire flock twice, killing them all near instantly.

"What's your name, weary traveller?" Kach asked the man.

"Morani," the man replied without opening his eyes.

"I am Kach," he inclined his head as he introduced himself. "Pardon me for saying so Morani, but you look like shit."

Morani, with his eyes still closed, snorted in amused derision, "I'd like to see you faring any better in my shoes."

A bright column of fire, wide enough to swallow a large village, exploded into being up ahead. Its shockwave ruffled their clothes and raised dust around them. Morani clicked his tongue in annoyance, opened his eyes and sat up, "To hell with it!" he shouted, "I've run this far, yet he has still followed me. He can have his wish and kill me then, but I'm not taking another step!"

He huffed and threw himself back against the wall with his arms folded and a scowl on his face. Kach studied the flaming pillar intently before it dissipated. "That", he said slowly, "is Suk's magical signature I sense."

"Oh, you know that bastard, Ker'man?" Morani replied as he scowled straight ahead.

Ker'man. The name given to everyone with skin such as Kach's.

"We're…acquainted."

Morani's eyebrows drew down, "My only prayer right now is for the depths to open up and swallow him whole."

Kach laughed softly, "I suspect that would have happened long ago, if only the god of the underworld wasn't so scared of him."

Morani turned to Kach with a puzzled frown, "Who or what is he that you speak of him so?"

Kach returned Morani's frown with a smile, "Suk is one of the most powerful shamans to have ever lived," his smile became wry, "and as you've discovered, he's a tad emotional."

Morani snorted in disgust and curled his lip, "Emotional," he invested the word with a heavy dose of scorn. A crack of thunder sounded, and they were both quiet until its echoes faded, then Morani finished his sentence, "Try bat-shit crazy!"

"He's about two kilometres away now," Kach

mumbled to himself. He returned his focus to Morani, his smile now amused, "Might I ask why he is so upset?"

Morani threw up his hands, "That's what *I* want to know."

Kach nodded sagely, "Right, right. His reasoning would confuse anyone in the best of times." He crossed his legs, folded his arms and looked out at the desert stretching before them, "Tell me how you met him, and keep it brief, he'll be here in a matter of minutes."

Morani muttered to himself in irritation, before sighing and narrating his story.

"I had just concluded business in Pancholan, when that fucker –" he nodded in the direction he had come from, just as several sand dunes exploded. The air became glittery with sand particles, "– appeared and started taking out my employees." Morani shook his head, "It's been three weeks since then, and I've lost two thirds of my crew. Plus, half of the profits!". His pitch heightened sharply when he said the word 'profits'. "In the beginning, I was convinced he was a demon, summoned by my ex-wife as a last fuck you from her to me. Or perhaps, some god had decided to shit on me for some perceived slight," he paused as he stroked his chin, then chuckled darkly, "maybe both?"

Kach found himself liking the man and his gruff, irreverent attitude, "Well", he said, "we can safely rule out the possibility he's a demon, hard as it is to believe." His side glance caught Morani's doubtful expression, and he continued, "I know Suk personally, and there's not many gods with the guts to use him in their schemes. Those that do are, mercifully, otherwise occupied for now." Kach dug into his bag, took out two peaches and handed one to Morani, then bit into the other. "Now," he said through a mouthful of juicy peach, "Suk is extremely eccentric, but he does have a kind of logic. Therefore, I can say for certain that he's not attacking you 'just because'," he swallowed.

Morani frowned sceptically as he bit into his peach, he gave his mouthful three brief chews before swallowing and replying, "Then why do you think he's doing this? Even now, my hired shamans are dying just to slow him down, and there's no damn explanation for it."

"Hmmm," Kach finished his peach and popped its stone from his mouth. It rolled down the stairs and settled onto the sands. He adopted an expression of deep thought while rubbing his chin. "Based on what you've told me, it's possible that you might have passed each other on the street one day, and he was offended by your body odour."

"Huh!?" Morani exclaimed, incredulity writ on his face.

"Or," Kach continued, seemingly oblivious to Morani's reaction, "maybe you happened to be in the same Qawa house on one occasion, and you slurped your tea too loudly."

Morani gave Kach's face a searching look, while Kach kept his gaze straight ahead. Now a kilometre away, a giant golem of desert sand and rock had risen up and was smashing its fists into the ground. Bolts of lightning shot out of the sky a moment later, crashing into the ground as well.

"Are you making fun of me?" Morani finally asked, his voice soft and carrying an edge of anger.

Kach waved a dismissive hand as he responded, "Of course not, this is a life-or-death situation after all."

"Then," Morani replied through gritted teeth, "you would have me believe that I've been chased across a fucking continent, for three weeks, because of my personal hygiene, or – or the way I drink my tea?"

"It's entirely possible."

"It's entirely bullshit!" Morani erupted in a shrill croak,

"What you're saying doesn't have a single lick of sense."

Kach shrugged his shoulders, "Of course, I said there must be a reason as to why he's attacking you," he turned to Morani with a smirk, "I never said, however, that it would be a sensible one. Where do you think you are anyway?"

Morani opened his mouth to give an angry reply but was cut off by the ground shaking. A mass of craggy stone rose up with a resounding boom, where the battle of elements had been taking place. It destroyed the golem in an instant, blotted out the sun and cast the entire temple in shade. Lightning sparked impotently around the stone mass, before ceasing altogether. Morani gawked, the partially eaten peach slipping from his fingers.

"This is the great continent of Kan'dilah, home of the greatest shamans in the world," Kach said, his tone and facial expression calm and casual. At his words, Morani shut his mouth with a click and gave his head a vigorous shake. For all the danger they were in, Kach spoke as one explaining that the sun was hot, or that water quenches thirst.

Kach stood up, straightened his attire and snapped his fingers. Geometric patterns made of golden energy materialized around them, interlacing with and overlaying one another, then solidified into a protective dome, surrounding them and the area immediately surrounding the temple ruins. Morani grunted in surprise. No more than three heartbeats had passed between Kach snapping his fingers and the dome forming.

Kach continued to speak as he looked over his handiwork, "Men, women and even children walk around this place as living gods." He turned to face Morani with a cold gaze, "If you insist on stubbornly clinging to such a boring brand of logic, you won't survive here long, Morani.

Even if you are a high-ranking member of the Osan Trader's Guild."

Morani flinched away from Kach, his eyes widened with alarm, "I don't remember telling you that, Kach."

Kach turned his head to look down at Morani and snorted, "Why would you need to, when you advertise yourself so openly?" he tapped his own middle finger as he replied.

Morani's eyes darted to the ring on his finger and he winced and turned his head away, grimacing and looking chagrined at the same time.

"Well, that does sound like...*reasonable* advice," he sighed then looked back up at Kach, tired resignation in his eyes, "It's such a shame, that I'll be too dead in the next minute to apply it."

Kach's face broke into a grin, "If you have truly accepted your death in this place, I will respect your decision. However, if you would rather live then help me and I can help you."

Morani turned to Kach with his mouth open to speak, but hesitated then turned back and scoffed instead, "Obviously I don't want to die here, but I don't see any way of preventing that." He looked up at Kach with a side glance, "Unless you're saying you're a match for a monster that just raised a mountain."

"It would be troublesome, true, but I doubt it'll come to that."

"What makes you so sure?"

Kach looked over his shoulder with a smile at the temple doors. "I've been making friends in high places. Or should I say deep places?"

Morani's side glance narrowed into a suspicious frown. "Why go through all this trouble in the first place? With a snap of your fingers, you cast a high level barrier that would take a first order shaman ten minutes of unbroken concentration to create. Escaping would be easy for you."

"Indeed, it would be," Kach agreed with a nod, "but like I said, we can help each other, so you're in luck."

The golden dome flashed and the air around them rang with a sonorous gong. The ringing reverberated, giving the impression of a massive bell struck within a cavernous building.

"Ah!" Kach exclaimed, his tone jovial, "our violent friend has arrived."

Morani shot a terrified look at the dome, which stopped flashing, and licked his lips, "H-how would we help each other?"

"I can help you get out of this mess. In exchange, you will help me get to Salmiran City. Unnoticed."

"Why?"

Kach chuckled, "Do you really have the time to ask me that?"

The dome flashed again and the gong was even louder this time, forcing Morani to clap his hands over his ears. The ground beneath their feet vibrated with a tremor and grains of sand jumped up from the impact.

The tremors ceased after a few moments and Morani cursed under his breath. He released his ears with a sigh and replied, "It seems that I do not. Very well, I will help you. Now, hold up your end of the bargain!"

Kach smirked triumphantly and pulled out a violet satin pouch from within his robes. It was small enough to fit in the palm of his hand and emanated a soft blue-purple glow. He crouched and loosened the drawstrings of the pouch, then overturned it. The contents of the pouch fell onto the ground with soft clacks and Morani's eyes flashed with greed. The contents were a handful of sapphire gems glowing with an inner purple light.

"Spirit gems," Morani whispered with awe.

"Offerings," Kach said as he straightened up. The glow from the gems brightened and they levitated up to Kach's eye level, where they arranged themselves into a slow spinning ring and remained suspended.

The dome was struck yet again, but this time, the sound of the gong was discordant. A network of thin cracks appeared all across the dome and it flashed continuously.

Morani's eyes darted around the dome as he turned round on the spot. "Now what?" he asked, his voice strained with barely contained terror.

Kach snapped his fingers and the dome puffed out of existence. Straight ahead, where the edge of the dome had been, was a pair of crumbled pillars with jagged tops, one pillar taller than the other. In between those pillars was a man with his fist drawn back, ready to deliver a punch. He let it fall and scowled up at Morani and Kach.

Beside Kach, Morani was huddled and trembling, whispering a mix of pleading prayers and desperate curses.

"Whatever you do, make sure to stay within a metre of my person," Kach said. "Now, let's go."

"Fuck," Morani whimpered as he rose.

They proceeded down the stairs. Kach's steps were measured and confident, while Morani limped down behind him and did his best to keep within his shadow, his breathing harsh and shallow. They reached the bottom of the stairs and walked to stop a few metres from the newcomer.

This man was short, bald, had big eyes and had a tanned, copper complexion. All his clothes were dark brown, from his shirt with a plunging V-neck collar, sleeves cut off at the elbows, to the trousers, whose hems stopped just above the ankles. On his feet were simple, black leather sandals, with a double-strap passing between his first and second toes. Other than his face, every other inch of his skin that could be seen was covered in flowing script that wiggled and swirled as if alive.

He glared at Morani, who did his best to completely disappear behind Kach, then shifted his glare to Kach himself and his lip curled into a sneer.

He looked up behind them at the temple ruins. For a moment his expression was unreadable, then his face twisted into a ghastly smile before returning his attention to Morani. "It's fitting," he said, his tone harsh and clipped, "that an insignificant insect like you, would give offerings to an equally insignificant god."

"Oh, spirits of my ancestors," Morani whined in a choked whisper. Kach's lips twitched into a small smile, but he otherwise remained silent.

"Regardless," Suk said as he walked forward, "you're going to die here today, you little shit." Kach took a step forward and held up his right hand in front of him, palm facing Suk. Suk stopped in place and scowled, spitting to the side as he did so, "Fuck out of my way, before I wring your balls," he snarled.

Kach, with his arm still up, raised an eyebrow and the smile on his face widened. "Now, now," he said in a mocking tone, "I know you're happy to see me, but let's not get too excited eh?"

Suk's scowl deepened and he bent his knees to a crouch. He held out one arm in front of him, fingers bent into a claw-like posture, the other was held closer to his body, hand closed into a fist. The wiggling, swirling script jumped from his skin and hung suspended in the air around him.

"Prayer of flame," Suk growled. The suspended, indecipherable script lit into flaming orange, indecipherable script, then zoomed back to his skin with a sizzle. His eyes flared momentarily with the orange flame, then he propelled himself forward, blazing a trail of fire behind him. He closed the distance in a heartbeat and threw a flame-covered fist at Kach. There was a blinding flash of orange-whiteish light and a boom, followed by a cloud of dust that billowed up around all of them. Moments later, a passing breeze blew the dust away and revealed Morani turned around, squatting on his heels with his hands held over his head and Kach, wearing a toothy grin as he looked down at the fist that had stopped inches away from his face.

The script around Suk's body had reduced in brightness to a dull glow. Suk himself was trembling as he stood still, his body leaned forward and his fist outstretched. Veins popped out on his neck and bald head. His face was a mask of rage, with lips pulled back to reveal gritted teeth. The deafening blare of a horn ripped through the air and Suk slammed face first into the ground. The sandy ground beneath him became depressed, as if it was bowing under the weight of a giant, invisible pillar.

Kach looked down at Suk with a smug smirk. "Suk, have you ever been to the deepest part of the ocean?"

Morani released his head and risked a peek over his shoulder. He gasped and fell backwards in shock at the scene before him. The singular cause of his terror for the past three weeks, was now lying down, face and belly on the ground, unable to even twitch a finger.

"I have," Kach continued, "the pressure alone can reduce a city to rubble in seconds."

He bent to one knee and hung his head over Suk's. "The deity of this temple is an ancient ruler of those very depths.

And what you are now experiencing is a taste of that same pressure." He chuckled. "Not bad for an insignificant god, eh?"

*

Suk growled wordlessly and the script on his skin flared brighter. The blaring horn call came again, and more pressure slammed down onto him, sinking him further into the ground and making the depression in the sand more pronounced. The air vibrated as the horn's call continued, on and on, and on. Suk mustered his body's strength and, with lots of huffing and grunting, managed to lift his head up to rest on his chin.

He looked up at Kach's face, and his growls stilled in his throat. The eyes of the man that knelt over him shone with a brilliant, all-consuming golden fire. It was not fear that gave him pause, Suk had not needed to fear anything for a very long time. But he still had cause to be wary. The traces of divinity he felt within this man were unknown to him, yet at the same time they were strangely familiar. Almost nostalgic even.

"Well," Kach prompted, his voice had taken on a deep, dark timbre quality, "should we take this further?"

Suk knew he could still win, that he probably would win. But not without cost. For him, now was not the time to pay that cost. The glow left Suk's tattoos, and the horn blared with a low, drawn note. The pressure vanished and Suk slowly pushed himself up to his feet. He dusted off his clothes and gave Kach one last glare, tinged with a hint of grudging respect.

"We will meet again," he said in his clipped growl. The script jumped from his skin, and he uttered a guttural chant in a now dead language. The script reconfigured itself into concentric rings, embedded with squares and triangles. The pattern zoomed back and as soon it touched his skin, he disappeared.

*

Behind Kach, Morani let out a breath he had been holding and clutched at his chest. He closed his eyes as he breathed in and out large, shaky intakes of air. When his breathing settled, he opened his eyes and looked at Kach with hope and anxiety.

"Is it over?" he asked, a tremble in his voice. "Do I get to live?"

Kach, his eyes and voice now back to normal, threw his head back and barked out a laugh, "Yes, for now. Next time you're around, make sure to leave some offerings."

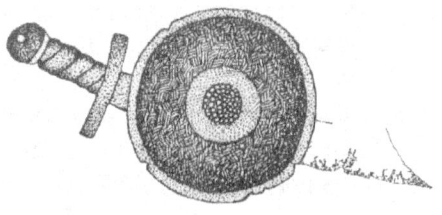

THE WYRM'S TONGUE
Daniel Mahoney

They rode in like they owned the road, five shadows stretched wide across the dirt track, dust curling from the hooves of their mounts. Pieces of armour glinted here and there—an iron pauldron, a dented breastplate, the rim of a rusted helm—strapped over worn coats and sun-bleached leather. Blades hung from some belts, crossbows from others. None looked like they belonged to the same army, which meant they belonged to something worse.

By the time they reached the farmyard, the sun was low and copper-red, throwing the whole place in bloodlight.

The woman stepped out onto the porch, drying her hands on her apron. She looked at them the way she might look at a summer storm—measuring the distance, gauging the damage it might bring. She was greying, but the harsh environment hadn't completely robbed her of her fading beauty.

The man in front reined in his horse with a tug and smiled, though it didn't reach his one remaining eye. A haggard patch partially covered the ragged scar on the other side of his face.

"Afternoon, ma'am." His voice had a slow curl to it, like smoke from a dying fire.

"You're a ways off the road," she said in a dusky voice that matched the fading light.

"We're looking for a man," he replied. "Old fella. Goes

by many names, but once they called him The Wyrm."

Her hands stilled. "'Tis not a name spoken much anymore."

The man spat on the ground. "Still too often for my liking. See, we tracked him to a cave nearby, hopin' to collect on a debt of honour. But the old bastard wasn't keen on payin'." His eyes drifted past her, toward the house. "Cut down my men before he vanished. My guess is he's got kin nearby. Has to be a reason he hunkered down here."

She didn't answer, her throat tightening, breath caught halfway.

The man swung down from his horse, dust puffing around his boots. "Now… we can have a polite talk. Or we can go searchin' on our own."

"Have at it. Nobody here but me and my three boys."

"Best fetch your sons," the leader said mildly. "The horses need tending to. We'll be stayin' here for a spell."

He looked at his men and nodded. They dismounted in a cloud of dust and creaking leather.

"Find the old bastard."

The woman turned, apron hanging limp at her sides, and stepped back into the shadowed doorway.

The stew on the hearth had gone cold. Her boots whispered over the worn floorboards as she crossed to the narrow hall. Only when the men outside could no longer see her face did the stiffness in her shoulders loosen. She pressed a hand against the wall, feeling the grain beneath her fingers, steadying herself.

Thom, the eldest at twenty-two, was already standing in the kitchen doorway, jaw set tight, a cleaver in his hand.

"Back to the table," she whispered, not unkindly.

"Ma—"

"Now."

Will, nineteen and all sharp angles, leaned against the pantry, trying to read her face. Cole, the youngest, had been dozing in the corner chair, long legs tangled under him. He pushed himself upright, blinking, still half in a dream.

"Some men are here," she said, voice quieter now. "You'll help with the horses. Do what they say."

Before any of them could answer, boots thudded heavy on the porch.

The door swung wide without a knock, and a man stepped inside—pale hair hanging out of a dented helm, the stink of road dust and stale ale riding his breath.

His gaze slid over the boys, pausing on Cole.

Cole was still shaking the cobwebs from his head when the pale-haired man stepped forward. The blow cracked across Cole's temple—hot breath, the taste of iron, white light—then the floor rushed up and swallowed him whole.

The woman's breath caught—but she didn't scream. Not yet.

The pale-haired man's grin faded into something colder.

"Let's not make this harder than it has to be. You two, horses—now."

The young men looked askance at their stricken mother, despite the act of violence against their sibling. She nodded at them.

"You," he said. "We're hungry. See to your boy and then make us some supper."

The door slammed shut as he left. Now she did cry.

*

Cole's world tilted sideways. The floorboards gave way to stones slick with moss.

Boots moved somewhere far away, voices leaking through the cracks—low, indistinct murmurs like threats whispered on the wind.

Then another sound rose up, close and steady: metal on metal, a whetstone singing sharp and cold over steel.

When he opened his eyes, the farmhouse was gone.

He was crouched by a narrow creek, water the colour of tarnished silver winding between mossy stones. The air smelled of wet earth and juniper, heavy with the scent of old secrets.

On the far bank sat an old man—older than the trees, by the look of him—hair gone white, shoulders still broad and carved like stone. No armour, just a long coat of dark wool that seemed to absorb the light. Across his knees lay a sword: narrow, single edged, black as night except for the silver line along its edge that shimmered like a sliver of moonlight.

"Come to gawk, boy?" the man asked without looking up. His voice had the rasp of dry leaves scraping across dead wood.

Cole remembered now—chasing a rabbit too far, sliding down a ravine, waking to find this man beside the creek.

"I… thought you might be a highwayman," he'd blurted, breath catching.

The man chuckled—a sound both tired and dangerous, like a blade scraping stone. "Highwaymen don't live long enough to turn grey."

Cole's eyes kept drifting to the blade. Something deep in him already knew what it was, and that frightened him.

The man sighed, as if he could hear the boy's thoughts, a slow sound like wind through a graveyard. "Recognize it, do you?"

Cole hesitated. "Yes, sir… Wyrm's Tongue."

That earned him a quick, piercing glance—sharp as the sword's edge. The old man went back to his whetstone, the scraping steady and relentless.

"Well, boy, you have me at a disadvantage. You know who I am."

"My name's Cole, sir."

"And what are you doing out here in these woods, Cole Sir?"

"Just… just Cole. I live on a farm, not far from here. Sir."

The sharpening stopped. The man's gaze pinned him like a spearhead, cold and unyielding.

"I'll make you a bargain, Just Cole. You don't tell a soul you saw me here, and I'll let you live to come back."

He rose to his full height—a craggy mountain of a man carved by years of war and wilderness. The sword seemed to drink the light as much as it caught it.

"You're ungainly now, but you'll be tall and quick one day. In return for your silence, I'll teach you how to use one of these."

The edge of Wyrm's Tongue gleamed silver in the fading light, and for a heartbeat Cole thought it might swallow the sky whole.

*

Cole slowly blinked his eyes open. The moss, the old man, the sword—all gone.

He lay on his mother's cot, staring up at the low, cracked ceiling. The smell of warming stew hung thick in the air, heavy with onions and fat, but beneath it lingered something sharper—sweat, leather, and the sour stink of unwashed men. His mouth tasted of copper. His head throbbed in time with his heartbeat, as if cleaved by an axe. A cold, wet rag pressed against his brow.

For a moment, he didn't know where he was.

Then the voices came—low, rough, seeping through the walls like dark water. Boots scuffed against worn floorboards, chairs scraped and groaned under heavy weight. A harsh, high laugh cracked the air, followed by the wet smack of something hitting the table hard.

Through the open doorway, he saw his mother at the hearth, ladling stew with careful, mechanical motions. Thom and Will were nowhere to be seen—their absence was a sharp hollow, like a pulled tooth. Three strangers sat at the table, one watching her with a wolf's cold stillness.

The pale-haired man lounged in Pa's chair, one boot hooked over the rung, flicking a knife idly in his hand. The blade's edge caught the firelight in slow, hypnotic flashes. Beside him, another rider gnawed on bread, spitting crumbs onto the floor with careless disdain.

Cole tried to listen, but their voices tangled into a muddled drone, words slipping past like minnows darting in a murky pond. His eyelids grew heavy. Then a voice cut sharp through the haze—

"The Wyrm."

The word burned hotter than the pain in his skull.

He pushed up onto one elbow, but the room pitched wildly, like the deck of a storm-tossed ship. The walls stretched, bent. His hands slipped beneath him.

He collapsed back onto the cot, the cold waters of unconsciousness swallowing him whole once more.

*

Cole opened his eyes and found himself back at the creek.

Mist clung low to the water, curling between rocks slick with moss. The air was cold enough to make his breath smoke.

The old man stood with his coat open, sleeves rolled to the elbow, Wyrm's Tongue catching the pale light as he turned it in his hands. His torso was a map of scars — fine silver threads and jagged white seams crossing the stone of his frame.

"You look half-dead, boy," the man said, almost amused—but with a dark undercurrent. "Good. You'll learn better that way."

Cole stood barefoot in a ring of flat stones cleared on the bank — a crude training circle. His makeshift wooden blade felt heavier than an anvil in his hands.

"Keep going, Cole. Time to see if you're made of more than wishbones and wind."

They had been at it since morning, as they had been for the past week. Every muscle in Cole's body ached; his palms were torn open, the blisters ripped and raw. Swinging a sword was proving worse than farm work — worse than threshing in midsummer heat.

All that time for one move the old man called Crow Wing.

Cole raised the wooden blade horizontally, arms trembling, and slashed from left to right. He rolled his wrist, reversed, and cut from right to left.

"Again."

He repeated the motion.

"Clip the feathers before the bird takes flight. Again."

The sun sank inch by inch, gold leaking into red. Sweat stung the torn flesh of his hands. His grip slipped.

"You look like a drunk holding up a clothesline," The Wyrm said, stepping forward to twist Cole's grip into place. "Now—again."

Cole swung, slow and clumsy. The sword spun from his fingers and splashed into the creek.

The old man laughed — a sound rich and unguarded, but with a sharp edge beneath it, like a blade hidden in silk. "I think that's enough for today," he said, eyes narrowing as he watched Cole's every move.

Cole sloshed into the shallows to retrieve the stick, water numbing his raw palms.

"Do you think I'll ever get it?" he asked, the words heavy with doubt.

"I think you had it hours ago," the old man said. "But knowing the move isn't enough. It has to be muscle memory — instinct. In a fight, there's no time to think. Only act."

His gaze drifted toward the sinking sun. "And I needed to know you wouldn't quit. I won't start something if you're not going to finish it."

Cole frowned. "Start? I thought that's what we've been doin'."

"No, boy." The Wyrm's smile was a bare flash of teeth, cold and sharp. "This is just the beginning."

*

Cole opened his eyes to shadows crawling along the ceiling. The training ring, the old man, the cold bite of creek water — all vanished.

From the next room came his mother's voice, low and careful, each word weighed before it left her mouth. A lazy drawl answered her, rough and edged with something cruel, followed by the scrape of boots over wood and the groan of a chair leaning back.

Cole shifted, trying to rise. Pain knifed behind his eyes, pinning him flat.

"You said he'd be nearby," one of the strangers said, voice rough like gravel. "An old man like that don't get far."

"He'll come," the pale-haired man replied, voice calm but ice-cold. "They always come back for blood."

The word made Cole's heart seize in his chest.

The door banged open. The one-eyed leader strode in, spurs ticking sharp and deliberate across the wood floor. His gaze swept the kitchen, the hall, the dark corners — as if the shadows themselves whispered secrets to him.

"Enough eatin' and jawin'," he said. "Check the loft, the barn, every shed and stall. Turn this place inside out if you have to. If he's here, we'll smoke him out — and burn whatever's left."

Two of the riders shoved back from the table and stalked outside, their boots pounding like war drums on dry earth.

"If he ain't here," the leader said, voice dropping low and hard like a blade sliding from its sheath, "you and I are going to have ourselves a little talk."

They were hunting The Wyrm — and they thought his mother held the map to his bones.

He braced an elbow against the cot and tried to stand, but the room tilted, black closing in from the edges. Somewhere far away, his mother's voice urged him to stay down. Then her words — and the world — vanished beneath the cold mist of the creek.

*

Cole turned the sword over in his hands, the morning

light running pale and cold down the length of the blade. It was nothing fancy—just good steel with a grip wrapped in plain leather, but it felt impossibly heavy compared to the carved branch he'd been using. Like it carried a weight beyond its metal.

"You've been swinging sticks long enough," The Wyrm said, stepping into the circle of flat stones. His coat was off, scars mapping his forearms like a battlefield. He moved with the quiet, dangerous ease of a wolf sizing up prey. "Time to see if you can keep all your fingers when it matters."

Cole was standing this time, not crouched. His boots squelched in the soft mud near the creek.

The old man circled him, muscles taut and coiled, holding Wyrm's Tongue as if it weighed nothing, the blade glimmering faintly like a shadow lurking at the edge of light.

"Widow's Guard," the old man said.

Cole tried to lift the sword The Wyrm had given him. His arms were already tired from holding it too long.

"High. Rest it on your shoulder, not in the air—you aren't strong enough to hang steel yet."

Cole did as told, but his stance wobbled.

"Now—Kingbreaker."

Cole swung. It was clumsy, slow.

The Wyrm shook his head. "That's a child hitting a rug. Kingbreaker's for when you mean to crack a helm in two."

He stepped close, looming like a predator about to strike. "Watch."

In one smooth, ruthless motion, he brought Wyrm's Tongue down in a crisp killing arc that bit deep into the log they'd been using for a target. The sword sank with a finality that seemed to echo.

"That's the difference between a swing that warns a man… and a swing that buries him."

Cole swallowed, nodding.

"Crow Wing," the old man ordered.

Cole slashed left, rolled the wrist, slashed right. The blade whispered through the air, heavier and slower than the wood had been.

"Again. Quicker. A crow doesn't ask permission before it flies."

They moved into other forms—Threshing Blow, Pike's Eye. Each one left Cole's arms burning hotter, the muscles in his back screaming for relief.

"You'll fight the blade before you fight a man," The Wyrm said, circling him like a wolf stalking the final stretch. "Best learn which one's your real enemy."

By the time the sun was low, Cole's shirt was plastered to his skin. The Wyrm took the sword from him, testing its edge against his thumb.

"You didn't drop it," he said finally. "That's something."

Cole, too winded to answer, only nodded. But the weight of the steel in his hands had stirred something deeper than pride—a quiet, dangerous hunger to see what he could do with it.

"How's your mother?" the old wolf asked unexpectedly.

"My… my mother?"

"Your father shat you out, did he?"

Cole turned red. "She's fine, I guess."

"Good. That's good." He levelled Wyrm's Tongue at the boy. "One more time for the road?"

*

He awoke to silence.

No clatter of pots, no murmured voices. Just the faint echoes of the world outside the house.

Cole's head throbbed in slow, deliberate pulses. When he moved, it felt like the floor tried to rise up and meet him. His stomach twisted. He rolled over the side of the mattress and retched.

Still dizzy, but better.

With sudden determination, he forced himself upright and leaned over the side of the cot again. He pushed until something came loose — not just from his stomach, but from the haze. The world steadied. His vision sharpened.

The ringing in his ears dulled. A crack of breeze moved through the open windowpane. Outside, faint voices carried — too far away to make out. Not his mother.

The pale-haired man's measured tone. The one-eyed leader's gravel rasp. The memory of bootheels like a clock ticking down. The smell of ash. The weight of failure.

Cole wiped his mouth and sat back against the bedframe. His legs still trembled, but his thoughts were coalescing. He reached up, touched the tender welt at the side of his skull.

They thought he'd stay down.

He wouldn't.

The barn. That's where he kept it all. That's where he'd hidden everything that mattered to him.

He crawled to the window and peeked between the curtain's frayed edge. No one in sight.

Cole drew a breath, slow and even. His body wasn't ready. But readiness didn't matter anymore.

His blood was all that mattered.

It was one of the many lessons his grandfather had

taught him.

*

Cole followed the narrow trail, uncertain where it led. The sky was still pink with the last light of evening, but the air seemed colder here—denser, as if the mountain exhaled with each step he took. When the path ended, he found himself standing before a narrow cleft in the stone, half-hidden by ivy and mist.

The Wyrm's voice called from within—calm, but commanding.

"Come in, boy. Don't dawdle."

Though he'd trained with the old man in the forest for nearly three years, he'd never been invited here—not once. He thought the Wyrm slept in the trees, like an animal, or vanished between lessons like a spirit.

He stepped into the cavern.

It opened slowly, like a throat swallowing him whole, the stone walls slick and close, the air dense with memory. The only light came from a soft glow somewhere down the narrow corridor. The deeper he went, the more the space widened, until he stood in a hollowed chamber carved into the mountain's heart.

It wasn't what he expected.

Cole had expected bones, maybe weapons—something crude and brutal. Instead, he found beauty. Shelves of old books and scrolls filled the stone walls, and the tapestries that hung in the gaps shimmered with fine embroidery, scenes of battle and starlight woven in impossible detail.

The Wyrm stood near the back, crouched beside a heavy wooden chest. He looked older here. Larger. The flickering light emphasized the sheer bulk of him—

shoulders like stone gates, arms coiled with muscle. He turned slowly as Cole approached.

"I used to be quick," The Wyrm said, his voice low and reflective. "Back when I danced."

"Danced?" Cole asked, unsure if he'd heard right.

"I was fast once," he said. "Quicker than thought. But speed fades, like memory. You get old, bones stiffen, reflexes dull. So I trained the muscle. Became something heavier. Slower, maybe—but just as unstoppable."

The old man stood slowly, lifting something from the chest. He turned. In his hands, he held a set of black leather armour—well-worn, supple, but reinforced at the joints. It gleamed faintly in the dim light.

He stepped closer, and for a moment, something shifted in his eyes. Pride.

"I wore this in my prime. Before I learned to carry my weight like a wall. It's yours now."

Cole reached out, fingers brushing the cool leather. It felt alive.

"Why now?" he asked.

The Wyrm looked at him long and hard. "Because you're ready. And because it's your birthday."

Cole blinked. "You know?"

"I know a great many things," the old man said. Then, quieter, "You look like her, you know. You have her eyes."

A silence stretched between them, heavy and ancient. Cole's throat tightened.

"My mother? She never told me."

The Wyrm looked into the distance. "She had her reasons. And I gave her more."

Cole looked down at the armour again. His grandfather's armour.

And slowly, reverently, he lifted it into his arms, the

weight of a legacy larger than himself.

*

The one-eyed man's patience was wearing thin. The sun had dipped behind the trees, and the shadows they cast stretched like long, skeletal fingers across the farmyard. Still, there was no sign of The Wyrm. His voice cut through the growing quiet like a whip cracking through the silence.

"Bring the woman and the two still able to walk outside. Now!"

Boots thudded heavy against the wood floorboards. Thom and Will appeared reluctantly, their faces grim beneath the fading light. Their mother's eyes were steady—cold, like a blade pressed to skin—though the set of her jaw betrayed a storm brewing beneath. They stepped out into the cold dusk, flanked by rough hands and the glint of cold steel.

Inside the barn, Cole's heart hammered so loudly he feared it would give him away. Every muffled word outside seemed to tug at him, urging him to move, to strike—but the part of him that remembered fear begged him to stay hidden.

He pressed his back against the wall, forcing himself to slow his ragged breaths. He could almost hear The Wyrm's voice: *If you hesitate, boy, the fight is over before it begins.*

He slipped to the far side of the barn, where dust clung thick and the shadows pooled like oil. The smell of hay and old wood mingled with the faint metallic tang of tools long unused. His fingers searched the rough timber, brushing splinters, until they found what they were looking for—a loose board, barely held by rusted nails.

With a careful push, it shifted inward. A cold breath of

stale air stirred the hairs along his arms.

Behind it, nestled in the shadowed hollow, lay the black leather armour. Familiar now, heavy with meaning. He hesitated, remembering the first time he touched it—his grandfather's eyes watching, weighing, finding him worthy.

He pulled it free, the scent of worn leather and old sweat rising like a ghost in the cool air.

Cole slid the armour over his shoulders, tightening each strap like a vow. The weight settled around him—not just protection, but a legacy carved into flesh and bone. It carried the shape of a man he'd never truly known, and the shadow of the one he was becoming.

His hand slid deeper into the hiding place, fingers brushing against cloth. He pulled free a long, wrapped bundle.

When he peeled back the covering, the curved blade drank the barn's dim light. Black, cold, and deadly—yet warm in his grip, as if it recognized him. His grandfather had called it a serpent's whisper in steel.

Wyrm's Tongue.

*

The old man lay propped on a mound of threadbare blankets, the fire's glow painting deep canyons in his face. His breath came shallow, like the bellows of a forge that had nearly burned itself out.

Cole sat watch in the single chair by the bed, the leather armour creaking when he leaned forward. This was no grand battle. No heroic last stand. Just the slow, stubborn ending of a legend finally outpaced by time itself. Death had come calling for The Wyrm.

"Well," his grandfather rasped, a crooked grin splitting

his weathered face, "Wouldn't you know it. After all the blades, all the arrows, all the men who swore I'd never see another sunrise... I'm going to die in bed. A perverse punchline, if there ever was one, eh boy?"

Cole tried to smile, but it felt wrong. "You beat them all."

"That's the trick, boy." The Wyrm coughed, still somehow amused. "Never let another bastard write your ending. Blood demands blood, and it never forgets."

"Are you... happy with yours?"

The old man laughed—a rasping sound that cracked like dry timber. "Happiness? I've known it only briefly, stolen like a thief in the night. But they took my happiness— your grandmother—from me."

Cole could feel the cold shadow behind the words. "What did you do?"

"I became The Wyrm, Cole. I littered the land with the bodies of those responsible. I brought an entire kingdom to its knees. And I would do it again. The stories speak of much, but what they're missing could fill volumes."

His grandfather closed his eyes, still for so long Cole feared the end. Then they snapped open again, the glint fierce and sharp.

"That's the last lesson. Blood calls for blood. It's a debt that can never be paid, only passed on. Do you understand what that means?"

Cole thought about his mother and brothers, imagined them in danger, and felt the cold steel rise in him. "Yes, grandfather. I think I do."

The old man smiled with satisfaction, though his eye clouded with sudden pain.

"One final gift. One you've earned."

From beneath the sheets, he drew a bundle wrapped in

oilcloth. His hands trembled, but the grip stayed sure. He set it on Cole's knees.

Cole peeled back the cloth, though his soul already knew the contents. Wyrm's Tongue. The dark steel gleamed, the curve of the blade like a question with only one answer.

"It's yours now," the Wyrm said, voice barely more than a breath. "Treat her right, and she will never let you down. Carve your own path, Cole. Write your own story—and make sure no bastard gets to write the last word."

"I will, grandfather. I promise." Cole's voice caught. "I will make you proud."

"You already have."

With those final words, The Wyrm's life left his body.

At twilight, Cole built the pyre himself. Flames roared to life, swallowing the body, sending sparks spiralling into the night like scattered stars. The air thickened with smoke and iron. His grandfather had feared his enemies would desecrate his remains—another lesson proven true.

For days, Cole remained alone in the forest. But he was no longer just mourning. He paced the shrine of stone and steel he'd built—a sentinel waiting, sharpening himself for the reckoning to come.

Months later, the men came, smashing the shrine to rubble.

They did not find The Wyrm alive.

But they found death waiting.

Blood calls for blood.

*

The family huddled just beyond the barn, flanked by five armed intruders. The one-eyed man's rough voice cut through the cold night air like a whip.

"Come out, Wyrm!" he barked, his gaze burning like hot coals. "We'll tear them apart if you don't show yourself!"

Only silence answered.

Then the mother stepped forward, blade flashing in her hand. With a desperate lunge, she aimed for the leader's throat.

His reflexes were quick — catching her wrist, tearing the knife away, and slamming his fist into her ribs. She gasped, staggered, but did not fall.

"Enough of this! I'll kill every last one of you," the leader snarled, breath sour with whiskey and rage.

"No, you won't."

The voice came low and steady from the barn's shadowed entrance.

Cole stepped into the moonlight. The worn leather armour clung to him like a second skin, Wyrm's Tongue resting at his hip. His eyes were cold, sharp — utterly certain.

For a moment, his mother's breath caught — she saw the father from his youth reflected there.

"I want The Wyrm, not a pup," the leader sneered.

"He's gone," Cole said, voice calm but edged steel. "I burned his remains last summer."

The leader's grin twitched, a flicker of unease. "And my men?"

"Them I left for the crows." Cole's words fell heavy, final.

The sneer faded. "Kill him."

Three blades hissed free.

Cole's stance shifted — not to meet them, but to invite them in. The Wyrm's lessons moved through him like muscle memory made flesh.

His opponents were already dead.

Cole danced.

Crow Wing intercepted the first sword, then opened its wielder's throat in a single, whistling stroke.

Widow's Guard came next — blade high on the shoulder, point angling back. The second man lunged for the opening.

The Wyrm's voice rang clear: "When they see this, it's already too late."

Kingbreaker fell like judgment, splitting helm and skull in the same breath.

The Wyrm: "Aim for the crown he thinks he wears."

Pike's Eye turned aside the last blade. A serpent's strike followed — one thrust, straight through the heart.

The Wyrm: "They are expecting two moves — not a single death blow."

Three men fell in as many breaths.

Cole stood over them, blood dripping from Wyrm's Tongue into the dark earth.

The remaining two outlaws — and his family — looked on in stunned silence, fear and awe warring in their eyes.

The pale-haired man stepped forward, rolling his shoulders, blade already lifted.

Cole matched him, calm, centred. The first clash rang like a bell through the yard.

Steel on steel. Step, turn, parry, thrust. The pale-haired man was fast, but Cole was faster — forms flowing into one another, each strike answering the last like lines in a song only he knew.

The pale-haired man knew he was outmatched. He stumbled, hand surreptitiously grasping a handful of gravel. He stood suddenly, launching the debris at Cole's face.

But Cole was no longer there.

He sidestepped, a blur of motion. His blade flashed in a diagonal line — Shedskin Step — cleaving the pale-haired man from shoulder to hip.

The Wyrm's voice echoed: "Be somewhere else when the steel comes."

He pivoted, flowing with the same motion, and crossed the space to the one-eyed leader before the man could finish drawing breath.

"You think you've—"

Wyrm's Tongue flashed.

The leader's head hit the ground before the word could finish. His body stood for a moment longer, swaying, then toppled beside it.

The Wyrm: "A dragon strikes, it does not talk."

The night held its breath.

Cole stood before the family he swore to protect. His mother met his eyes—no child left in them, only the steel and shadow she once feared in her father. His brothers looked at him as if he might devour them at any moment.

Cole said, "More men will come. I can't stay here." He adjusted the black leather armour, its weight fitting him like a second skin. The old man's sword hung ready at his side, gleaming faintly in the dying light.

"Where will you go?" she asked, though she already knew the answer.

"To make sure no one ever threatens you again."

She watched as his silhouette faded into the darkness— the black leather armour moulded to him like a second skin, the cold weight of Wyrm's Tongue at his side a steady promise.

From beyond the trees came the faint sound of hooves, slow and deliberate.

"My father may be gone," she whispered, "but the Wyrm's shadow will never fade."

As the first stars blinked awake above the silent farm, Cole disappeared into the night, ready to carve his own path through the coming darkness.

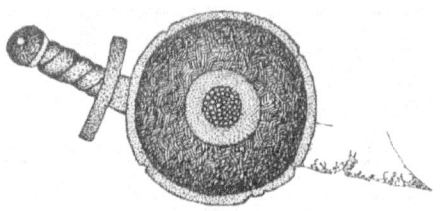

WARDARK AND THE SANDS OF SERPANAM
Craig Herbertson

The desert of Serpanam was bounded by the forest to the north. To the northeast the lower slopes of the mountains of Moerland edged the desert of Serpanam in a great half circle reaching out like grey corpse-hands on the burning sands of the arid south-face. To the West the desert expanded into the great river Sperta which created an alluvial plune with sprawling farmlands that led to the coast of Serpania, to the hills on the edge of the port of Serpanam and the wide and unknown oceans. Far to the south, the fiefdom of Serpania true emerged from the tributary waters of Sperta: A land gifted to religious orders by the emperor Franken; a pleasant fiefdom of small fecund villages and farms, of the two citadels of Serpanium and Feralium and uncountable monasteries. Beyond this lay the empire of Franken on the edge of the Sudron which waged continual war on the Tyranny of Jalca and, beyond that, lands unmapped and unknown to our people where there be monsters.

From "A history of The Age of the Gilded Swan" Monk Gaunilo of Feralium

Blessed are the sands of Serpanam
Unbounded grave of the heroine
No More Jwain of Jalca
No more her swirling sword

'The Epic of Jwain of Jalca' Fragment by the unknown rebel

THE CLOAK OF XIANTHUS

The dying man fell to his knees and with difficulty held his body upright. The wind was beginning to whip up, the sand shifting and eddying in the air like fragile tendrils of mist. But there was no mist in the air, only a baking heat, sucking all moisture and life from a world where the sands stretched to infinity and a searing light bored into the eyes from a pitiless sun.

The man slowly raised his head revealing a face almost blackened by that sun; blonde hair blanched white, grey retinas staring from orbs of dusty marble in hollowed sockets. His hands, caked in blood, made a vain attempt to shield his tortured eyes from the blazing light as the dry air hissed through parched and tortured lips and his rasping lungs, bereft of moisture, pumped like a blacksmith's failing bellows.

The man was naked but for his leather britches. His upper body muscled like a bronze statue, chiaroscuroed with lines of blackened blood, smudged with dark bruises and scarred with recent wounds, seemed almost inhuman. His back-scabbard was empty and so with weaponless hands he hollowed his palms still trying to shade the hellish light and to look ahead on to the undulating plains of unending desert. Soon the sun would drop. The cold would creep like a leper over the sands and in his weakened state he would die, and over time his bones would be picked clean as would the bodies of the nomad warriors he had killed three days before.

There was nothing ahead, only unyielding, unbroken desert. The man dropped his hands to his waist. What he had hoped to see was not there and he grasped a handful of the sand only to open his hand and let the grains slip slowly through his fingers like the whisper of the *death caravanserai* intruding on his fading consciousness.

And then the wind dropped and a stillness engulfed his world. He raised his eyes again. How long before the bitter cold? The rictus of a grin spread across his face. At least his death would release him from the burden of his damnable quest. He would fight to the last, of course, straining every muscle and every fibre of his being to survive. But without water the end was inevitable, and without warmth the end was inevitable. He had neither. Not even the manner of his death was in his hands.

Oh, to have a bright sword and a last battle.

Time passed. The man remained immobile as though frozen to the ground. His mind was fading into the *caravanserai*. He saw glimpses of his past, his mother smiling with love of her only child, her blonde hair and grey eyes, a mirror of his own. The strength and pride of his father, Wevan, headman of the tribe. The recent past where he had achieved the heights of glory: Lighting the Vandergan mountain fires to save his people from the Gobeln, the monstrous siren queen beheaded, the Smagardeen tyranny destroyed, the Pirate King strangled on the deck of his own ship and all captives freed.

And all the dead warriors he would rejoin if there was a life beyond.

The man had brought these events to pass by his will and his spirit and by the strength of his sword arm. In the extremis of pain, he spoke his name through parched and crusted lips. "I am Wardark," he whispered.

Wardark would be remembered in story and song long after his death. Another man of his time would be gratified.

But Wardark was not another man. He was Wardark, a reiver of the North, a killer; a survivor, a cursed, doomed and warlock-bound warrior.

The air was cooling, the sun now spreading a trailing orange glory in the skies as it dipped to become a half cup on the horizon.

With the cooling of the air the desert began to stir. Some distance away a shape formed, the height of a sword, and then another and another. At the Tavern of Balthus in the port of Serpanam Wardark had heard talk of wizards who wrought mirages which could twist a man's mind to seeing things that were not there. Now in every direction, clouds of sand began to rise like spouting waterfalls. The whole of the barren desert became a checkerboard of ethereal fountains. Was he succumbing to the ramblings of the already dead?

Like ghostly corpses the sands began to swirl and sway, spinning and weaving across the barren desert. The legendary sand jinns of Serpanam, born of the witch-world of the desert, were rising before his eyes. And of a sudden it seemed that they had gathered like an armed host and began to sweep towards him. Then all at once they began to weave and reform, some collapsing, some joining like veiled Serpanian dancers, until at the end of an interminable time, a single sand devil, which towered above the others, hovered a short distance from him.

Slowly, as all others collapsed, this whirling devil seemed to solidify, almost like water turning to melted ice. A great head composed of swirling sand appeared on the ethereal body. And a rasping voice filled the air.

"Wardark, can you hear me?"

Wardark, despite imminent death. smiled inwardly. It was Xianthus the warlock of the Vandergan mountain come apparently to remonstrate with him as he died.

"Wardark. Answer me! This shape will not sustain!" Even as the warlock spoke, the shape glimmered and gurned out of sight and then reformed.

Wardark tried to croak a response, but his parched lips could hardly open. Eventually he hissed, "Dying."

"Dying? Dying! You cannot die. I have commissioned you." There was no reply. "I see you cannot speak. I must communicate directly with your mind. This will hurt. Do not be alarmed."

Again, Wardark smiled inwardly. Close to death as he was, he had almost gone past the point of pain.

Or so he had believed. The sand devil projected a phantom arm to his head and a blast of fire crackled from his forehead to his feet. His body jerked like a man hit with a volley of arrows, piercing pain impaling him to an astral void. Time stopped, the world disappeared and Wardark had a vision again of Xianthus caged and suspended under the eaves of the Vandergan mountain; held in a cage composed of swirling silver light. A cage that flickered like a glow of fireflies. No sign now of silken robe of red and gold or the ancient face with hair that hung a spear's length below his prison, no sign of anything but an unspeakable gaze from eyes that had seen appalling horrors and watched the death throes of uncounted enemies. Eyes that glared at Wardark from a face, indistinct but recognisable, now emerged from the darkness. The lips moved.

"I see you have clothed my voice with my appearance, Wardark. Perhaps some of my power is invigorating your spectral existence. Unusual, but then you are an unusual man."

Wardark said nothing. He was still wrestling with the concept of an inner voice, not his own.

"You thirst; soon you will die of cold. In this perpetual

prison of multidimensions I forget these visceral things. I forget the inadequacy of your temporal body. Let me adjust the temporalities." There was a moment's pause in which Wardark felt his thoughts spiral away. In that pause an intimation of the chill of the desert began to slowly descend on his body. He observed with a moiety of his mind, that the sun had fallen. It was like the presentiment of the harsh winters of his youth. He raised his head about to deride the wizard when the ethereal arm of swirling sand drew back and raised to the sky. The palm opened and the taut fingers flung upwards. There was an explosion of noise as though a tree had been struck by lightning, and the blackening sky was suddenly alight with tendrils of electricity.

To his astonished eyes a grey cloud enveloped him. A sudden squall of rain poured in a tempest above his head, drenching his body and filling his open mouth with life-giving water. For an unknown time the water swirled about him. It soothed his aching body and cooled his burning face. He drank until his parched lips gagged on water and he threw up, cupping streams of water in the palms of his outstretched hands. Slowly the rain stopped and the cloud dissipated.

And then the wizard did something which implied a power utterly beyond human understanding. As Wardark's body began to shut down, his stomach contracting and his muscles bulging with an inner agony born of freezing cold, the desert winds stirred and the very stars wheeled in unnatural speed above his head. Xianthus was tampering with time itself. In what seemed moments the wheeling stars drew light from the universe; the half-moon revolved like a spinning arc racing across the sky and the darkness dissipated as a silken dress draws in the spreading stain of red wine. The cloud whipped up and disappeared; the rain was utterly gone. Wardark fell forward, barely holding his body up with one hand. He raised his head. The wizard's ethereal shape, composed of grains of sand, was slowing, falling.

In the distance a strange object appeared. It was tiny but growing at every second. It flapped like a bird and then span like a tiny dancer. It grew and grew. Wardark watched it with a mind so unbalanced by amazement that he hardly noticed his own existence. Somewhere far away and fading, Xianthus spoke. "We cannot have you freezing to death before your time comes, warrior. When you awake you must go to the east, a small detour which will be of great service to my...to your... journey. this cloak will take you there. You will know what to do..." The voice disappeared and even as it did Wardark saw the strange object grow from a scrap of cloth, driven by an unfelt wind to appear as a red cloak hurtling and fluttering towards him as though it had a mind of its own.

The whole expanse was lit in dawn's light. Xianthus had propelled time forward and restrained the hours of night into a few seconds. The desert was awakening to a new sun. The cloak flapped eerily towards Wardark and then with a final sluggish movement wrapped around his torso. Wardark fell forward on his face. Even as he fell, his instinct for survival rose up against death and he pulled the cloak about him.

Bereft of thoughts and shrouded in the warmth and protection of the cloak he was instantly asleep.

THE GAUNTGORGON

Wardark slowly opened his eyes. From beneath the cloak, he was first made aware of the burning sun which had risen to the roof of the clear blue sky. The cloak had warmed him in the cold early dawn and now served to protect him from that sun. But a noise had awoken him. A faint stirring on the wash of sand.

Any stirring in a desert presaged danger of some form. A spear's length from Wardark's face a creature was sloping towards him, intent it seemed on sustenance. In short, like every creature in that land of horror, it desired his flesh. The creature paused mid-step. It bore a crest of elongated scales running from its head to its tail. A dewlap at its throat flicked in the light breeze. Above the dewlapped throat the thin-lipped mouth opened fractionally as a red tongue flicked like a worm between a set of gnarled teeth. Five large claws extended from its toes. It was half again the size of Wardark and now stared at him through two slitted and layered eyes. Despite his wide travels, Wardark had never encountered a gauntgorgon. They were rare. Had he known it was young and barely grown he may well have considered himself already dead. In that moment where both beasts, the man and reptile, stared at each other Wardark found himself caught by the bulbous eyes of the gauntgorgon. He had never encountered such a creature and had no idea that its main strategy was not its powerful talons or wide mouth but its ability to hypnotise its prey.

Now Wardark felt the effects of the eyes. He was sinking, sinking into a strange world of contradictions. Fragments of memory resolved and then he was being drawn back to the recent past. What was happening? The image of the gauntgorgon snapped out of existence and again, he was in the dockside quarter in the port of Serpanam. He sat in glum silence at a great oaken table carved from some monster tree. How had he returned to this time and place?

After the death of the pirate king the Northmen had celebrated for three days and nights in the Tavern of Balthus on the seafront. Here they had sat before him, their swords propped against the wall, in their hands the large wooden flagons of strong beer, gorging on pickled fish and stewed rice, singing the ancient songs; songs of victory and martial glory of great deeds, some true, others somewhat inflated. The air reeked of musk, ripe perfume, sweat, dried hops and the ever-present aroma of rotten fish. In the shadows seamen lolled in half slumber resting in the arms of sleeping whores, burly Serpanite dockers whispered to the throw of the die and the exchange of silver. But the spirit of his companions was ineffable. The defeat of the pirate had caused an outbreak of local public celebration as would any execution, lewd exhibition or public infamy but deeds of renown had been achieved, and this added a romantic spice to the celebrations. No one liked a pirate, and the Northmen were popular. The name of Wardark, their leader, would whistle across the desert and over the seas to become part of myth and song.

Then with time his name would fade as the figures of his companions faded to be replaced by the straw-strewn floor on which stood a pair of black leather boots. Wardark shook his head as past events came in fragments. A day or night had passed. His companions were gone, sailing with his father back to the Vandergan, back to their homes. For a brief second the impression of bulbous reptilian eyes intruded on his vision and then he was back in the tavern.

Why was he here alone?

Wardark's eyes rose to take in the owner of the black leather boots. He saw a large man clad in deep crimson-red pantaloons and an emerald smock with gold embroidered sleeves. He bore a great chain of gold and amantadine jewels almost buried in a swathe of chest hair. Above this a thick neck masked by the blackest of beards. Wardark rose to meet the gaze of the brown, piercing eyes of a man, strangely ebullient in this glum place. What was he saying? He was the merchant, Branleran. But more than a merchant. The eyes of this merchant had surveyed the world, and his ears heard the talk from the port of Serpanam to the great cities of Franken and beyond. He knew the trade routes and the slave routes, the mercenary runners and their camps, the hilltop forts of the barbarian tribes, the castles of the knights, the demesnes and the monasteries and the secret paths and ways of the hunter and, of greater importance, the men to trust and the men to avoid.

Directed to a snug the merchant pulled forth a stained and browned parchment. With a sweep of his bejewelled hand, he scattered the empty flagons and wooden plates from the table and laid out the parchment: an ancient, tattered map. With a flourish, he placed weighted candlesticks on the four corners of the map.

Wardark stared at the unfamiliar script and smiled inwardly to observe that his own land of the Vandergan was unknown to the merchant, but, despite his broad reiving, other lands were unknown to Wardark himself. Dominating the map was a vast, empty waste where landmarks were few: an oasis here, a ruined village or fort there. This, explained Branleran, was the great desert of Serpanam. The merchant's spatulate hand made a wedge on the western side of the map. "Here," he said in a deeply timbered voice, "the river of Sperta crests the port and flows two days travel by camel until it expels into the sea to the south where the alluvial plain stretches inland by the river until it ends beyond where the cliffs become lower and lower hills and finally, we reach the plains. Here," he said thumping the table, "where the great river spreads to the plain it creates a coastal desert where the sea winds send a chilling fog to the land and the ancient gods have made a paradox: a land where one can drink the air, but no rain ever falls. Here past this humid barrier a crescent of ruined villages of lost ages edges the inland desert, and beyond, in this massive desolate region, no moisture-laden winds can come."

The merchant knew the secret ways. And for a price he could show Wardark the ways of the slavers and the route they must take.

For an instant Wardark became aware that he was staring into the eyes of the gauntgorgon. The beast was closer now, the tongue flicking in and out of its skull-like grimace. He tried to move but found that movement impossible.

Then he was back in the past again. Why did he need to know the way? And then it came to him in a flash of understanding. His cousin Evern, the lovelorn boy and the girl they had rescued from the Pirate king.

Besotted, in the midst of the reveries, his cousin Evern had disappeared with the girl. No doubt some rendezvous where he could hide from the bantering eyes of the reivers whose merciless baiting had amused them all. But there was no amusement when the two lovers had failed to return. The Northmen had scoured the village to no effect. Three days of questions with no answers. The ship waited in the harbour, those on board, the freed Vandergan women, the wounded and able warriors all with a fervent wish to return home. His father had finally made the decision. Return they must. And he, Wardark the doomed, had insisted he would remain, despite all protests.

Already his people had sensed that there was something subtly different about Wardark. He was a hero, a warrior, almost a legend, but none knew of the secret quest he was condemned to fulfil. None knew of the warlock, Xianthus, and his doom. This talk was madness, but they saw the reasoning behind a single warrior who might work better alone.

All his companions, Banen the Bald, Vayan the Red and the other reivers had volunteered to remain and continue the search and although Wardark had pointed out that it was simple and logical for one man to do so they had, at first, been reluctant. Finally, persuaded by his obvious obduracy and his reasoning that a single warrior might work better alone, they had desisted and it was agreed, as he knew it must be. Wardark knew that he must continue on his quest alone but not for the young lovers. Sadly, that was merely a consideration. The quest that had been determined many moons before by Xianthus the warlock, whose soul had been imprisoned on a whim by the witch, Meredith. The tainted soul lay under the Vandergan mountain condemned to ten thousand years of agony, but the body lay in a grave in the catacombs of Menolops on the southern shore of Franken in a casket of marble and gold beneath the bowels of the sacred altar in the arch cathedral of Menolops the Gaunt.

Wardark, to pay his debts to the warlock, must, for reasons beyond his understanding, remove a silver chain from the corpse.

Again, time slipped and slid and Wardark retreated into a new scenario.

"As I have told you, this boy, your cousin I understand, and the girl of the Vandergan, very beautiful, they were taken by nomads. These nomads are slavers from the eastern desert." Branleran opened his arms in an expansive gesture. "Not pleasant men."

Slavers!

And with that realisation, Wardark was sent rushing back through the lanes of memory to the Serpanam desert and the moment of truth. A handsbreadth from his face the bulbous eyes of the gauntgorgon pierced his own and the gaping jaws opened wide exuding a foul breath. The red tongue flicked once, the armoured body tensed. With a sheer effort of will, Wardark released the hypnotic paralysis as the huge reptile leapt forward like a toad to snap the flesh from his face. With lightning speed born of his reiver soul, Wardark drew back, twisting his body to grasp the open jaws in two hands. And then there began a titanic struggle as both man and beast engaged in the primaeval contest of life and death. Wardark's whole body, weakened by hunger and exhausted by strife, battled to keep the jaws apart as they hovered over his face. The beast twisted to left and right, trying to dislodge the fingers from its jaw as Wardark was thrown backwards, his feet kicking in the sand and tangling in Xianthus' cloak. The gauntgorgon thrust forward and Wardark felt his grip weaken as he fell under the heavy weight of its body in an explosion of sand.

One chance. In a sudden burst, he thrust up with both hands. The gauntgorgon shifted and then bore down. And then in a flash he withdrew both hands, the jaws clamped and opened wide in a fraction of a second. With a grunt and an impossible speed of movement, Wardark balled a fold of cloak in both hands and punched it into the open mouth, drawing his forearms apart as they thrust into the throat. The creature bore down, jaws opening and shutting, clogging on the cloak as Wardark withdrew one arm and in staccato movement, punched more and more of the heavy cloth into the drooling mouth. The creature tried to draw back and Wardark twisted, leaping onto its back, fingers in the flaring nostrils, pushing the reptile's head into the sand. For an age he pummelled and shoved with his full weight until the gauntgorgon weakened and stilled. The breath laboured a little longer and with a final shudder all movement ceased.

Wardark waited and then with a grunt rolled from the beast. But he was not done. With his last failing strength, he slowly pulled the sodden cloak length by length from the creature and with only a hint of revulsion, drew the dead tongue out between the dead jaws. With a steady movement he crushed the beast's jaws onto the tongue, severing it piece by piece until he could pull the bloody stump no further.

Lying on his back, with the sun rising above him in a clear blue sky, Wardark began to chew on the pieces, drinking the acrid blood and hoping with a sour smile that he was not about to die of poison.

THE SLAVER

Again, Wardark awoke to the vision of a pair of black leather boots. There was no straw beneath them, only white sand.

Wardark raised his head. Although his head beat like a drum at least he had not died in the night.

The merchant Branleran had discarded the red pantaloons and emerald smock in favour of the black loose-layered tunic of the nomads. With a headcloth held in place by a thick agal, his face was shielded from the sun. Nothing could disguise the piercing brown eyes.

Silently, Branleran handed Wardark a goatskin sack of water. Wardark sat up and carefully drank a few sips. He handed the sack back to the merchant.

"It appears," said Branleran, "That you have

encountered a gauntgorgon. Something of a marvel in these times. More marvellous that you have killed the beast with your bare hands."

Wardark did not reply. He watched as five tall men clad in similar garb to the merchant unsheathed their swords and approached with caution. He recognised the nomads. He had killed several of their comrades a few days before when they had attacked him in the night, only fleeing when his sword had snapped as it sheered a man's spine and embedded itself in his pelvis.

Branleran said abruptly, "Shackle this man."

Wardark took another piece of tongue and chewed on it carefully. He watched as the nomads added their curved daggers to the swords and began creating a half circle around him. They had learned of his strength and speed. If his sword had not been broken in their previous encounter. If he was not weakened by hunger and thirst... Wardark stood. He recognised the futility of resistance. He still considered it.

"I know now how you are so well versed in the paths of the slavers, for you are one yourself," he said.

"Yes," said Branleran. "I bewitched you in the Tavern of Balthus. A simple concoction slipped into your drink. It was easy to send you across the desert alone to a rendezvous you would never succeed in achieving. The map was true, but I am not."

Branleran eyed the figure of Wardark as he might a prize beast. The sun-blackened, bruised and wounded body was taut with iron muscles and despite the exhaustion, starvation and deprivation the warrior seemed as though he may be about to fling himself across the distance to kill him. The merchant took a step backward. "You have cost me three of my men already. But such are the trials of business.

A warrior has many valuable qualities to the rich potentates. You should at least fetch a price that will cover that loss. But more interesting is the beast you have killed. The gauntgorgon is extremely rare; the bones have medicinal uses for the monks of Feralium; the skin will be stuffed and exhibited; the skull will decorate the walls of a potentate in the south."

"And what of my cousin and the girl. Was that another lie?"

"Oh no, they are far ahead across the desert of Serpanam. You will follow their trail in a similar cage." Branleran smiled "Perhaps you will meet again in the slave auction."

Behind the five nomads in the far distance, Wardark now saw a Caravanserai approaching across the sand. A string of camels bearing burdens and horses bearing the tall black-clad nomads, half-naked archers with sun bronzed bodies and a few mercenaries whose armour glinted in the sun. There were many wooden cages and wagons bearing slaves, and women walking, some in britches and smocks with gallant headdresses. These carried swords in back scabbards and spears on their shoulders, others, mere girls, veiled and clad in white loose-fitting robes and traditional kufiyah. Their pace was slow, and the image of them glimmered and wavered in the heat like a fragile mirage. Wardark had considered. He was brave but no fool. His body was weakened with privation, his defeat inevitable. There was a time for fighting and a time for cunning. His time would come soon enough. He picked up the cloak, now tattered and stained with blood and gore, and wrapped it around his upper body. He felt a strange convulsive, almost sentient pull of the cloak but there was no breeze. He smiled and proffered his hands.

"Come," said Wardark, "if you shackle my hands instead of my feet, it will save you carrying me to my new accommodation."

Branleran hesitated and then spoke words of command. "Do as he says. He is exhausted. It will save time."

But they did carry him, as when shackled, Wardark took one more breath and keeled over, unconscious in the sand.

THE OASIS

Wardark examined the bars of his cage. It was larger than most and constructed of mahogany rather than the wicker of the women's cages. He looked thoughtfully at the joints, the floor, the roof, then turned his gaze to the scene outside the cage.

Branleran had set up camp three days before in an oasis with the cages set in a circle on the edges of the trees where they made a defensive circle, which created a penumbra of shadows on the white sands. Guards were set at intervals between the cages. They were a mix of nomads, the odd armoured warrior and light archers distinguishable by white headbands and canvas pantaloons. These guards had been taking turns between their fires and their duty since Wardark had been roughly woken in the afternoon. One, a female mercenary, a quiet solitary individual, had given him water from a skin bag, gruel and a plate of some hard fruit each day. Once an archer had stared at him in silence for some time before returning to joke with his comrades. A huddle of children had thrown stones at him before being shooed away by an old woman.

There were a few campfires set at intervals between the

cages where these guards, mercenaries and archers, squatted, gambling and laughing as the sun disappeared behind the horizon. In the inner circle he could see many more campfires where the lilt of a flute could be heard extemporising the gypsy melodies of the nomads. The smell of roasting lamb wafted tantalisingly through the date trees, and shadows of slaves darted around serving meat, wines and sherbets, lemons, oranges and dates.

Wardark tested the shackles on his wrists. The metal was strong, unfamiliar to him.

"Franken steel, once mined on the eastern slopes of the mist-clad mountains of Moerland." The voice was low, gruff, the accent thick. "Tough to break."

Wardark looked up. The mercenary who had fed him gruel and fruit in the afternoons stood with one foot on the footboards of the cage. She leaned with her hands on her bare knee.

Wardark crouched so his face was level with the mercenary. She was a woman of middle years with a broad chest and unusually large forearms for one of her sex. Her broken nose and scarred face spoke of a hard life. She had once been beautiful but under her greased-back, black hair, two haunted eyes spoke of the all-pervading ugliness and brutality of the world. This was the woman who sat apart. She proffered her hand, several strips of dried flesh in her palm. Wardark reached out. He took the meat. He chewed a strip carefully and stashed the rest in the sheath of his back scabbard.

"We were told you are from the Northwest coast. They say there's another of your kind, a youth, some days to the south. I've seen your women on occasion, feisty things when trapped by the slavers, but never one of your warriors." The mercenary examined Wardark frankly. "You look handy and they say you slew three of the nomads. Not an easy task."

"I would have slain a few more but my sword snapped in-between a big fellow's bones," said Wardark.

"Well, between you and me I don't have much time for these slavers. They'll as like have me in a cage when we get further south. I took the job because it's a long way to Franken and the desert is not a place to be out and about alone. Too many predators, mostly people."

"So I have found."

"The gauntgorgon. I overheard Branleran say you killed that with your bare hands. Impossible, of course," she scoffed. Wardark had no desire to correct the woman. It seemed impossible to him. She continued, "Branleran has a taxidermist working on the corpse in the big wagon. I caught a glimpse of its head as they brought the thing in, carried in under sacking. If I hadn't seen the head, I wouldn't have believed it. There are bones scattered in the desert, of course, but no one has seen one of these things alive since my tribe's age-set were grandfathers. And that beast set the whole village astir. They say it took a hundred men to kill the thing and many died in the battle. We have songs about it."

"Fortune was on my side," said Wardark

The mercenary shook her head. "You don't strike me as a man who relies too much on fortune." She stood up, seemingly making some kind of decision. "My name is Jwain. I'm a half breed, born in the south of Franken near the Sudron of a Sudronese mother, a slave, and a minor Franken noble whom I killed with my own hands." She smiled ruefully. "Who knows where fortune takes a man... or a woman."

"Wardark, son of Wevan, a reiver from the North."

The mercenary proffered her hand. Wardark extended his hand as best as could with the impediment of the shackles.

When the mercenary had left, Wardark drew the tattered cloak around his body and seated himself in a corner of the cage. The cloak again seemed to move independently, a butterfly movement on the edge of consciousness.

For a long while Wardark waited until the campfires were smouldering and the noise and bustle of the camp had settled to whispered voices and the calls of guards marking the changes. As the camp died to a silence, broken only by the light wind of the desert fluttering through the date trees, Wardark opened his palm. In its centre was a metal pin, a gift from Jwain. Wardark examined the pin. It was the key to his shackles.

THE DESERT GOBELN

In the night, they came. Wardark, who had remained awake, testing each of the bars and the panelled roof and floor of his cage without any great success, was the first to see the dark forms stealing like a swarm of locusts across the landscape. They came silently with deadly purpose. In an instant, Wardark's cage was enveloped by the horde, some reached with hands into the cage, others leapt to its roof, faces peering down with ghoulish madness. Even as he rose to his feet, Wardark saw a guard dragged by the smouldering campfire, throat torn open, blood spouting out onto a spent fire to steam and hiss.

Gobeln! The arch enemies of the Vandergan, but a form of the species which Wardark had never encountered.

The Gobeln of the Vandergan were huge creatures, towering by a head over a man. They carried clubs and would rip the sword from a warrior with their bare hands to use as an improvised weapon. They were cunning, malicious, intelligent, Wardark had spent his entire life reiving on the borders of his Northern land to protect the villages from this relentless enemy, but these creatures were smaller, quicker, half the size of their giant cousins, yet terrifying, nonetheless. They had no weapons, only teeth and clawed hands, some desert breed who had grown apart from the mountain herds.

Now the bugles of the guards rose in pitying crescendo, quickly stifled as men and women drew weapons or were silenced by death.

Wardark, inured to horrific sights and protected by the cage, observed the ambush with a practised eye. He was impressed. When the chance came, the Gobeln would swarm a man, pulling and clawing from every side, grabbing limbs and disembowelling with teeth and claws as the man fell like a prisoner being hung drawn and quartered. But the men of the caravanserai were astute. The tall, black-clad nomads knelt in groups of three with sword and curved dagger forming a mesh of steel. The archers paired with the armoured mercenaries, and as the mercenaries swept their swords in a dancing circle of protection, they fired dart after dart into the teeming horde of Gobeln. Some archers, their white headbands dancing like fire trails against the black sky, leapt to the roof of cages, while their companions thrust with spears at the encroaching Gobeln.

It was clear that Gobeln attack was a frequent occurrence. Those who had time to erect their well-tried defence kept the creatures at bay and by a process of attrition diminished their numbers rapidly with little loss. The warrior women formed circles thrusting with their spears and swinging their curved blades. Some were not so fortunate; surrounded and alone, caught unarmed, the

Gobeln would rend and tear like ants pulling apart an invader. In the wicker cages desperate slave girls, naked and unarmed, crouched screaming as hands clawed at their flesh, and older women threw nets and jabbed with spears. Lone archers had no defence but a short dagger, and they fell thrusting and hacking, their backs to these cages, protecting their merchandise with grim yet futile purpose.

It was like a man stamping on carnivorous ants, the myriad versus the one; a question of numbers, of slow destruction, or indiscriminate slaughter; a question of who or what would die. And the man, if he could not slaughter in numbers, once overwhelmed, was finished.

Wardark watched dispassionately. He had no weapon and no exit from his prison. He must simply wait.

And then another factor. From the darkness came a body of nomads, bearing torches and casting firebrands as they moved. They marched in phalanx, the firebrands littering the ground around them and casting eerie shadows. At the head of this elite company, Branleran the merchant wielded a great two-handed sword. The nomads held some form of halberd. Some thrust with point as others swept with the axe head, mowing through the Gobeln like scything peasants in a field of corn.

It was clear to Wardark that for the greater part the Caravanserai had an advantage. Their fight was organised, disciplined and born of vast experience. Even now the Gobeln were retreating, some wounded, limbs missing, black blood spouting from wounds, some in a kind of blind panic.

But that was only the greater part. Wardark had also observed that the Gobeln, driven by animal instinct, would immediately feed when they had slain. Their jaws dripping with blood, their claws ripping flesh from bone. He had watched as several of the company fell in isolated incidents, caught alone and surrounded. Their brief screams rang through the air as their bodies were torn asunder. It was with this realisation that he observed a figure backing towards his cage.

Jwain, the mercenary.

She had clearly been caught unawares, or perhaps she was simply a woman who had no desire for company and felt no need for protection. Wardark had sensed her emptiness and isolation and had seen her solitary campfire, set apart from the others not far from his cage. This now became her downfall. He watched as she swirled in a desperate circle, her sword sweeping in undulation motion, slicing heads, legs, and arms from the circling Gobeln who thrust and grabbed like horrific children, jumping forward and retreating in a surreal game of hunt the witch. Jwain was naked except for britches, and her upper body was rent with wounds and lacerations. She leapt and crouched, keeping a perpetual motion against impossible odds. Somehow, she had failed to secure her armour and, as effective and skilled as she was, her speed and her blade were a poor defence against a horde. The Gobeln, in a mad frenzy for flesh, sensed the kill and dove forward, increasingly bold.

Even as she stumbled, turning towards Wardark, a thrown firebrand struck the ground and lit her face in a flickering orange glow. The broken nose, the scars, the haunted eyes, staring in shocked appeal, rippled in the dancing light. She fell to her knees directly before him and, with one last effort drew her sword back and with a mighty yet despairing blow, smashed the bars of his cage,

Wardark, with an even greater speed had struck his shackles with the stolen pin and, with the war cry of the Vandergan, crashed through the damaged bars in a tumbler's leap. Wardark landed on his feet just beyond Jwain. Swirling the chain like a mace he swept a circle of protection around them. Gobeln were flung into the air, limbs smashed, heads turning like leather pig skins in the air amidst a welter of blood and guts.

But they came again. The chain was torn from his hands, and he faced the horde unarmed. Wardark glanced swiftly behind him. Jwain had turned onto her back and lay like an entombed knight with her sword clutched in prayer hands. With failing strength, she held her sword up. Wardark took it up with mighty oath and began laying about him with the strength of a madman. All around, the screams of desperation, the oaths and cries of warriors, the dreadful crunch of steel on bone and the smell of blood and gore, played like the dark symphony, the eternal dance of life and death. On they came, relentless and awful, and time became an illusion of endless conflict and inexhaustible weariness.

And then it was over.

Amidst the smouldering charcoal of spent fires, the blood drying on the sand, the torn flesh scattered like meat and bones on a slaughterhouse floor and the smell of blood and death, the desert wind sounded its own peculiar voice to augment the dreadful silence as, slowly, the hint of a dawn suffused the landscape. The oasis seemed small and contained in the vast landscape, a cemetery for half-sized Gobeln who lay all around in heaps of slain, a place of horror.

Wardark, again on his knees with a broken sword in hand, felt nothing. And then a broad forearm came from behind to hold him in an embrace, the skin soft and yielding, the breath on his neck sweet.

Branleran approached at the head of his men.

"So, northern barbarian, the Gobeln have been kept at

bay yet again and the losses were not significant." Branleran barked an order to his commander and then contemplated Wardark and Jwain with interest, "It seems this woman has freed you from your chains. She will be sold then as you will be sold, a small recompense for the breaking of faith and, I see, the breaking of your cage, an expensive item which can be repaired, nonetheless. As a first task and a welcoming to your new status, you can both help with the clearing of the bodies. They will foul the oasis otherwise."

With an effort Wardark rose to his feet. He lifted Jwain. Her head lolled forward. She had become limp in his arms.

"I have taken a great dislike to you, Branleran," said Wardark.

The merchant laughed. "Your likes or dislikes are not my concern. Only your value as merchandise. Unfortunately, it appears that I have lost another sale. You hold a dead woman, Wardark."

Wardark had felt it even as they spoke. Jwain had died in his arms. He looked down at the scarred face, the broken nose, the naked, wounded torso a maze of blood and wounds on the bare skin. It was a pitiable sight.

She had sensed some fellowship with him. Had his doomed quest set him apart? Was his isolation recognised by one doomed? Was he drawing lost souls to him as candle draws a moth? *Xianthus. The curse of Xianthus.*

With care he lowered the limp body to the sand and gazed impotently at his hands with their bloody palms. He turned his head. Behind him, the sun had just begun to rise, and the light began to roll out like a vast golden carpet, flooding across the desert.

Even as it did, there was a strange discombobulation of air. Branleran stepped back, startled, his eyes growing wide with alarm.

From behind Wardark, a noise like a squeaking bat penetrated the air. It seemed to come from a far distance, and yet it grew swiftly into a wail and then a roar as of dreadful winds, of hurricanes, of tornadoes, of god-like dimensions beyond the ken of man; an immense wind gathering up from the netherworld, sending flurries of sand like thrown dust to cloud the air. A sand jinn sprouted, grew, grew more and enveloped the cage, sending the tattered, gore-stained cloak to spin. The cloak hit the broken walls of the cage for a second and then bundled through the shattered bars to swirl like a ghost caught in some localised storm. It flapped around Wardark like a ghost seeking a body, maddened by air.

"Xianthus," whispered Wardark and he smiled grimly. To the astonished gaze of Branleran the world around Wardark began to spin. The black clad nomads dropped to the sands, wailing in maddened prayer, the cloak swept up into the air, thrashing wildly in the impossible wind. The sand began to swirl; a sand jinni forming and reforming and swirling the cloak in a frenzied ellipse around Wardark. Wardark spread his arms as a man crucified. But his face held no agony, only a wry expression of triumph.

The cloak hit Wardark with an immense force, he clutched it in an iron grip and, like a red sail winching on his outstretched arms, it gusted forward, blowing the merchant over and sending Wardark to fly like a kite over the oasis and beyond.

THE DOOM

Wardark was closer to the mountains of Moreland. Their misty peaks could be seen beyond a series of undulating hills, sparsely covered in shrub and strangled weeds. He had landed in gulley under an overhang of great volcanic rock where a small spring trickled in a tumbled mass of boulders, the spillings of a cataclysm a million years distant in time. Xianthus' tattered cloak lay by his body, a spent force. Wardark had been thrown into the sky like a rag, tossed and buffeted by aethereal winds for incalculable distances, until he had spilled out onto the desert floor, rolling like a ball wrapped in the cloak. He had come to rest finally in a pile of gorse brush, his body bruised and battered, but his spirit unquenched.

The dark night was drawing in, the sun lowering. A small green snake slid down the gulley, hesitated and then drew towards a shamble of rocks.

Wardark lay a long time in silence, listening to the slough of the desert wind. Later, when the night grew so cold that the air began to mist, he drew the cloak around him and thought again of the mercenary, Jwain, of her life, of the pattern of choices that a living entity takes. Had she recognised her own doom, had she seen his? He thought of his cousin Evern, caged and bound for slavery far to the south. Whatever fate had woven for Evern, Wardark could only try to align his doomed path so that it crossed the path of the boy. The fate of others was now truly beyond him and indeed his own was in the balance. Weaponless, without the means to make fire and still weakened from privation he was prey to every misfortune.

Even as this thought struck his mind, he felt the almost imperceptible presence of magic. Rolling his eyes towards his shoulder he observed the small green snake coiled on the rock at his head. The snake was classically poised to bite, but it remained static, exuding a faint glow.

A sibilant whisper, almost out of the range of hearing, joined with the wind.

"Ah, Wardark. You are safe?" Xianthus, the wizard.

"I have been safer," replied Wardark ironically. "Without warmth I will likely die, without a weapon I will likely die. In fact, the progress of your quest seems to have stalled as I am in much the same condition as when we spoke last."

"Gather the small sticks and gorse from around you and place them in a pile."

Wardark did so. He felt a rip in the fabric of time and the small pile burst spontaneously into a spark, a flame which grew to a tolerable fire. He threw a larger stick on the fire and then another. It blazed nicely.

"You have fire and water. Your immediate needs are met," whispered the wizard. "As to a weapon, go to the south. Two days and nights you must journey. You will find the pyramid of Miniata, a daughter of Meredith. A sword lies at its centre, a powerful weapon. Obtain the sword and journey south, south to the catacombs of Menolops on the southern shore of Franken…"

"…Yes, yes," said Wardark wearily, "the tomb, the sarcophagus, the silver necklace around the neck of your ancient corpse. So, I must journey again across the desert where I will doubtless die of hunger."

The voice of Xianthus had faded to the volume of a mosquito.

"There are berries in the gully. In the meantime, I have exhausted the spirit of this creature, but the flesh is edible. The snake will supply your immediate needs."

Wardark watched as the snake's head dropped to the ground like a hanged man and the glow surrounding it died. With a sigh of exasperation, he picked up the body and thrust a stick through the mouth.

Sitting on his haunches he pulled the cloak around his shoulders and began toasting the reptile over the fire.

ALSO AVAILABLE *from*
PARALLEL UNIVERSE PUBLICATIONS

Carl Barker: *Parlour Tricks*
Charles Black: *Black Ceremonies*
Benjamin Blake: *Standing on the Threshold of Madness*
Mike Chinn: *Radix Omnium Malum*
Ezeiyoke Chukwunonso: *The Haunted Grave & Other Stories*
Irvin S. Cobb: *Fishhead: The Darker Tales of Irvin S. Cobb*
Adrian Cole: *Tough Guys*
Adrian Cole: *Elak: Warrior of Atlantis*
Adrian Cole: *Elak: King of Atlantis*
Adrian Cole: *Elak: Sea Hawks of Atlantis*
Andrew Darlington: *A Saucerful of Secrets*
Kate Farrell: *And Nobody Lived Happily Ever After*
Craig Herbertson: *The Heaven Maker & Other Gruesome Tales*
Craig Herbertson: *Christmas in the Workhouse*
Erik Hofstatter: *The Crabian Heart*
Andrew Jennings: *Into the Dark*
Samantha Lee: *Childe Rolande*
David Ludford: *A Place of Skulls & Other Tales*
Samantha Lee: *Childe Rolande*
Jessica Palmer: *Other Visions of Heaven and Hell*
Jessica Palmer: *Fractious Fairy Tales*
Jim Pitts: *The Fantastical Art of Jim Pitts*
Jim Pitts: *The Ever More Fantastical Art of Jim Pitts*
David A. Riley: *Goblin Mire*
David A. Riley: *Their Cramped Dark World & Other Tales*
David A. Riley: *His Own Mad Demons*
David A. Riley: *Moloch's Children*
David A. Riley: *After Nightfall & Other Weird Tales*
David A. Riley: *A Grim God's Revenge: Dark Tales of Fantasy*
David A. Riley: *Lucilla – a novella*
Joseph Rubas: *Shades: Dark Tales of Supernatural Horror*
Eric Ian Steele: *Nightscape*
David Williamson: *The Chameleon Man & Other Terrors*

www.paralleluniversepublications.blogspot.com

Phantasmagoria Magazine
HORROR, FANTASY & SCI-FI

AVAILABLE from **AMAZON**

FORBIDDEN PLANET INTERNATIONAL (Belfast)

Phantasmagoria
Mag.co.uk

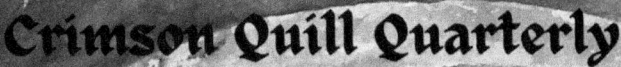

Crimson Quill Quarterly
Volume 8
October 2025

Featuring the talents of:

Tom Doolan

Malcolm North

R. K. Olson

Nik Patrick

C. W. Stevenson

McKay Wadsworth

L. D. Whitney

READ FREE

JANUARY 21

SAVAGE
REALMS
M O N T H L Y

TALES OF
SWORDS AND SORCERY

FEATURING THE TALENTS OF:

WILLARD BLACK   STEVE DILKS

DAVID SIMS AND   KELL MYERS

https://bit.ly/SavageRealmsFreeMag

Available from *www.TuleFogPress.com*

Available in paperback and kindle eBooks

Artwork by Jim Pitts

PARALLEL UNIVERSE PUBLICATIONS

New
Sword & Sorcery
from
PARALLEL UNIVERSE PUBLICATIONS

ELAK WARRIOR OF ATLANTIS — ADRIAN COLE

ELAK KING OF ATLANTIS — ADRIAN COLE

ELAK SEA HAWKS OF ATLANTIS — ADRIAN COLE

CHILDE ROLANDE — SAMANTHA LEE

SWORDS & SORCERIES TALES OF HEROIC FANTASY — Volume 1

SWORDS & SORCERIES TALES OF HEROIC FANTASY — Volume 2

SWORDS & SORCERIES TALES OF HEROIC FANTASY — Volume 3

SWORDS & SORCERIES TALES OF HEROIC FANTASY — Volume 4

SWORDS & SORCERIES TALES OF HEROIC FANTASY — Volume 5

SWORDS & SORCERIES TALES OF HEROIC FANTASY — Volume 6

SWORDS & SORCERIES TALES OF HEROIC FANTASY — Volume 7

SWORDS & SORCERIES TALES OF HEROIC FANTASY — Volume 8

SWORDS & SORCERIES TALES OF HEROIC FANTASY — Volume 9

SWORDS & SORCERIES TALES OF HEROIC FANTASY — Volume 10

THE CURSED

David A. Riley

In 2025 Tule Fog Press published my Welgar stories under the title Welgar the Cursed.

From his raw beginnings as a carefree mercenary, Welgar had no idea that his future would lead him into a dark, demonic nightmare. Although he had always instinctively hated sorcery, it was into the depths of what magic could create that he found himself entangled when he unwisely crossed swords with some of its most malign practitioners

Follow Welgar's quest as he struggles to rid himself of his horrific curse, which brings death and terror to anyone close to him, friend or foe. Travelling from the hot jungles and grim temples of feared Agrypt in the far south to the forbidden demon-haunted city of Cyramon in the arctic north, Welgar is willing to sacrifice it all to become again the man he once was.

"For those enjoying the current surge of interest in Sword & Sorcery, David Riley's Welgar is definitely one to follow. Skillfully crafted, spiced with lively action and a healthy dash of humour, these yarns are a delight, and stand out on a crowded battlefield." – Adrian Cole, author of *The Voidal Trilogy*, *Dream Lords Series*, and *Elak, King of Atlantis*.

Avaialble as a paperback & kindle eBook

Welgar the Cursed is a novel broken up into 6 stories that chronologically tell the saga of Welgar from his aw beginnings as a mercenary to the terrible curse of being possessed by a demonic god.

www.ingramcontent.com/pod-product-compliance
Lightning Source LLC
Chambersburg PA
CBHW051523260626
47170CB00003B/758